POTOMAC BEACH

By

Eron Shosteck

PublishAmerica
Baltimore

First printing

At the specific preference of the author, PublishAmerica allowed this work to remain exactly as the author intended, verbatim, without editorial input.

ISBN: 1-4137-8348-1
PUBLISHED BY PUBLISHAMERICA, LLLP
www.publishamerica.com
Baltimore

Printed in the United States of America

Dedication

For my daughter, Leah, who already loves being read to at bedtime, and whom I hope will develop her father's lifetime love of books.

Acknowledgements

I want to thank my wonderful wife Lisa, who over the years has acted as editor, sounding board, counselor, technical support troubleshooter, coach, motivational speaker and emotional rock, sometimes serving in several of those roles concurrently. I also want to thank my spirited daughter Leah, who allowed me to feed her bottles as I balanced her in the cradle of one arm while typing with my other hand amidst the gloaming of the computer screen. I wish to show my appreciation to my mother, Patti, for her editorial advice borne of her experience as a published author; my step-father, Harvey, for his financial advice; my sister, Debbie, for her candid assessments of an early draft; my in-laws, Mort, Ruth & Jeff, for their laughter at the right times; and the good folks at *National Journal* for giving this material a chance to be seen and read by political junkies when it was in an early, raw form.

Chapter 1:

The Congressman Who Didn't Know His Own Position

For such an astute politician, Idaho Congressman Charles Lattan was engaged in a seemingly foolish exercise, squandering valuable time addressing people who couldn't deliver a single vote. Here it was, the heat of the election season, and the freshman Republican was delivering the standard palaver on the calling of public service to a stuffy gymnasium filled with fidgety middle school kids.

At first he'd scoffed at his campaign manager's suggestion that he speak to students. But impressing a roomful of youngsters with the responsibility of elective office, sharing with them the adventures of life as a Congressman, discussing the duty of accepting the sacred trust of the people, would be a good workout, a chance to get back on message, talk about anything but the picayune nuisances that had dogged him recently. So what if his top fundraiser had served time for vehicular manslaughter? That was years ago! And it didn't have anything to do with him!

Damn the media and their gleeful stories condemning Charles Lattan through guilt by association!

It was a non-voting audience, yes, but at least it was one free of ciphers who would badger him with only more of the same tired questions. Maybe if he reached a few kids, showed an interest in Our Nation's Future, he might even score a nice feature photo in the paper. Smiling with a young one, how touching. Maybe it would make the voters forget these damn non-scandals, help them to remember why they elected him in the first place. It's so clear how much Congressman Lattan cares, you can see it in the way he's listening to that child. He really should be re-elected.

After weeks of weakening self-confidence, he finally had some positive thoughts charging through his head. Here he was, talking to row after row of kids perched on fold-out wooden bleachers, the pre-pubescent funk of a middle school gym enveloping him, and he felt invigorated. Renewed. He was back on message, back to fighting form. Sure, some of the students were poking each other and fussing, as kids will do, but some were listening. Yes, he was reaching them. They were fascinated by the machinations of government and his role in it.

"I wasn't always a Congressman," Lattan said, his confidence growing with each platitude. "Before serving on Capitol Hill, I served in the Idaho state legislature, a sort of miniature Congress for the state. Each state has its own little Congress to work on local issues, the way Congress works on issues affecting the whole country. And I even had another job before that. I was a small businessman, and I helped people even back then by running a company that made sure all of the sinks and showers and toilets in their homes worked well."

There were a few sniggers at the mention of toilets. Boys will be boys. But they were listening!

"My job back then was to unclog pipes that were jammed up," Lattan continued. "And I enjoyed helping people that way. But more government rules began making it harder and harder for me to do my job helping people. All of their new rules and laws began to clog up my business. Pretty soon, I was having trouble staying in business. So I did what any person in this country has a duty to do under our democratic government."

The continuing references to plumbing seemed to pique the young ones' interest. To an age group fascinated by bodily functions, his speech was nearly as titillating as a sex education class. The attention further boosted his confidence, and he began thinking Photo Op. Yes, he'd told his personal story, polished this stump speech so many times, that he could deliver it while thinking about more important concerns. Such as where the photographers were, and which kid was photogenic enough to serve as a prop.

"And so I said to myself, I've spent my life up until now unclogging appliances that were stopped up. Where better to use that training than in the legislature, where red tape and misguided regulations are stopping up the little guy's ability to run his business and help people."

Scanning, scanning. Three hundred kids now waiting to hear him say more about toilets, to share some details about septic tanks and sewers. A dozen or so teachers, probably teachers union members. Where was the press? Where were the cameras?

He tried to catch his campaign manager's eyes, but the tubby southerner was busy riffling through a folder, bored by a familiar story. Was there anyone writing, taping, filming? Scribbling on a reporter's pad? Eyes sweeping the gym. All pimply-faced kids and teachers. Good God, you can't tell me there isn't one reporter here! For godsakes, this speech better not go to waste! Scanning, scanning. Surely, there must be—

But there were no stenographers, no photographers, no microphones to be seen.

How could it be? The press had been swarming him for weeks to cover scandal. But now, a Congressman addressing the leaders of tomorrow on the importance of public service wasn't news? The insolence of the media!

But then—yes!—he eyed a woman writing on a legal pad. Perhaps. ...

"And so, students, it is because of my passion to help others, to use the tools of government to serve people and to better their lives, that I chose a career in public service. And the work I've started for the people of Idaho, I want a chance to finish. That's why I hope your parents, uncles, aunts, older brothers and sisters, and teachers, will give me that opportunity."

He finished with the usual bilge about encouraging students to volunteer, "get involved," "make a difference," "change the world," and "give something back." All the while he focused on the one reporter, his conduit from this stuffy gym to the voting public, his lone chance to make this event worthwhile.

"Thank you for listening, and I'll be happy to take your questions."

The kids began squirming once more, as though disappointed they would hear no more about clogged toilets.

Then a hand went up. A cute, reedy girl, at the awkward age between growing taller and developing physically, holding up a tentative hand.

"Yes, young lady in the third row."

"You talked about a lot of stuff about government and all, but my dad said he's not voting for you because of a lot of stuff about you we saw on the news."

Lattan winced and tensed his jaw. No relief! Even from children! The assault continued!

"Congressman Lattan, if I may," interrupted the principal, a rotund woman with a beehive hairdo and horn-rimmed glasses. It was the one who had introduced him earlier, and who had been gracious enough to read verbatim from his official campaign bio. But what was in store now? Was she going to bludgeon him with the youngster's question rephrased more tactfully?

"Congressman," she repeated. He braced himself, his muscles tightening as if suddenly corseted. He ran his hand down his tie, smoothed his mane of white hair. "I'm sure we're all aware of the various press reports you've been the subject of recently. While we may have discussed these issues around our kitchen tables, or heard our parents talking about them, I don't think it is necessary to revisit these issues, which hardly seem relevant to the focus of your remarks today."

Thank God! He exhaled audibly. Finally, someone who agreed that these stories were nonsense!

And a teacher, yet! Not some businessman or bible-thumper he'd expect to come to his defense. Hardly seem relevant, she said! Maybe the public wasn't listening to the media after all! Bless this woman! Sign her up to work a phone bank!

"But what does seem relevant, in light of your comments today about helping people, is your position on abolishing the Department of Education. Last year, you said you supported the Republican Platform of Principles, which included dismantling that agency. I wonder if you might explain to our students how your support for eliminating the Department of Education jibes with your commitment to serving people, investing in future generations, and the other themes you articulated today."

The corset squeezed him again, only much tighter this time. Axe the Education Department? When ... I don't remember ... I never said ... the thoughts caromed around inside his head like pinballs ... trying to remember ... had he ever agreed to that stupid platform thing? It sounds plausible ... how would he defend himself to a gym full of students?

The campaign manager looked at his boss in alarm, then began tearing through his brown attaché, is if the answer was contained in some position paper they toted around for just such occasions. And he hadn't even read his own position papers! Too busy for such drudgery, leave it to the staff.

The campaign manager soon looked up from the briefcase. His fat face inflated with panic. He didn't know, and he must have sensed that the candidate didn't know either. And the person who would know, the chief of staff, was god knows where on Capitol Hill.

Chaos reigned inside Lattan's skull. He never recalled endorsing such a scheme. But he could have signed it to please some conservative group. And so many bills had so many amendments tacked on to them, who could know? Only those attorneys, the legislative counsels, could translate the things. And there were so many papers he signed every day: letters, petitions, pledges, statements, Dear Colleagues, not to mention all of the flotsam produced by his staff, who signed his signature on his behalf. And then there were the other members who cornered him in the cloakroom, on the House floor, in committee hearings, in the hallways, in the can! Charlie, will you sign our pledge, we really need ya on this one ... Charlie, will you co-sponsor this bill, we'll throw in some pork for your district in the next appropriations bill ... Charlie, you sign mine, I'll sign yours.

He didn't know! Why didn't someone prep him on this, give him some talking points to review on the ride over? Then he remembered: the campaign manager had asked if he wanted briefing papers, and he'd been too proud to admit he needed any prepping. He stared again at the woman scribbling on the legal pad, who stopped writing and returned his gaze.

What do I say!?

"Of course, I support education," Lattan began, his voice changing octaves on every syllable in education. "That's why I'm with you today. But with regard to the Department of Education, you have the question of what is the proper role of the federal government. Education is an issue best left to the states, not the bureaucrats in Washington telling teachers in Idaho how and what to teach."

"But Congressman," the principal interjected, "don't you believe that eliminating the entire department, removing it from the cabinet, is a bit drastic? Can't we reduce federal influence without axing the whole department? What kind of a message are we sending to our children if we say education isn't as important as defense? How can you stand in front of all of these students and claim we don't need an education department?"

She was having nothing of his explanation. Now Charles Lattan was suddenly the enemy of education.

The reporter would certainly lead with this angle. She'd run to her editor, dreams of front-page bylines waltzing in her head, and say Have I got a story for you. "Lattan Tells Students He Supports Abolishing Education Department." Page one! Oh, they'll have a field day! They'll gleefully editorialize about how a man with questionable judgment before has now erased any doubt about his complete lack of common sense. *To tell an audience of students and teachers that he favors eliminating their department reinforces the editors' view that Charles Lattan is not Congressional material. What's next, a visit to a soup kitchen to announce his opposition to food stamps?*

Oh, it'll be disastrous! The press has been waiting for the death blow, and now they'll have it. He grimaced again, braced himself for one last defensive strike.

"No, of course I'm not saying the government doesn't have a role in promoting education," Lattan stammered, desperately trying to regain his equilibrium. "I've never said that I favor eliminating the federal role in education. What kind of fool would I be to come before an audience of students and teachers and claim — "

"So you're saying you favor retaining the department?" the principal interrupted again. Every teacher was glaring at him in silent support of their principal. The kids had long since lost interest. They were monstrously bored, swinging their legs, making faces, wondering when it would all end, probably thinking about rushing home to play Nintendo. The campaign manager continued to stand there helplessly. And the woman continued to scribble away on her pad.

"I support education, yes, of course," Lattan said, spluttering.

"So you've changed your position since signing that pledge," the principal said sarcastically. "Now you support keeping the education department? Please, Congressman, we'd like to know what exactly your position is on this issue."

Lattan's brain was on fire. Please, Congressman, we'd like to know. Can't have headlines saying I favor nuking the department ... but flip-flopping for a hostile crowd is no good either.

Then the strangest thing — the words came out of his mouth seemingly without effort, as though his subconscious was ready to spew anything to end this ordeal.

"I support education, as I said, and I support the continued important role played by the U.S. Department of Education."

He heaved a sigh ... the interrogators seemed placated ... the reporter scribbled. God, what would tomorrow's headlines bring?

"Thank you for having me," Lattan said, flashing a weak smile, then stepping from the podium. Again, he seemed impelled to action without knowing exactly why. The principal took the stage and immediately began rattling off a list of announcements. The students began chattering, sensing they no longer needed to behave. And Lattan, already forgotten by the crowd, headed straight to the reporter to commence damage control.

"Hello, miss," he said, holding out a hand to shake, trying to smile and appear calm. "Any questions you have that I can clarify for you?"

"Uh, no," she said, rising nervously to shake hands. "I think I got everything I need."

No! Can't let her go without giving her my side! Stall her!

"So, what paper are you with?"

"Paper?" she asked incredulously. "I'm not with any paper."

Lattan was baffled. Was she taking notes for a radio broadcast? "Well, then, whom are you with? I mean, what's your affiliation?"

"Affiliation? I'm not sure I understand," she replied. "I'm a student working on my senior thesis at Boise State. It's on public speaking. I was just taking notes for my research. I hope you don't mind. My aunt is a teacher here, and she told me you were coming today. I needed to hear some public figures for my paper. I guess I should have asked you first."

"A student! Senior thesis!" Lattan said, laughing with relief. He turned to his campaign manager, now at his side. "Did you hear that? Her senior thesis. On public speaking." He laughed again.

"I heard her, sir."

"Well, that's just marvelous," Lattan said, delighted with the news.

"Don't be too hard on me," he said, winking at her.

"No sir," she said. "I'm not even using real names."

"There goes my chance for publicity," Lattan said, laughing again. "Not using real names," he said, turning again toward his campaign manager.

"I heard, sir."

"Well, I have to go. Thanks again. Sorry I didn't ask first," she said, and disappeared.

Suffused with his own aplomb, he turned again to his aide. "Damn it, find out what the hell I signed. And don't let this happen again. We might not be so lucky next time."

Chapter 2

Broiling From The French Fry Tax

Lattan left the Steve Symms Middle School in Boise feeling relieved. Though he didn't get the photo op he'd wanted, he was glad no press had shown up. Had the media been there, they would have gotten a juicy story about the Congressman who couldn't remember whether he'd staked out the courageous position of calling for elimination of the Department of Education. But since there were no camera crews to chronicle his hemming, hawing and backsliding, he'd been saved by the iron rule of political earned media: Without press coverage, the event never took place.

Lattan even allowed himself to entertain thoughts that this was a sign things in his tight race for re-election were turning in his favor. After the firestorm caused by the revelation that his top fundraiser had served time for DWI vehicular manslaughter, there was nowhere to go but up. Perhaps this was the beginning of his ascent out of the vortex.

So when his chief of staff suggested he accept an invitation to appear on "Larry King Live" to talk about potatoes, he was excited. Sure, as an obscure freshman Member from a small state, he'd not had much experience on national TV. But the recent media attention on potatoes had made him a must-guest by virtue of geography.

The recent media attention... it was all so absurd. Since the tobacco tax pact had fallen through, liberal do-gooders had been on the hunt for a new consumer product to demonize, ascribe social ills to, and, of course, tax. So now Congress was about to debate the Potato Tax, which would slap a $1 user fee on each order of french fries. A Potato Tax, its proponents claimed, would discourage over-consumption of french fries, thereby reducing health care costs. And it would hold the french fry industry liable for all of the fat Americans whose health had been imperiled from too much super-sizing.

As the man representing Idaho's 17th Congressional District, the largest potato-growing region in the country, Lattan found himself, by default, the go-to guy for opposition to the Potato Tax. He held out the hope that being seen as a nationwide stalwart for that all-American starchy vegetable, that staple of so many dinner tables, the bakeable, broilable, fryable, slatherable, versatile spud, would make voters forget about his recent problems and see him as a statesman.

So instead of the normal campaigning at the Kiwanas, Knights of Columbus, Chambers of Commerce and women's sewing circles, Lattan found himself sitting in the LKL make-up room getting his forehead powdered as his 22-year-old legislative assistant briefed him on the issue.

"Remember, the key point you want to make over and over again is that with potatoes, there is a difference between use and abuse. With tobacco, all use is abuse."

"Right," Lattan said, distracted by the hypnotic motion of the young woman buffing the bald front of his head. It was so embarrassing! A once regal mane, his hairline seemed to be receding as quickly as his favorable poll numbers. But only in the front ... now he merely had more forehead, that's all. ...

"And don't get drawn into the arguments about protecting Idaho farmers. The tobacco guys make the same points. It'll increase the perception that potatoes and tobacco are similar, when our whole message is how they're different."

"Right," Lattan said, shifting his gaze to his aide. Look at her, so self-important, so convinced of her primacy to the machinations of Congress. A 22-year-old advising him! Congressman Charles Lattan! I know the issues, young lady!

"That's fine," he snapped, a little more abruptly than he meant to. But it was enough to remind this kid who was the Congressman and who was the assistant.

"Sixty seconds, Congressman," a headsetted cameraman said, sticking his head in the make-up room. His head looked weird, craning in the doorway, disembodied from the rest of his body.

"Do you want to take these talking points?" the aide asked, rattling background papers in her hand.

"No, no, I'm fine. I know what I need to know," he said, flinching slightly as he recalled the recent trouble with remembering his position on education. Following that fiasco, his Legislative Director had finally determined after ransacking countless files that Congressman Lattan had indeed signed a letter in support of such a move. His aide had signed the Congressman's name and merely forgotten to tell him what his position was. Thank goodness no media had been at that middle school speech to document his flip-flop.

Lattan was whisked out of the make-up room and on to the set. All at once, the white-hot kleig lights blazed on, a camera crew person attached an earpiece to him, and King began his introduction.

"Tonight we look at the proposal for a Potato Tax," King told the camera, leaning forward, his suspenders stretching over his shirt. "Recent government readjustments of how we define obesity have focused new attention on how many Americans are overweight. This, despite a country seemingly obsessed with dieting, evidenced by the hundreds of diet books on the store shelves to the explosion of low-fat and fat-free products.

"Some are arguing that our national spare tire is placing a costly burden on our nation's health care system. That treatment for obesity and related illnesses, from heart attacks to cancer, is producing bills as big as super size fast food meals. Who should pay? There's a new movement to bill the producer of the foods that are making us fat. In the tradition of holding gun manufacturers and tobacco producers liable for the damage caused by their products, some say we should hold fatty food manufacturers responsible for overweight Americans."

"I'm joined tonight by Congressman Charles Lattan, Republican of Idaho, whose Congressional District includes the country's largest potato growing region. Congressman, welcome."

"Thank you, Mr. King," Lattan murmured, intimidated by the cameras and the lights, feeling his forehead begin to glisten with perspiration.

"Congressman Lattan, you've heard the statistics. Americans are fatter than ever. Why shouldn't the people who make these fattening foods pay up?"

What a leading question! This was not standard fare for Larry King! Christ, this guy was supposed to be the Class A relief pitcher of the softest of softball questions! The nerve! Thinking he can intimidate me just because I'm not used to the talkie circuit!

"Larry," Lattan began testily, "you make it sound as if the potato producers in my district are holding poor slobs at gunpoint and forcing them to inhale plate after plate of french fries. This is the problem with this proposal, and any government proposal that seeks to hold an industry of hard-working Americans responsible for the behavior of the public at large. Personal responsibility is the issue."

"I see," King said, nodding sagely. "Please continue."

Continue? Where? ... Then Lattan grabbed the first random thought that flashed through his brainpan.

"It's like Ben Franklin said, and I'm paraphrasing here, 'A man who can't mind his own belly can hardly be expected to mind anything else'."

"Ben Franklin?" King asked, bewildered. "He was a rather large gentleman himself, wasn't he, Congressman?"

Yes, he was! What was I thinking? Stupid, Charlie, stupid! Got to get out ...

"But the point is that we're responsible for our personal behavior, how many hash browns we eat, whatever, not the industry that makes the product for the public."

"I see, Congressman," King said, with a smooth confidence and booming voice inflection that signaled the unmistakable prelude to a rhetorical ambush. Lattan could spot it a mile away. But always when it was already too late.

"Using that logic, Mr. Lattan, would you say then, sir, that the tobacco companies have been unfairly targeted in the same manner, when smokers are the ones who should bear the consequences of their actions?"

Ambushed! A hell of a stretch, from discussing the salt-of-the-earth Idaho spud farmers to backing the interviewee into sounding like an apologist for the cancer stick conglomerates, but the weasel did it! How could I have not seen this coming? How could I not have realized that this is what the media do? Guilt by association! Got to get out, got to get out. ...

"There's a difference between use and abuse with potatoes," Lattan said. "Not so with tobacco."

"Please explain," King said.

"Well, with potatoes, there is some nutritional value if they are consumed in moderation. You can't say that about tobacco."

King nodded, as if placated, or satisfied he'd asked enough probing questions to look like he was a serious journalist.

"Let's go to your calls. Durham, North Carolina, you're on the air."

"Hello?"

"Go ahead, caller."

"Am I on the air?"

"Yes. Do you have a question for our guest?"

"I'm a long-time listener, first time caller. I love your show, Larry."

"Thank you, Durham. Do you have a question about the potato tax?"

"Yes, yes I do," the Durham caller said, in a voice that sounded as if it had been scorched by three packs a day for decades. "My husband is gettin' so big he can't hardly move around the house anymore. Every day, he's driving through those burger joints and eating second and third helpings of fries. And then he has mashed potatoes with ham on Sunday, and eats chips during sports on TV, and — "

"Thank you, caller," Larry said, turning toward Lattan. "Congressman, any reaction?"

Lattan thought better of saying, *yes, Larry, the American viewing public is a bunch of blithering idiots ...* But he restrained himself.

"Yes, Larry," Lattan said, clearing his throat. "I feel for this woman and the pain she and her husband must be going through. But why punish Idaho farmers for the personal choices we all make? I would suggest that the answer here is to eat a more nutritious diet—"

"But wouldn't that mean less demand for your constituents' products?" King asked.

"Uh, it, well, not if people, er ... altered .. the way they prepared potatoes, perhaps boiling them instead of frying ... " Jesus, now I'm sounding like Martha Stewart ... "Potatoes are a very nutritious food."

"But why not a tax?" King insisted. "Won't that encourage people to eat more healthfully, and raise money for health care at the same time?"

"Larry, I've seen the research on this," Lattan began, knowing he was about to inevitably make something up, but somehow helpless to stop himself, as if intoxicated on the First Law of Political Thermodynamics: If the Congressman sounds like he knows what he's taking about, no one will challenge him. "And what study after study shows is that the abuser of any product is not price sensitive. Anyone who is addicted to french fries will go to any length, even stealing, to get money to finance their habit. All a french fry tax would do is cause the vast majority of Americans who consume spuds responsibly and in moderation to reduce their potato intake."

"Interesting analysis," King said. "I'd like to see those studies."

"I'll have my staff courier them over to you tomorrow." And at that moment, Lattan knew his staff members, undoubtedly clustered around the TV in his office watching his appearance, were cringing and making notes on how to find any studies that remotely backed his assertions. But that was their job, wasn't it?

"Rochester, New York, you're on the air!"

"Hey, Larry, I wonder if your guest can spell potato, or is he as stupid as Dan —"

"Thank you, Rochester," Larry said, abruptly severing the line. "McLean, Virginia, go ahead."

"Yeah, I wondered if Congressman Lattan would be so opposed to this tax if he wasn't in such a tough re-election fight."

"Caller," Larry said, "If you don't mind my curiosity, why would someone in Virginia be following a race in Idaho?"

"Let's just say I like to follow politics."

"OK, McLean," Larry said. "Congressman, any response?"

"Let me say this," Lattan said, wondering whether it was a Democratic Congressional Campaign Committee intern or liberal interest group type on the phone. McLean, affluent area ... had to be a liberal do-gooder. "My record on opposing taxes is clear. I have never voted for a tax increase as a matter of principle." Again, he pictured his aides scrambling to check the *Congressional Record* to verify.

"Congressman Lattan, thank you for being our guest," King said, turning back toward the camera. "In our next segment, we talk to the president of the National Business Expense Form Association about increased paper costs, and what it means to you, the consumer."

"OK, we're clear," yelled a cameraman from the darkness beyond the set. The kleig lights switched to dark.

"Thanks again, Congressman," King said.

"My pleasure," Lattan replied.

"Hey, try that Viagra? I recommend it highly."

And instead of being worried about all of the specious claims he'd made on national television moments ago, the lone thought that charged through Charles Lattan's mind at that moment was ... do I look so old and wizened that I need Viagra?

Chapter 3

Special Ordering A Load Of Troubles

Had he the strength to lift it over his head, Congressman Charles Lattan would have hurled the podium, and its tangle of microphones and wires, at the empty House seats in front of him. Mere minutes into his Special Order speech against the french fry tax, the few remaining members had left the House, turning his Moment of Glory into an empty echo chamber.

Lattan had entertained visions of delivering his remarks to a rapt television audience and a House full of supporters. The freshman Republican was offering plenty of warm and fuzzy platitudes, the usual prattle about the hard-working potato farmer in Idaho. But no one was listening! The prima donnas of the press gallery were nowhere to be found.

No, they weren't interested in anything positive he had to say about his constituents. But if this had been a campaign event, they would have been ready to chronicle his impending demise. Their ears would tingle when the phrase *my distinguished opponent* left his wizened lips, knowing such words were a familiar preface to the cataloguing of a rival's incapacities. But now that he was extolling the wonders of the spud — being genteel, talking about his vision, his ideas, his love of the starchy vegetable — no one cared!

The C-SPAN cameras were rolling, sure ... but who was watching? The usual kooks and loons who called into their programs, no doubt. ... Christ, he wouldn't even have the honor of fielding viewer calls, the way he had recently on "Larry King Live." No, it was Charles Lattan alone in the House chamber, alone in front of the bored camera crew of the Cable Satellite

Public Affairs Network, talking about potatoes. ... Maybe if he mentioned kleptomania or alcoholism. ...

Then he realized ... if there were reporters around, they'd be asking, "What makes you think you can win re-election?" "How do you plan to stop the french fry tax?" "Are you still close with your top fundraiser who was convicted of DWI vehicular manslaughter?"

Why didn't they ever write a story about Congressman Lattan working 16 hour days, scrambling from hearings to votes to constituent meetings? Or Congressman Lattan jouncing between Capitol Hill and Idaho, from bridge dedication to high school civics assembly to a tour of some industrial plant? ... Putting on those silly goggles, acting interested in whatever manufacturing process they were showing. Why was his service never acknowledged?

Where was the respect for someone who surrendered any semblance of privacy or of ordinary life, who gave up his weekends to address the VFW and the Knights of Columbus? Who relinquished time with his wife and kids, who couldn't even go out to dinner on his wedding anniversary because of late votes on the floor? All to serve the public, the good people of Idaho who'd elected him ... acting on their best interests, voting his conscience ... and for what? To have them be so ungrateful for his work on their behalf? To have the world ignore his Special Order speech?

Didn't they realize how powerful he was? A Member of the greatest deliberative body in the history of civilization ... a representative of half a million people ... congressional and campaign staff, Washington and Idaho offices ... I vote on their futures! Did they realize how many people waited to meet with him every day? Did they know how many speaking invitations, party invitations, wedding invitations from campaign volunteers, he turned down every day because there were so many people competing for his time, for his ear, who wanted to sway his vote on legislation, who wanted to hear his views on the issues? They should have been honored he'd blocked time out of his schedule to do this Special Order!

But he knew it was pure folly to expect the media to treat him as royalty when there were 434 just like him doing the exact same thing. It was the Inside-the-Beltway mentality of the media. You could bet that if he was speaking at a church dinner in Idaho, people would be listening, every paper in the state would be recording his every word!

The story of Charles Lattan — it was such a great story! Obviously, the media who ignored him were just jealous, underpaid journalists envious of a modest man who'd started his own plumbing business and built it into a chain. ... A self-made man who'd promised the people he'd bring his business know-how to Congress, and who did. Envious journalists, contemptuous of anyone who captures the American dream. ...

And where were his distinguished colleagues? Out getting loaded at some reception, no doubt. ... Did Charles Lattan stand alone against the french fry tax? Oh sure, when they needed his vote, they were button-holing him, back-slapping him, *Charlie, we really need ya' on this one* ... but when he needed the favor returned — on something as banal as a Special Order speech, nothing incriminating like a recorded vote — he faced an empty House chamber!

Oh yes, if he could have lifted it, he would have heaved the podium right into the empty seats.

Lattan knew he had to remain stoic. After all, the C-SPAN cameras *were* recording this charade. So he tried to appear prim, proper, dignified. But he knew his spit-shined rigidity was an obvious facade, masking his inner anxiety. He was uncomfortable in the spotlight, even if no one was watching. Charles Lattan, the plumber turned Congressman, had always shied away from the press. But now, in a tight race with the election only weeks away, the klieg lights were scorching him. After he won, he pledged to himself, he would no longer deal with the media. That's what his otherwise worthless staff was for.

The vein in his temple pulsated. He hunched over the podium, his spare frame shriveling. Should he continue? He rolled the idea around in his cranium ... was there a point to this theater?

Of course he should! He didn't need a phalanx of well-wishers to boost his confidence, nor a retinue of staff to feed him sound bites!

He jutted his jaw and raised his long nose. He ran his hand over his snowy hair ... jeez, could've sworn there was more there just last week ... He stiffened his posture and smoothed his scarlet tie, impeccably coordinated with his crisp white shirt and regulation suit, the perfect shade of political blue. He still felt fit, was still thin and wiry, even at 59. He flashed the wooden campaign smile for the cameras. Must appear composed! I'm a Congressman! This is my Special Order!

"And so, Mr. Speaker, when we think of the potato, let us think not of soggy, greasy slivers served at fast food restaurants, but rather a power-packed food full of complex carbohydrates and fiber."

Just then, out of the corner of his eye, he caught a figure entering the House chamber. Now, in addition to himself and the Speaker slouched in the chair, there was a third person in this cavernous hall ... sort of staggering toward the well.

The unidentified figure, creased and rumpled in an ill-fitting suit, made his way to the Democrats' podium. And he had a cigarette planted between his lips! The effrontery! The impertinence! Smoking during my Special Order! The House floor was non-smoking, wasn't it? Who even knew? Lattan continued staring at this short, unkempt man, who, despite his appearance, bore the inimitable lapel pin identifying him as a member of this august body.

"Will the gennelman yeel?" the unidentified Member asked.

Christ! What do I do? ... the thoughts zinged around Lattan's skull ... who is this guy? ... he's a little tipsy, at least, maybe worse off than that ... decide! Cameras rolling! ... Hell, I'm tired of talking anyway.

"I yield to my distinguished colleague from—"

"The great sate of Kassas."

"My colleague from the great state of Kansas."

"Misser speaker, this isn't about potatoes." The cigarette continued to dangle from his lips as the Kansas member spoke. Quite a feat. "Iz about all vegables, like the corn in my sate."

Lattan was stupefied ... the guy, whose name he didn't even know, was clearly drunk. But, sober or not, he was still a Democrat opposed to the french fry tax, and an ally of Charles Lattan!

"So, we should not raise tasses on patoes, because corn could be next. You know, slippee slope. Thank you, misser Speaker, and I yeel back to the gennelman from Montana."

Montana? Lattan was instantly enraged ... Montana! You corn-eating bastard! You interrupt my Special Order, think you're being of some help, and you get my state wrong! You drunken fool! I could strangle you with these microphone wires! Would that cigarette still be in your mouth then, Mr.

Kansas? Go back to whatever trade association reception you just stumbled out of!

Lattan then realized the cameras were still rolling — on dead air! He instinctively straightened himself, clenched his jaw. Must maintain balance.

"Thank you to my distinguished colleague from the great state of Kansas," Lattan said through gritted teeth. Now what? Got to get out of here! "And Mr. Speaker," he began concluding, throwing in a few more anti-tax bromides, "I yield back the balance of my time."

Lattan finished by flashing his campaign smile, then stepped away from the podium and retreated to return to his office. Now he'd get his headlines, wouldn't he? Mr. Kansas made sure of that, the lout! Now, instead of a Special Order no one watched, those damned wire reporters were no doubt already crafting "isn't it funny a drunk Congressman made a scene on the House floor" stories, complete with the angle, "and he was so drunk he got Rep. Charles Lattan's state wrong."

Chapter 4
Fighting The Doubts

Lattan was convinced that news of his colleague's drunken interruption of his Special Order speech would be fodder for the political reporters. But this morning's papers had reported ... nothing. And that made him less worried about negative press than the only thing worse — no press!

Now he had worked himself into a dither that the media were ignoring him because they'd collectively decided his loss in November was a *fait accompli*. So he was suffering from an acute case of the doubts, and he needed to boost his flagging spirits. And what better way to do that than to fly back to Idaho and be among his constituents?

So a mere 12 hours after his speech, Lattan found himself hustling through the doors of his Pocatello Falls campaign headquarters, ready to let the sycophants engulf him.

Upon his entrance, as if on cue, the roar immediately dissipated. The Congressman had arrived. The candidate has graced us with his presence!

The receptionist first, and then the young volunteers, all looked up from their phones, their computers, their notepads, to fix their eyes on the man they were working to elect. *Hadn't they ever seen a Congressman before?* Then he remembered. It had been awhile since he'd been in the campaign office. So let them look. Let my countenance inspire them to greater effort. He nodded to everyone, smiling the campaign smile.

He turned and gamboled down the corridor toward his office. But he couldn't help pausing to examine new posters on the walls blaring "Re-Elect Congressman Lattan," complete with his smiling face. *Such a handsome,*

Congressional face. He smiled again at the silent, stolid volunteers, whose numbers grew as word of his arrival spread. *Such looks of determination on their faces! And looks of admiration!*

These moments made it all worthwhile. The endless handshaking, the forced listening, the fundraising, the 18-hour days, the speeches, the shameless vote-seeking ... this was why he sacrificed. When a plumber for rural Idaho could walk into a room and have everyone stop to gaze at him ... when a modest man could induce people he didn't even know to work for him to get him elected to national office ... when an ordinary citizen had a campaign headquarters festooned with posters bearing his handsome photo ... it made it all worthwhile.

"Good morning, how are *you*," Lattan said, suddenly emboldened by his own fulsome self-talk. He reached to shake the hand of a student volunteer. "Thank you for all of your hard work." How he loved to edify, to see the awe in their young faces.

He nodded at the others who'd stopped to watch him, then resumed his way down the corridor. He passed the fundraising office, where blue-haired old ladies cold-called Republican donors, reading a standard sales pitch printed on "Committee to Re-Elect Charles Lattan" letterhead.

Frenetic interns weaved past him, carrying reams of paper and phone messages. He passed the issues office, outreach office, coalitions office, strategy office, press office, bulletin boards of clippings and schedules, fax machines spewing papers, phones ringing, campaign staff *tap-tap-tapping* on computers. All working to get him re-elected! Oh, yes, it was well worth the sacrifice.

He arrived at his private office and rushed in to find his campaign manager and press secretary seated in front of his desk, engaged in serious conversation.

"Good morning, Alex," he said to his campaign manager. "Kentrell," he nodded to his youthful press secretary, then walked around to sit behind his desk.

"Mornin' Congressman," said the campaign manager, as if startled to see him, though Lattan was expected.

Lattan put his elbows on the edge of his desk and steepled his fingers. He smiled jauntily at his aides — *his* aides! "What's the latest?"

Alex glowered at Kentrell, then turned toward Lattan. "We've got ourselves a situation," Alex said. "Nothing major, but we need to put some attention on it."

"Let me guess," Lattan said blithely, still high from the adulation heaped on him by his volunteers. "Someone used a campaign car to pick up his dry cleaning."

"I'm afraid it's a little more serious than that," Alex said.

A pang of tension pinched Lattan's forehead. ... It was just like staff to ruin his good mood.

"Seems we didn't completely dodge the bullet from that drunk Kansas Congressman who interrupted your Special Order speech last night," Alex said tensely. He then brandished a familiar publication in front of Lattan's face. "Our sassy friends at the *Daily Political Briefing* put a snide little story in about it. I don't know how they got it, seeing that none of the wires had it. Musta' seen it on C-SPAN."

Alex continued to explain the situation, but Lattan was no longer listening. Once again he was consumed by an acute case of the doubts ... the doubts about overcoming this latest fiasco .... the doubts about his electability ... the doubts about his worth as a U.S. Congressman.

Maybe all of the pundits, all of the prognosticators, even those insolent bastards in the press, were right!

No! Must exorcise the doubts from his head! ... *I'll be damned if this story jeopardizes what I've spent so much time striving for ...* putting my interests aside to serve the public ... all this time listening to old ladies at church luncheons, surrendering my evenings and weekends for meetings and hearings and markups and parades and press calls and speeches and smiling, *always* smiling, even when I have every right to tell someone to go to hell ... I'll be damned if the years of sacrifice to keep the seat I deserve is going to be negated by some drunk Congressman spoiling my special order and some political tip sheet's story on it. ... Who could care about this? Only the effete elites in the media, who can't stand it when a working man makes good, *that's right, a plumber,* instead of some egghead from the Ivy League, is entrusted by the public to represent them in Congress. Only the media care, not the voters.

But as his aides were going over their damage control options, and though he tried to crowd the distress out of his cranium, the doubts were all but consuming him.

And so he was propelled into the rest of his mirthless campaign day with nary a twinge of enthusiasm ... affecting his campaign smile ... waving at highway medians, knocking on doors ... he tried to be enthusiastic, but he knew he was just slogging along the campaign trail ... Charles Lattan, the unfettered insurgent? Fighting for the commoners against the Washington elite? It was all so trite. But he still made his appointed rounds, blustering with a farrago of crowd-pleasing lines that drew felicitous (if hollow) applause at rallies, town hall meetings, senior centers.

Lattan tramped into his campaign office at 9:30 that evening, enervated from a long day of campaigning. He took off his shoes and put his aching feet on his desk. Poured a snifter of brandy. Clicked on the television and watched distractedly, sipping his drink.

After a few minutes of local news and the requisite mindless banter between the anchor and the weather forecaster, they moved into their political stories ... that's how bad it had be become ... he'd been bumped down below the weather ... An "Election Update" graphic, displaying a computer-generated image of his head, took form on the screen behind the anchor. He groped for the remote control to increase the volume, nearly spilling his liquor.

"A new poll of likely voters in Idaho's 17th Congressional District shows incumbent Charles Lattan slipping," the anchorwoman started. "Only days before the election, a survey of 1,000 registered voters has Democrat Rich Cooper ahead of Lattan by a margin of 47 to 36 percent.

"Less than a week ago, the race was a statistical dead heat—"

Lattan clicked off the television and rubbed his temples. He was too tired to hurl the remote control at the tube. How could those numbers be right? Most of the people he'd met on the campaign trail said they were supporting him. Were they all liars? Or was Alex merely steering him into friendly territory to boost his confidence?

He recalled his first campaign for state delegate. The party chairman had told him not to be fooled by people who say they love you, because almost everyone you meet will. Few people will be openly hostile to your face. It was much easier for people to tell you they support you than to tell you they oppose you. Spend too much time on the campaign trail, and you start believing your own press releases. Spend too much time around your staff, and you start believing you're a born leader. The adulation could be intoxicating. Debilitating, if you weren't careful.

Christ! A 59-year-old man — a Congressman! — should know better than to succumb to sycophants. But he'd so wanted to believe in the ultimate redemption from the voters that he'd begun denying reality. Lying to himself had forestalled his acceptance of the inevitable. Lights off except for his desk lamp, leaning back in his desk chair and staring at nothing, Lattan for the first time acknowledged that he could lose.

Chapter 5

Protest At Campaign Headquarters

Lattan awoke from a brandy-induced sleep to find his campaign manager, Alex Macro, standing over him, clutching a copy of the poll that had convinced Lattan it was all over. Slowly Lattan pieced together the events of the previous evening, and remembered the TV report on his falling poll numbers that had driven him to drink the bottle of cognac now laying empty on the floor.

"Charlie, get up!" Alex said.

"I must have dozed off," Lattan said, his eye catching the empty bottle beside the campaign office couch, wondering if Alex had seen it and what he thought. "What time is it?" He rubbed his eyes, tried to smooth his wrinkled shirt.

"It's a little after six. We've got to get you home to shower and change. Big day on the campaign trail."

"Why bother? If you've read the poll you've got in your hands, you know it's all over." He ran his hands over his snowy mane.

"The hell it is," Alex said. "That's the kind of talk that I, as your campaign manager, will not tolerate."

Lattan peered at his potentate through red-rimmed eyes. "How much coffee have you had?"

"Oh, only about a couple of gallons since four a.m."

"Do me a favor and get me some, would you? Then I want you to help me write a dignified concession speech."

"I'll get your coffee, Congressman, but you'll first have to agree to dispense with the gallows humor." Alex spurted out of the room, and Lattan took the opportunity to tidy himself. Then Alex returned with the coffee, scalding hot. The steam rising from the mug was thick in the rays of the early morning sun.

"Now, what's got you so geared up?" Lattan asked.

"This," Alex said, taking his copy of the poll, thick with cross-tabs, from his side, and holding it in front of his chest like a maitre d' displaying a wine list.

"What?" Lattan said, staring at the poll, unappreciative of the cruel joke. "That shows us down 11 points. That's my obituary."

"Have you read it?"

"Saw the news last night. Besides, I pay you to read polls so I don't have to."

"Right," Alex said. "Well, lucky for you, there's a question buried deep within the survey that could help us out." He flipped through the bound document. "The one they didn't report on the news, this one right here. Take a look." He handed the report to Lattan.

Lattan read the question aloud. "Do you think the media have spent enough time covering real issues affecting Idahoans, or have they focused too much on side issues? Enough time on real issues, 24%, too much on side issues, 70%, refused/don't know, 6%."

He gave his campaign manager a searching look.

"That number, 70%, is the most one-sided response in the poll," Alex said.

"So what? That doesn't change the other numbers."

"Last night I felt the same way. I looked at the poll and figured it was all over. The question on the media was just small consolation. But then I woke up and it hit me. That question tells us that people are fed up with the press. So now, we run against a new opponent. We no longer run against Rich Cooper—his favorables are too high anyway—we run against the media."

Lattan stared with disbelief. "You sound drunker than that Kansas member who interrupted my Special Order speech."

"Think about it," Alex pleaded. "Remember that old saying, 'He who sets the agenda wins?' We're reeling because we've let the press set the agenda. We've let them make the potato as evil as tobacco, and they've made you as evil as tobacco companies for opposing a tax on spuds. Well, this is our chance to seize back the agenda." He tossed the poll onto the couch, then pantomimed a frame. "Charles Lattan, underdog, victim of a media smear campaign. Charles Lattan, man of the people, fighting a tyrannical, irresponsible, pro-tax press. Charles Lattan telling voters, 'We're not going to let the media decide this election, we're going to let *you* decide this election'." He pointed his chubby finger straight at Lattan, who recoiled. "You look at this poll and see defeat. I look at it and see something that gives us a fighting chance. What do you think?"

"I think you've seen too many movies, that's what I think."

Alex sighed. "It's far-fetched. I'll acknowledge that. But what else have we got? If we continue like this, we'll be dead by November. It's only July. It could be embarrassing. I know you're not a quitter. Let's at least give it a shot. What have we got to lose?"

"Why the hell not?" Lattan asked audaciously. "In a way, it's liberating."

"Like that line from the Janis Joplin song, 'Freedom's just another word for nothin' left to lose."

"Janis who?"

"Never mind," Alex said, chuckling. "The important thing now is to regain some momentum. Let's give the troops a confidence builder. I've already taken the liberty of scheduling a pep rally here this morning for the staff and volunteers. They need to hear it from you, Charlie, that we're not going to get off track. They need to be inspired. Then, after a few words from you, we'll send them out to spend the day passing out literature at shopping malls."

"What made you so sure I would agree to your recommendations?" Lattan asked, half-angrily, but more relieved that his campaign manager was taking charge of a bad situation.

"Like you said, that's what you pay me to do, sir," Alex said, smiling.

Four floors below the campaign headquarters, the streets of downtown Pocatello Falls were virtually empty, and the stillness of the scene was more pronounced given that only a skeletal staff roamed inside. The few volunteers at the office this early began executing instructions Alex had given them the night before on the assumption they would be accepted by Lattan.

One volunteer directed others on placement of the podium, flags and banners. Another placed stacks of pamphlets and bumper stickers in plastic bags to pass out to the canvassers. Others answered the phones. Then the paid staff began filing in. An advance man, a woman from the issues office, a couple of people from finance. When everyone finished preparations, Alex commandeered the candidate to speak to the masses in the conference room. "Let's go fire up the troops," he said to Lattan, leading him toward the podium.

Lattan basked in the practiced applause of his staff and volunteers. When it subsided, he prepared to give a rousing speech designed to rouse his own forlorn spirits as much as that of his staff.

But—

... there was a noise coming from somewhere ...

It was a garbled voice. Everyone started looking around to see where it was coming from ... it was high-pitched, shrill. Shrieking, sort of. Did someone have a radio tuned to a punk rock station?

Then the shrieking became more rhythmic. The whole roomful of people was baffled. Everyone craned their necks this way and that, trying to figure out where the caterwauling was originating.

Now the shrieking had a cadence. Like a chorus of voices, shrieking in time. A chant, perhaps. Where was it coming from?

Lattan, Alex and everyone else looked around the conference room, utterly bewildered. Alex rushed to peer in the hall, which was silent, and where the shrieking seemed more distant. It reminded Lattan of that child's game, searching for a hidden object, his opponent providing clues as he walked closer to it or farther from it: *colder, colder, warmer, warmer, hotter*. Then Lattan stepped away from the podium and toward the windows at the far end of the conference room. There, the shrieking got louder, more intelligible.

Lattan looked out of the window at the street below. His eyes swelled as he gawked at the sight. His heart leapt into his throat. Perspiration spangled his forehead. "Oh, good lord!" A huge throng of people waved placards, shaking their fists in the air as they chanted in unison with a woman on a bullhorn. At the perimeter of the crowd, reporters surrounded them with microphones extended on booms, cameras rolling, recording every word and movement, itching for footage of confrontation. A few protesters were speaking into microphones, providing interviews. Several police officers stood stiffly, billy clubs ready.

Lattan figured they numbered at least a hundred, mostly women, waving signs, clogging the sidewalk, spilling into the street. He squinted to read RAISE FRENCH FRY TAXES NOW! FRY LATTAN! DEFEAT MR. POTATO HEAD! LATTAN IS A HYPOCRITE! LATTAN FAMILY VALUES = FATTER CHILDREN! NO FAT PUSHERS IN CONGRESS! PUT LATTAN OUT TO THE SPUD PASTURE! Then he realized what they were shrieking: "One-Two-Three-Four, Kick Lattan Out The Door! Five-Six-Seven-Eight, No Congressmen Who Stand For Gaining Weight!"

Lattan felt his underarms moisten. How did they get here so fast? How come no one warned us? His breath quickened. He gulped air into his parched throat. His heart fluttered. His skin grew clammy. He turned around to face the volunteers, instantly embarrassed by the absurd contrast of being besieged by protesters while red, white and blue balloons hung on the walls, yard signs were stacked on the floor, and mounds of literature bags sagged on tables. Lattan stood there helplessly. His jaw was tight, revealing an almost Nixonian underbite. Had to remain calm!

"It seems we have some visitors outside." Trying to smile his campaign smile, the carnival fun-house smile. "Everyone sit tight until we figure out what we're going to do about them." He and Alex then whisked away to his office to survey the situation from their perch.

"What are we going to do? Answer me!" Looking out the window.

"Let's take a deep breath," Alex said. "We're not in physical danger, so let's relax."

"Relax? A thousand angry potato taxers out there and you want me to relax? Every goddamn TV station in the state, and you want me to relax? Think of something!"

Chapter 6

Confronting The Protesters

Lattan paced in his office, periodically pausing to glower at the protesters chanting and gesticulating outside of his campaign headquarters four floors below. His campaign manager, Alex Macro, stood with his flabby arms folded against his chest, rifling through his mental files for the right response to the burgeoning political disaster.

"Let's relax, first of all," Macro said. "Let's take the time to come up with the right response."

"Relax?" Lattan snapped. "Are you out of your southern-fried mind? We have to do something!"

"You know, Congressman, we don't have to do anything," Macro said, attempting to be calm, though his voice was quavering. "Doing nothing is a policy, as they say. If we engage them, it'll become a bigger story."

"Not engage? Do you realize how bad that would look?" Lattan was incredulous. "They'll be all over the news, with their sound bites about how french fries are as bad as tobacco, and we need to raise potato taxes. And I'll be portrayed as the puppet of Big Potato Interests, hiding in his bunker!"

Just then, their youthful media consultant, Kentrell "Alt" DeLeet, darted into the room. A ratty tan suit hung off of his rangy frame. Perspiration-soaked blond bangs clung to his forehead. He was barking orders into a cellular phone and gesturing to whomever was on the other end of the line, as if the person could see him.

"That's right, line up the Young Republicans for the radio talk show," DeLeet said into his phone. "I want to make sure that when Charlie is on that call-in program, only *our* people get through. OK. Right. Talkatyababe." He clicked the cellular closed and jammed it into his coat pocket. "Awright, let's figure this out."

"DeLeet," Macro said with just a hint of a sneer, "'Bout time you got here."

DeLeet ignored the taunt and rushed over to the window, ignoring Lattan as if the Congressman was only incidental to this enterprise, properly being led by the cynical handlers and their associate lackeys. He peered out at the crowd with the calm detachment of a doctor assessing the prospects of a gunshot wound victim.

"Well," he said confidently, knowing the campaign manager and candidate were hanging on his every word, "we have to do something. If we let these demonstrators drive the stories, the media will report it as if these nutballs represent the average voter in Idaho. You've gotta go out there and confront them, Charlie."

"Now hold on just a sec," Macro said. "If Charlie goes out there and makes a statement, it becomes a bigger story. Let's think strategically here. What headline do we want? 'Lattan Snubs Potato Taxers', or 'Potato Taxers Fry Lattan'?"

"How about neither?" Lattan snarled, taking his eyes off of the spectacle to glare at his aides. "How could you have let this happen? Couldn't you have done something to stop it?" He stormed from the window and sat in his chair ... *Wasn't it always the aides' fault when something went wrong? Weren't they supposed to be able to control crap like this?*

Macro stood at the window with his hands on his hips, scowling at the sight below. DeLeet stood next to him, sweating and ruminating. Now Lattan got up from his chair and joined them at the window.

Without looking at either, Lattan asked faintly, "Well, gentlemen ... do I go out and try to soothe the savage beast?"

"It doesn't look like they're leaving," Macro said.

The crowd began a new chant: "IDA-HO-ANS HAVE A PLAN ... IT'S TIME TO CAN CHARLES LAT-TAN!"

DeLeet sighed. Lattan resigned himself to the inevitable.

"I guess you'll have to go and try to diffuse this," DeLeet said.

Moments later Lattan, Macro and DeLeet emerged from the building. The police bounded to the front of the crowd, making room for the triumvirate, holding the protesters at bay. The mob fell silent. The placards came down. Lattan could feel every eye on him. Reporters scurried to the front of the crowd. Clumsy camera crews followed.

Lattan cleared his throat. Put his hands in his pockets, then at his sides. Then crossed his hands behind him. Not used to working without a podium. Fuzzy microphones in his face. Police having to exert more force restraining reporters than protesters.

"I want to thank everyone for coming out here today." He kicked himself for going on campaign rally autopilot. Crowd silent. "I'm glad you're here, because it gives me the opportunity to clear up this matter."

"No deep fryers in Congress!" A female shriek from the back.

"Yes, well, I agree," Lattan said, holding his hands straight up with his palms out. "Ladies and gentlemen, I believe this issue has gotten seriously distorted by the media. We're all interested in health issues—"

"Tax french fries now!" Another shriek from the back. "Make the fat industry pay!"

"Well, let me get to that. I understand your concerns about health issues, about the possible abuse of potatoes. But you have to understand the difference between moderate, responsible use of potatoes as part of a nutritious diet, and the abuse of potatoes—"

"Hey, Charlie, do you let your kids eat french fries?" yelled a male heckler. Laughter from the audience.

"What would you do if your wife didn't make you mashed potatoes because she was on a diet?" A female scream from far back.

"Now hold on a minute," Lattan said, trying to regain control of the unruly crowd. He squinted into the bright midday sun. Cameras documenting everything. "Potatoes are a healthy food, an integral part of this state's economy—"

A chorus of boos drowned him out. His mind reeled. His brain was inflamed with visions of defeat. ... *What would I do?* I've been in public office for twenty years! I'm not about to take a pay cut and go back to unclogging drains! Or living in this two-bit state! With its militia kooks on the right and potato tax kooks on the left! ... I like Washington! Fancy receptions! Georgetown cocktail parties! Capitol Hill bars! *Washingtonian* best restaurants! Playing golf with lobbyists! I'm not afraid to admit it ... to myself, at least! *I have Potomac Fever!*

"Let me finish, please! Fellow Idahoans — I've listened to you, now please listen to me!"

More boos, louder and more intense. Lattan's pulse roared in his ears. The insanity of these people! Whoever heard of protesting *for* higher taxes! He shuddered. His heart felt as though it could flee from his chest at any moment. Defeatist thoughts careened in his head. I can't be a private citizen! I'm an elected official! A public servant! Legislator! Lawmaker!

"But please ... fellow Idahoans ... "

The crowd was clamoring now, shouting incoherently. ... At least they weren't chanting, at least no one could understand their jeering. ...

The next few moments were a fog, a total haze ... an eruption of activity ... jostling ... soggy french fries bouncing off him ... people caroming off of him ... Christ, they were pelting him with french fries! ... a policeman's badge catching the sun's glint ... *please, Congressman, let us escort you back inside for your own safety* ... arms and legs intertwining everywhere ... the crowd ... reporters scribbling furiously ... Alex Macro shouting to Kentrell "Alt" DeLeet ... DeLeet shouting something back, then shouting into his cellular phone. ...

The next thing he knew he was lying down on the couch in his office ... his wife, Ariel, standing over him ... looking at him as if he were a sick child ... then she turned toward Macro ... he heard her words, and he knew he was finished for the day: *better cancel his two o'clock at the veterans group* ... dare he admit it to himself? He was actually relieved. No more campaigning for the near future.

Then it hit him like an anvil. ... That tireless Rich Cooper, damn him ... he's undoubtedly out there shaking hands somewhere, or waving from a highway median strip, or holding a press conference, or knocking on doors, or speaking to a women's sewing circle, or addressing guys wearing funny lodge hats ... can't lose any ground! Gotta get up — gotta get back on the campaign trail!

Chapter 7

Dreaming Of A Press Conference

Lattan, winded and woozy from his confrontation with the angry mob, stretched out flaccidly on his campaign office couch. His attempts to muster the strength to get up and continue with the rest of his schedule seemed futile. The melee with the pro-french fry tax protesters had left him enervated. He sank into the creamy cushions of the sofa, his limbs as heavy as steel beams. His head throbbed like a speaker on a nightclub dance floor. Soon he was fading in and out of consciousness, into that strange blurry half-sleep that precedes dreaming ... he tried to rally his strength ... *got to snap out of it, Charlie, got to get up, get back out to talk to voters* ... but then his eyelids became so heavy ... maybe just a little power nap. ...

He could hear his campaign manager, Alex Macro, and his media consultant, Kentrell "Alt" DeLeet, caucusing about what to do, trying to choreograph the next move, while his wife, Ariel, beseeched them to let her haggard husband rest. ... So sleepy ...

Then he drifted away ... into a deep slumber ... or so he thought ...

Suddenly Lattan found himself standing outside of the main room of the National Press Club in downtown Washington, tugging at his suit coat. Brooks Brothers, navy pinstripe, the consummate shade of Republican blue. He smoothed his tie, also Brooks Brothers, flaming red. Both were set against a rigid white pinpoint oxford shirt. He ran his hand over his white hair. Busying himself, trying to appear unruffled, while he figured out why he was here.

Next to him were Macro and DeLeet, standing at either side like sentries.

They fidgeted, jangled change in their pockets. Lattan craned his head inside the doorway to survey the scene. Inside the room, video crews lined up their stands in the back, cameras facing the podium like firing squad rifles aimed at a man sentenced to death. Reporters seated themselves, note pads open, pens and mini-cassette tape recorders ready.

"How do you feel?" Macro asked.

"Fine," Lattan answered mechanically.

"Just read the statement, then take Q&A," Macro said. "Only a few questions—enough to make it seem like we're being open and forthcoming. Give 'em terse answers, then smile and wave and exit." Macro tugged at left ear, as if a baseball manager signaling a play.

Lattan again ran his hand over his snowy, thinning hair, then again smoothed his tie. He felt like a skydiver about to leap from an airplane.

With a full head of steam, Lattan walked in swiftly, straight to a podium laced with microphone wires. Man on a mission for personal redemption. Macro and DeLeet crept in behind him.

The reporters' buzz stopped at once. The white hot lights of the cameras blazed on. All eyes focused on Lattan. His two handlers stood along the wall, out of camera range.

"Good evening," Lattan said, his hands gripping the edge of the podium. "I appreciate your coming tonight. I would like to say a few words first, then I will be happy to take any questions you may have."

He cleared his throat, then retrieved a script prepared by Macro from his jacket pocket and unfolded it on the podium.

"Ladies and gentlemen, I stand before you tonight as a man troubled by the course of events in the 17th district congressional campaign," Lattan began, reading from the script. "I have dedicated my life to public service, working for the people of Idaho to create jobs, control taxes, promote traditional values and keep our streets safe. I chose public life because I believe it is one of the highest callings in a democratic society."

"I have always tried to be a model citizen. I have conducted my personal and professional affairs with the utmost integrity. Not only because I believe in adhering to high standards of personal conduct, and being the best father and husband I can be. But also because I believe that, as a duly elected official entrusted with representing the interests of my constituents, I have an obligation to comport myself in a manner that ensures I never transgress the social contract into which I have entered with others. I believe Charles Lattan the man and Charles Lattan the politician are inseparable."

"My friends, I subscribe to the belief that public officials have to avoid placing themselves in situations where even a perceived lack of judgment could be an issue. Personal responsibility, especially on the part of public officials, is a hallmark of a free society. We cannot achieve our goals without it. Public officials must set an example for moral conduct ... they must be above reproach."

"Yet, at the same time, I believe that all of us, public servants and private citizens, are but mere mortals, with human frailties and shortcomings. There is no magical state of virtue we achieve when we are sworn in as Members of Congress. We try our best, use our best judgment, to do what is best for our constituents, our states and our country as a whole. But we are people, with the same qualities and imperfections as the school teacher, or the truck driver, or the grocer. We are every bit as capable of rising to meet great challenges, and occasionally failing to meet those challenges, as everyone else in our great country. That's the beauty of democracy. Government of, by, and for the people — not by mythic beings possessed of superhuman strength."

"Ladies and gentlemen of the press, it is not my purpose tonight to provide a rebuttal to those who favor the french fry tax, or to respond to what is an obvious pro-french fry tax bias in your publications and on your programs. No, my friends, I stand before you tonight to say I believe the people of Idaho deserve better. A frank and fair discussion of the issues affecting their lives."

"I ask tonight that my friends in Idaho, who have elected me to represent them, look about my record of service. Think about who has worked for you to keep your taxes low, promote traditional values, and control the scope of government intervention in your lives. Because, my friends, these issues are too important to Idaho's future, and the country's future, to allow a french fry tax to obfuscate them. Thank you, and I have time for a few questions." He folded up the script and returned it to his jacket pocket.

The room instantly erupted with a cacophony of reporters' questions. Lattan took a deep breath, steeling himself for the hard part of the press conference — the one he couldn't script.

"Congressman, what is your reaction to the latest polling figures showing you down 11 points —"

"—why not tax french fries—"

"—how do you feel—"

"—you've said you haven't done anything wrong, so why this conference—"

"—what will you do if you lose—"

"—how does all of this make you *feel*—"

"—I have a follow-up—"

Lattan's confidence evaporated like tides receding from a hot sandy beach in an undertow. He was thunderstruck ... where were the plaudits for bearing his soul to this packed room? He began hunching over the podium, felt his face flush. The vein in his temple pulsed.

The supplications continued ...

"—how do you respond to charges that—"

"—how do you really *feel*—"

"—and I have a follow up—"

He continued to hunch over the podium; his posture was now more of an old man's stoop, as if he was ducking from incoming tomatoes. He gripped the sides of the podium, his knuckles turning white, his fingernails scraping the woodgrain. He felt powerless. He attempted to loosen his facial muscles, an effort that seemed to drain the last of his strength. ...

Lattan barely flashed the political smile, then waved an arm over his head.

"Thank you, thank you all for coming. That's all I have time for tonight. Thank you."

He turned from the audience, looked at his aides, and then hurtled out the back door—

Then everything went black —

And he was staring into the faces of Alex and Kentrell. Only it wasn't at the Press Club ... they were looking down on him ... he was lying down ... in his office ... in Idaho ... what the hell had happened?

"Charlie! Charlie! It's OK! It's a dream! Charlie!"

Lattan could smell Macro's foul coffee breath as the campaign manager gripped his shoulders and shook him.

"Where ... what ... reporters ... where'd all the reporters go?"

"Reporters?" Macro asked, his face contorted in confusion. He looked bemusedly at DeLeet, then back at Lattan. "You were sleeping. You've been asleep almost six hours. It's almost ten p.m. We're the only three people in the building. There are no reporters!"

"Reporters! Asking me all these questions—"

"A dream, Charlie, just a bad dream."

"But it seemed so real," Lattan said. "I was at the National Press Club, and I was holding a press conference to address something, and the reporters were having nothing of it, and they were attacking me, and—"

DeLeet smirked. "No more Kafka for you, Congressman."

A dream, only a dream ... Lattan repeated the words to himself ... and as it dawned on him that it was only that, he felt relieved for the first time in weeks ...

Until he realized he was acting like a child who'd had a nightmare, and his campaign aides were roll-playing the reassuring parents.

"Only a dream. Right," Lattan said, standing and running his hands through his hair, trying to regain composure. "Right. So."

"Let's get you home to pack," Macro said.

Lattan was baffled. "Pack? For what?"

"You're on the next flight back to DC. You're a Congressman, remember? Votes? Speeches? And most important—Political Action Committee donations! The french fry industry reception is coming up, and you're their guest of honor!"

Chapter 8

Reception Is Reality

Lattan tried to stanch his trepidation with positive affirmations—*be cool, relax, everything's fine, you're in control* — but nothing was helping. Here it was, less than three hours before the annual Federated Association of Taters (FAT) congressional reception, and his entire House staff was in a panic over the expected attendance. Never mind that Lattan, as the guest of honor, was supposed to enjoy the luxury of being free of such concerns. Or that it was the FAT government relations staff who was responsible for populating this event with bodies. Oh no ... who was responsible, whose division it was, *not my department* ... none of that mattered. All that mattered was that Lattan had reviewed the list of RSVPs moments ago and had worked himself into a dither when he learned that confirmed attendees numbered fewer than a dozen.

So now, shortly after three, Lattan sat and stewed behind his desk in his fifth-floor Cannon office while his staff scurried around in a last-minute effort to pack the reception in the Rayburn Foyer, the Hill equivalent of a swanky hotel ballroom. If an industry seeking influence was going through the hassle and expense of orchestrating an event to lure Members of Congress, it was the Rayburn Foyer or nothing. An event there, replete with tuxedo-clad bartenders serving premium distilled spirits and white-hatted chefs cooking up delicacies in portable fryers, could mean the difference between earning 10 minutes with the Member to pitch the industry spiel, or merely five with an overworked aide dreaming up excuses to swing back to the free buffet. Members intuitively accorded the status of Serious Lobbying Organization to those groups who hosted Rayburn Foyer receptions, far above the rank awarded unions and interest groups offering rail liquor in obscure committee rooms converted after hours by spreading vinyl covers over witness tables.

The Rayburn Foyer boasted steps down to its sunken entertaining area, soaring ceilings, floor-to-the-sky windows and plush red carpet — the perfect environment for trade association receptions, the raw currency of lobbying. Sure, they had tightened the ethics laws in 1996 to prohibit gifts and forbid the wining and dining of House Members and staff. But the reception was sacrosanct. How else were the hundreds of different associations in Washington, representing every imaginable business interest, supposed to get the attention of lawmakers in positions to affect the rules by which their industries engaged in commerce?

The trade association was a uniquely Washington by-product, a cottage industry of the federal government. Every industry, from the french fry industry to the business expense form industry — any business that provided a product or service to the public — had its own association representing it in the capital. Sure, individual companies battled each other for the consumer's dollar. But when they were faced with an issue that threatened their collective bottom lines — such as the proposed french fry tax — they dropped their weapons to unite for the common good. Hence the Federated Association of Taters, the trade association of the potato industry, the cartel that existed for the express purpose of trying to convince Congress to give its members a break.

Time was when the trade association — populated with former Hill staff who, having chucked public service for shorter hours, longer pay and expense accounts — would take Members to lunch to discuss why the french fry tax would hurt industry, drive up consumer prices and destroy jobs at fast food franchises in their states. One boozy lunch at a chic restaurant could do more to sway a Congressman's vote on an issue than thousands of constituent letters.

But when concern about influence peddling began to register in public opinion polls, the House banned *quid pro quo* dining. Fortunately for the associations, the reception remained unaffected, governed only by considerations that it be a "widely attended" event remotely connected to legislation pending before Congress.

The Federated Association of Taters reception certainly met that criterion. Every year, FAT put on its party to showcase its products, ply Members and staff with free drinks and hors d'oevres, and talk about the issues. This year's fete couldn't have come at a more critical time. Even in an election year, when Congress' most prodigal taxers would bridle their passions to spend other people's money, the french fry tax hovered over the potato industry like a sumo wrestler ready to pounce. FAT had to get its message to the lawmakers who had the power to control its companies' profit margins.

But FAT's event planners had flubbed it! Either they hadn't mailed the invitations on time, or the interns hadn't followed up with phone calls, or everyone assumed people would attend, based on previous success. So, upon arriving back in Washington, guest-of-honor Lattan had asked to see the list of attendees ... and ... he couldn't believe it! A dozen RSVPs for a gala in the cavernous Rayburn Foyer? With its soaring ceilings and squishy red carpet? FAT's ice sculptures, fully stocked bars, potato fryers, and washtub-sized bowls of every conceivable salty spud mutation gracing the linen-cloaked tables. ... It couldn't go to waste! There had to be a packed house on hand to watch Congressman Charles Lattan receive the Spudman of the Year Award!

Lattan was incredulous. Who was responsible for this impending calamity? Recriminations could be handed out later. But now every staff member had better scour her Rolodex and wangle some bodies for this event!

Lattan's DC chief of staff, Rachel Emmell, had been on the phone with the FAT folks all day in an effort to round up some bodies. ... She'd been yelling "six RSVPs from everyone" over and over to Lattan's staff, urging them to call every friend in town with the offer of free booze and french fries. Everyone assured her there would be a crowd. So shortly before six, Lattan and Emmell walked over to Rayburn for his big honorific.

"How many does that give us?" Emmell screamed into her cellular phone as the two made their way through the tunnels under the Longworth Building. "No, I don't care who, just how many ... are the girls there? And the ice sculpture? How about the bartenders?"

The girls ... Lattan recalled them from last year's FAT reception: bikini-clad coquettes, so thin they couldn't possibly be chip eaters, posing like beauty pageant contestants in front of the food tables, enticing paunchy Congressmen to inhale fistful upon fistful of snacks, the implied message being, "I'm hawking these delicious chips, and look at me! Not an ounce of fat on this figure! So you don't have to worry, big boy!" Capitol Hill, the epicenter of lawmaking for civilized society, also serving as the final, shameless bastion where elected officials and corporate front groups could still perpetuate such political incorrectness.

"Well, looks like we're making progress," Emmell said, clicking off her phone and turning toward Lattan. "Christ, we've done more to get people there than their whole event planning staff!"

Up the elevator, around the corner, faster, faster ... Emmell's heels were clicking and echoing on the hallway floor as she raced toward the reception. Lattan was a step behind ... always let the staff blaze the trail for your entrance ... and suddenly they were upon a packed crowd.

"Congressman, how are you?" beamed the FAT president, Flip Screen, shaking Lattan's hand as he stepped into the foyer. The hired photogs flashed away for the stock newsletter pictures. Lattan was introduced to about a half-dozen FAT board members, smiling away, remembering none of their names. He pretended to listen to a paunchy fast-food entrepreneur from Texas, but focused on the bodies filling the foyer. It was actually getting crowded! Members of Congress, whose schedulers had failed to RSVP, stood at the various troughs of chips, stuffing themselves the way they stuffed legislation with pork barrel projects.

Others stood in line at the custom potato bar, where chefs cooked up french fries, cottage fries, home fries, hash browns, mashed potatoes and steak fries to order. Still others, apparently having forgotten "Member of Congress" lapel pins were shining on their jackets, swigged booze and hit on the chip girls. Lattan felt sorry for the poor lasses, who endured it with fake smiles sewn on their faces, trying to disguise thoughts of "Is it worth a hundred bucks to spend two hours fending off fat slobs drunk on free swill *and* power?"

Congressional staff and interns, always eager to supplement their meager salaries with free food, hung over the giant plastic bowls, scooping piles of chips into their mouths between sips of their drinks. And the FAT lobbyists, charged with using this gathering to proselytize against federal excise taxes on potatoes, dutifully cornered every identifiable elected official to give each a good browbeating. Members of Congress, accustomed to this used-car salesmanship, nodded thoughtfully and pretended to listen, remembering who was slaking their thirst and filling their expansive guts with complementary samples of the industry's fine products.

"Congressman Lattan, I'd like you to meet our chairman," said Screen. Beside him stood a tall, gaunt man with sunken cheeks, mid-sixties, wearing a grey worsted wool suit, a starched white tab-collar shirt and a striped repp tie. "John Tucancel, this is Congressman Charles Lattan, recipient of this year's Spudman award."

"A pleasure, Congressman," he said, shaking hands.

"The pleasure is mine," Lattan said. God, how he hated this interminable small talk.

Tucancel, his thumb and forefinger cupped around his chin, nodded as he gazed at the Rayburn Foyer environs. "Lovely room."

"Yes. We like it," Lattan said sophomorically.

"Well, shall we?" Tucancel said. He signaled to an aide, who produced a box. All eyes were on the aide as he ripped open the top, reached in to a sea of styrofoam peanuts, and then retrieved a giant brass bauble in the shape of a potato. Lattan's name was etched on a small plaque affixed to the front, with the words "1998 Spudman Of The Year" embossed below it.

"May I have everyone's attention, please?" Tucancel asked. The photogs fell in formation, creating a semi-circle around Tucancel and Lattan. But no one else seemed to realize the gravity of the impending ceremony. The crowd continued to eat and drink and roar away with their conversations.

Emmell pulled a few folks aside to watch the proceedings, but it was clear there was no way, short of using a bullhorn, that this crowd's attention could be had. When there were enough bodies fill in for photo background, Screen nodded to Tucancel.

Lattan was livid. Was it too much to ask for a minute of attention in return for such a lavish spread? But the crowds continued to mob the bars, staff circled the tables of chips, people had to push to get anywhere ... the curtains were flecked with chip crumbs, splashed with dip and spotted with grease. And the noise! Lattan couldn't even hear himself receiving an award!

Tucancel, obviously resigned to the sad fact that the crowd was not to be corralled, proceeded with the ceremony. He said some obligatory remarks about Lattan's hard work on the issue, nodded and smiled for the cameras, handed the award to Lattan, and that was the end of it.

Lattan held the brass chip and smiled. A few more flashes went off. A few people shook his hand and thanked him, and then they disappeared toward the bar. Lattan was left standing with the award, his chief of staff the only person still in his vicinity.

"OK, Charlie, let's get out of here," Emmell said, turning and walking toward the steps. Lattan paused for a moment, as if hoping for a spontaneous display of approbation from the crowd. When it became clear that wasn't going to happen, he reluctantly followed.

No appreciation ... no respect ... the thoughts swirled around in his head ... chips crunched under his feet as he tried to make his way out.

Chapter 9

Focus Group Fiasco

The next morning, Lattan sat and fumed as a Washington Ledger story lay on the desk in front of him. He had a good mind to drive down to their office and give them a lecture. The nerve! Reporting his humiliating award ceremony! Those smart-alecks in the media, scoffing at everything ...

"I really think we ought to pay them a visit," Lattan said to his chief of staff, Rachel Emmell, who sat beside him, trying to calm him down.

"What good would that do?" Emmell said. "If anything, it would antagonize them more."

He knew she was probably right ... those scoundrels in the press! But still! "Is it too much to ask that they treat us with respect, if not for the man, than for the office?"

"Come on, Charlie," Emmell said. "You've been in politics long enough to know the media are a bunch of sourpusses angry that they have to report on other people's lives rather than enjoy their own."

Lattan reflected on that for a moment. She had a point. But everyone reads the *Ledger*! People all over the Hill are probably snickering right now!

"But don't you think this can affect people's perceptions of me? Every reporter, pundit, pollster, consultant—"

"But no one whose vote you need," Emmell said. "I mean, come on, Charlie. No one in Idaho reads the Washington press. You should be more worried about things like Rich Cooper's fundraising numbers."

Lattan twitched with panic. Had he lost so much perspective that he could no longer tell what was important in the campaign?

"Maybe you're right," he muttered, hating to concede the point.

"Please, Charlie. Journalists are the only people viewed with less esteem than politicians, and it's because they focus on this kind of stuff. Journalists are bitter people to begin with. They don't make much money, they hear complaints from both sides in stories all the time, each accusing them of being biased in favor of the other, and no one ever pats them on the back when they actually do a good job. No wonder they're so cynical, no wonder they sneer through every headline and story they write. Let's not give them another reason to pick on us."

Lattan nodded. Suddenly a trip to the Ledger seemed like the most idiotic idea he'd ever entertained.

"You're right. We'll forget it," he said, smirking. "OK, what's next on the agenda?"

Emmell riffled through a stack of papers on her lap until she located the one she needed. "Well, since we're done with this Congressional session and we're now officially in recess, Macro's taken over your schedule. From here on in, you'll be campaigning in Idaho."

"Recess. Thank God!"

"But remember to refer to it as a 'district work period.'"

"Right. Of course. District work period. So what am I *working* on first?" he winked.

"According to Macro's e-mail I printed out, you're going to a focus group. Tomorrow at two in Boise."

"Focus group? Why? On what?"

"To see how the average voter feels about the french fry tax."

Lattan was stupefied. Of course the average voter supported him — didn't they? Then he remembered those damned protesters ... and the falling poll numbers ... maybe a focus group wasn't a bad idea after all.

So the next afternoon, Lattan found himself sitting next to his campaign manager on folding chairs behind a one-way window in the Boise headquarters of their pollster, Ward Purfict. They watched in silence as Purfict instructed six carefully selected Idahoans on what was going to happen.

"This is what we call a voter focus group," Purfict said, sitting at the head of a metal table with three people on each side. The room was small and rectangular, resembling a police interrogation room. The six likely Idaho voters sat and listened as Purfict delivered his standard pitch. He looked up from his notes occasionally, peering through thick Coke-bottle glasses to make sure everyone understood.

"There are no right or wrong answers here," Purfict said. "We want you to be completely honest, and tell us exactly what you think about the issues we discuss. This won't take more than an hour, and you'll each receive checks for $150 on the way out. Any questions?"

"Yeah, I got one," said an immense man in a Seattle Mariners baseball cap, twirling the end of his handlebar mustache. "Who's payin' for this? Who wants to know what we think?"

"I'm not at liberty to disclose my client," Purfict said, making eye contact one at a time with all three women, then all three men. "Besides, if I told you, it could bias your answers. We're looking for your honest feelings. Don't worry about who wants to know. Just realize that sharing your heartfelt feelings on the issues facing Idaho and the country today is the most important thing. OK, let's begin."

Lattan leaned back in his chair, arms folded on his chest. Now this seemed like a complete waste of time ... and money! As if these idiots had enough brain cells to vote intelligently!

"I don't know what you hope to get out of this," he said, without looking at Macro.

"The media have blown everything out of proportion, right?" Macro said, looking at his boss, who continued to stare through the window. "Reporters and professional opinion-givers are the only ones who want a french fry tax, right? The voters don't want it, right? Well, this is our chance to confirm our hunches." Macro held out his arm toward the window. "Here's our chance to see if we're running on the correct issue, or if we'd do better by trying something else."

Lattan nodded absently. Macro returned his stare to the group on the other side of the glass.

"What do you think are some of the major issues facing our country today?" Purfict asked.

"High taxes," said the fat man with the mustache. "They're a disgrace, is what they are."

"Affordable health care?" a slight middle-aged woman said, as if seeking approval for being concerned about the topic.

"The degradation of the institution of the presidency," said a swarthy man in a ratty tweed jacket.

Purfict continued along this line for 10 minutes, being as general as possible to disguise the specificity of his client. But he could tell everyone in the group was looking for clues. He worked from general questions on Washington calumny, then to the Idaho House race.

"About time," Lattan said testily. "How much are we paying for this?"

"Listen, this is what we've been waiting for," Macro said without looking at his boss.

"Has everyone been following the Congressional race between Charles Lattan and Rich Cooper?" Purfict asked. Six nods.

"And if the election were held today, do you mind telling us whom you would support?"

The three men said Lattan, the three women said Cooper.

Lattan glared at Macro, as if to say, *I'm waiting to hear something I don't already know*. Macro's eyes remained focused straight ahead.

"Going back to some of the issues you brought up earlier, which of those issues do you think are the most important in that race?" Purfict asked. "Or are there *other* issues that are important there?" Purfict had told Lattan and Macro it was best not to raise the potato tax issue, but see if the voters brought it up. That was the only way to gauge whether the average Idahoan cared about it.

"The representative we elect has to take the lead in reforming Social Security," said the man in the tweed jacket.

"Prescription drug prices for seniors," said the baseball fan. "My pop can't pay for his blood pressure medicine with his pension."

"I'm concerned about Charles Lattan's policy toward the French," said a young woman, possibly a college student, who had been quiet until then. Lattan tensed at her response.

"You mean Mr. Lattan's policy on french *fries*?" Purfict tried to clarify.

"French fries? What do french fries have to do with anything?" the woman said dismissively. "I want to know why Congressman Lattan thinks our French policy is more important than what's going on here at home. I don't care about the French. I care about the Americans!"

Purfict stared at the mirror for a moment, then back at the young woman. "Uh, you must be referring to Congressman Lattan's policy toward ... french *fries* ... not the French, or, er, the country of France. As far as I know, he has not made foreign relations with France, or any other country, an issue in this campaign."

"You mean he isn't sending our tax money to France?"

"No."

"Well, I'm still not voting for him. It still sounds to me like Lattan isn't taking care of business at home."

Macro shut his eyes and slapped his forehead. Lattan rubbed his temples, sighing. Had his campaign possessed the cash on hand to pay for the damages, he would have flung his chair through the window.

Chapter 10

Stay On Message

Lattan sighed and sank into the creamy cushions of his high-back leather chair. His suit jacket bunched around his shoulders. His flaming red tie was twisted backwards, revealing where the narrow end tucked into the wide end. His white shirt was already creased for the day. His bad combover had fallen from atop his balding pate and hung limply on the side of his head.

Behind him, white curtains covered a floor-to-ceiling window, flanked on its sides by the American flag and the Idaho flag. Teak bookcases, full of thick, leather-bound U.S. Codes Lattan had never read, stood next to each flag. Framed pictures and plaques — photos of the Congressman with the governor, awards presented by various potato interest groups for votes in their favor — covered the walls of his Pocatello Falls district office.

Lattan's media advisor, Kentrell "Alt" DeLeet, sat on a leather wing chair across from his boss, *click-click, click-click, click-clicking* his pen. He stared at Lattan, waiting for a response.

Lattan was wary of talking to the reporter DeLeet had placed on hold moments before. Sure, after the focus group fiasco, he wanted a new issue to campaign on besides the french fry tax. And now he had one. But did he really want to talk to the press about the president's scheduled testimony to the Ken Starr Grand Jury?

"Run it by me again," Lattan said to DeLeet, like a felon squaring his alibi with an accomplice. He pursed his lips, trying to disguise his eroding patience.

"Stay on our message, no matter what he asks." DeLeet leaned forward, gesticulating with his pen. "You don't have to speculate about the president's sex life, just take the moral high ground and say these proceedings are damaging the institution of the presidency. It's not, 'We don't believe in the Independent Counsel's investigation,' but the real question is, 'Do we want to drag the country through this mess'?"

Lattan was incredulous at this advice. "You make it sound like it's *our* fault that crooked bastard couldn't keep his hands off his interns! I can't understand why I can't score any political points by attacking the scoundrel!"

DeLeet sighed. "You've seen the polls. The public doesn't care about it. As long as the economy's cooking, as long as people have their 401ks and their sport utes, nobody cares. So we don't use it as an issue. Got it?"

"OK," Lattan nodded, his forehead wrinkled. "I got it. Put him on."

DeLeet reached forward and pressed the speaker button on Lattan's desk phone. A reporter from the *Idaho Informer* waited patiently on the line.

"Sorry to keep you on hold for so long," DeLeet said. "I know you're on deadline. The Congressman's just getting out of his meeting. He'll be right with you." DeLeet signaled thumbs up to Lattan.

Lattan leaned forward to turn up the volume. He smiled, hoping his facial expression would debouch in his voice. "I apologize for keeping you on hold for so long. Thank you for being so understanding," he said, his voice husky from the months of campaigning. "What can I do for you?"

"As I explained to your aide, we're doing a story on what candidates in the congressional race think about the president testifying in the Monica Lewinsky case," the reporter said, his voice disembodied through the speaker. "Tell me, Congressman Lattan, what is your reaction to the president testifying?"

Lattan grimaced. "Well, that's an excellent question, and I'm pleased I have the opportunity to address it." He hunched over the phone. "It's a relevant question, and it's a critical issue ..." Lattan winced at his own sputtering, as if bracing himself for a crash and burn.

DeLeet yanked a legal pad from under the stack of papers on his lap, spilling the pile on the floor. He scribbled WAIT FOR RESULTS OF DNA TEST in huge letters, ripped off the page and stepped over the mess. He held the paper in front of Lattan, who grabbed it. Man overboard reaching for a life preserver.

"Well, I think we should wait for results of the FDA test," Lattan said, eyes surveying the sheet, placing it on the desk. "Until the lab results are conclusive, I really can't say—"

"You mean DNA, Congressman?"

"That's what I said."

"You said FDA, as in Food and Drug Administration."

"The hell I did!"

"Sir, with all due respect—"

"Now listen here, I know what I said—"

"Why don't we move on to the next question?" DeLeet said into the speakerphone, his voice rising a few octaves.

"OK by me," came the reporter's response. "Congressman, could I get your opinion on all of the buzz about whether the president should do a *mea culpa*?"

Lattan grimaced again. He rubbed his temples. "A what?"

"A *mea culpa*. A lot of people, even some of his advisers, are saying he should do a *mea culpa*. Your reaction?"

DeLeet scrawled HE SHOULD TELL THE TRUTH on another sheet. Again, he tore the page from the pad. He placed it in front of the Congressman, on top of the first sheet.

Lattan looked at the cue card but couldn't focus on the letters. What was a *me gulpa*? French? Spanish? Why couldn't this whippersnapper speak English?!

"Ah, well, I, uh, don't know anything about that, I mean, I don't make it my business to be dispensing advice to the president, so, but, I think —" ... then, in desperation, he looked at the cheat sheet ... "—I just think the important thing is for the president to tell the truth."

"Got it," the reporter said. "Thanks for your time, Congressman." Then the speakerphone clicked off and the interview was over.

But Lattan knew he'd blundered again. The pained look on DeLeet's face, the silence of his media adviser, said it all ... God, when would this ordeal end? Why was it always so difficult?

Just when he permitted himself to entertain visions of a raucous election night re-election party, he would backslide, appearing as the dullard everyone suspected he was. He knew he wasn't an inspiring orator, a revolutionary thinker, or a visionary. He was a back-slapper, a schmoozer.

Compensated for his lack of Ivy League erudition with a bond to the common man other politicians could only fake. But he *was* a common man! What else could an ex-plumber be?

"I think that went well," DeLeet finally said. "The only line that matters is the one about saying the president ought to tell the truth. That's what you'll get quoted on. Don't worry about that *mea culpa* stuff. That's all DC political jargon. No one in Idaho talks like that, except for reporters who aren't from the state."

"Right. Thanks," Lattan said, wondering whether DeLeet was being honest or spinning to try to make him feel better. He handed the stack of yellow sheets back to his aide.

Then suddenly the intercom beeped. "Some woman from a radio station is on line three," the receptionist said.

Lattan looked at DeLeet, who nodded. He punched the speakerphone button. "This is Congressman Lattan."

"Who?" A smooth, mellow, cigarette-cured, seductive radio voice.

"Congressman Charles J. Lattan! *May I help you?*" Annoyed.

"This is Paige Downe from KSTR in Pocatello. I was trying to reach the Congressman for an interview."

"Well, you got him!"

"Oh! A pleasure to talk to you, Congressman."

"What can I do for you?"

"I'm doing a story on the Clinton testimony for our noon update, and then I want to run it several times today on our top-of-the-hour report. May I run some tape during our interview?" Downe asked, in a phony radio talk show host tone.

Again, Lattan looked at DeLeet, who nodded. "Fine."

Lattan heard some clicking and clunking and switching on the other end, then: "OK, ready?"

"Go ahead."

"I just interviewed Rich Cooper, who criticized the Republican party, and you in particular, accusing your party of a witch hunt to get the president at a time when we should unite as a nation to find the terrorists who bombed the U.S. embassies in Africa. Your response?"

"Accused me of a witch hunt, did he?" Lattan snarled. He ran his hand through his thinning white hair. "When have I ever attacked the president? Hell, I just off the phone with one of you people. All I said was that the president should tell the truth!"

"Well, Cooper said you, as part of the Republican party, are by extension attacking the president at a time when all Americans have to unite against terrorism. How do you respond to that?"

Lattan cleared his throat. "Well, let's just say I've heard there's a movie called 'Wag the Dog.' Next question."

"Could you elaborate, Congressman?"

"Elaborate? You want some elaboration? I'll give you some elaboration!" Lattan said angrily. "Let's cut the crap right now, all right? You know it, I know it, the people of Idaho know it, that this is just Rich Cooper's way of trying to divert attention away from the fact that this president is a goddamn sleazebag who's sleeping with interns young enough to be his daughter. This is the weakest, most pathetic attempt at spin I've ever seen. You know goddamn well he's using this tragedy overseas to try to make it look as though he's above the fray. It's venal as hell!"

Lattan winced at the words that had escaped from his mouth before he had the chance to stop them. His stomach constricted. But he felt strangely powerless to stop his righteous indignation from consuming him.

"Why don't you ever do a story on how I've promoted economic growth?" Lattan continued ranting. "Or how I'm getting federal funding for Head Start, or fighting for Idaho potato farmers against the french fry tax? Only time I hear from you is when you want me to answer my critics. ... Lemme tell *you* something, I'm tired of answering the critics. I'm doing my job, and doing it *well*, I might add, and I'll keep doing a great job when I'm re-elected, and you'll be lucky if I ever take calls from *you people* ever again ..."

He was as if he was on auto-pilot, unable to control this discharge of pent-up anger at the media flowing out of him like a volcano spewing lava in every direction ... But just as soon as he'd realized he was losing control, the radio host got off the phone with a perfunctory thank you ... and it was all over. ...

He slumped in his chair. He put his hands over his eyes, rubbed his head.

DeLeet didn't say anything, as if he was shocked into silence. But he didn't have to. Lattan realized what he'd done. Now the whole state of Idaho was going to hear his rant. Why hadn't his staff done their job and stopped him? When he screwed up, it was always their fault!

Chapter 11

Where's The Outrage?

Lattan sat at his desk waiting with trepidation for delivery of the *Idaho Informer* and the other state papers to read the accounts of his rant about the day before. Surely all of those insolent reporters would have a field day! Paranoid thoughts caromed around in his skull ... he could only imagine the headlines ... *Lattan Loses His Cool On Lewinsky ... Lattan Shows Immaturity Of A Freshman ... Lattan Finding 'Loser' Label Hard To Shake*. ... God! How bad would it be?

At 8 a.m., the papers had not yet been delivered to his Pocatello Falls office, so he tried to calm his nerves with breakfast. He opened a desk drawer and pulled out a box of French Toast Crunchies, an old plastic bowl, a bent metal spoon and an unchilled can of Diet Mountain Dew. He poured the cereal in the bowl, then closed the box and returned it to the drawer. Then he opened the can of soda and poured it over the cereal. He ate in silence, then set down the spoon and brought the bowl up to his mouth to drink the last bit of soda and flakes. Finally, he wiped the bowl and spoon clean with a paper towel and placed them back in his drawer.

A loud *plop!* outside of the office door set Lattan's adrenaline surging. He sprang to the door, opened it, and picked up a stack of newspapers bundled with string. He dropped it on his desk and grabbed a scissors. With a firm snip he freed the papers, and promptly plucked the *Idaho Informer* from the middle of the stack. His heart clanged against his sternum as he braced for the inevitable blow.

But then he read the headline: Clinton Admits Relationship With

Lewinsky, Apologizes To Nation... then he scanned the article for his name ... and found it only at the end, where he was quoted — one line! — about the importance of the truth, followed by a quote from his opponent, Rich Cooper, something about Ken Starr's "witch hunt."

And that was all the ink for Lattan.

He was so outraged, and on so many levels. Reactions to the various indignities, affronts and offenses were all percolating, swirling around in the crenulations of his head ... clamoring for his indignation, demanding his venom ... he scarcely knew what to get enraged at first.

He started with the *Informer*'s headline ... Clinton didn't apologize one bit! That slick bastard did it again! What was it? He had *regrets*, he *misled* people ... for godsakes, it was as if the crafty SOB *knew* he wouldn't have to apologize because he *knew* the headline writers would write that he did! It was ... pardon the expression, scandalous! The dumb crooked hillbilly had snowed them again!

And then ... his mind was aflame ... the nerve ... one quote from *me,* Congressman Charles Lattan, after *I* granted this little *skunk* of a reporter *a whole interview* on the topic ... followed by another zinger from that young whippersnapper Rich Cooper!

Then he scanned the related stories ... interviews with people at bars ... how predictable ... "We should get on with the business of the country" ... "We're sick of this story." ... Well, what else would a bunch of drunks say at 11 p.m. on a weeknight at a bar!

Then he realized ... he should be grateful Clinton pre-empted any possible coverage of his radio rantings. ...

At a quarter to nine, Lattan's media guru, Kentrell "Alt" DeLeet, gamboled in with a styrofoam cup of coffee, two donuts and a stained tie. "Mornin' Charlie," he said, walking in.

"Morning," Lattan said, in an early-morning baritone. He noticed a manila folder under DeLeet's arm, with tell-tale newspaper clippings sticking out. DeLeet stood there silently, licking sugar powder from his lips.

Lattan feared the worst. "Whatcha got there?"

Lattan could see DeLeet's Adam's apple throb as he swallowed and took a deep breath. "Well, a couple of papers took a little, er, editorial license with your radio broadcast on Lewinsky." He paused. "But don't worry. It all kind of got buried with all of the coverage of Slick Willie's speech."

Lattan stared for a moment with a look of a fourth grader who didn't get the teacher's first explanation of how a bill becomes a law. "Lemme see 'em!" he snapped.

DeLeet walked over and placed the newspaper clips in front of Lattan. Lattan eyed the stack of papers as if seeing an auto repair bill for the first time.

And ... they were all practically the same as the *Idaho Informer* report ... a snide subhead to the Clinton story ... *Lattan Quibbles As Clinton Talks ... Charlie's Frown, What A Clown ... Lattan Radio Tantrum A Stark Contrast To Clinton's Somber Speech ... Charles Lattan, The Char-La-Tan?* ... He didn't know whether to be more outraged at the paucity of the coverage, or the tone of what little coverage there was. ...

Then he had an idea—

"Let's cancel that hand-shaking event at the potato farm this morning," he said.

"What for?" DeLeet asked, reaching into his jacket pocket for his cell phone.

"I want to seize the initiative on this. I want to hold a press conference to demand that the president resign."

"You want to *what*?"

"Take the high moral ground. Demand the sleazeball take a hike. Great idea, huh?"

But DeLeet was already talking on the phone with the campaign manager, Alex Macro.

"No, Congressman, I don't think it's a good idea," DeLeet said, snapping his phone shut and placing back in his jacket pocket. "With all due respect, sir."

"Why not? Dan Coats has, Dan Quayle has, Oliver North has."

"A retiring senator and a guy who can't spell our state's number one crop. And of course, that nutball ex-Marine colonel. Not a compelling cast of characters."

"And so has Paul McHale, and Ben Jones, and Bob Smith, and Tom DeLay, and a bunch of editorial writers outside the Beltway," Lattan pleaded.

"A no-name Democrat, a defeated Democrat and defeated actor, an unknown Senator and a guy who wears so much hairspray it looks like he's sporting a Kevlar helmet. Still not an impressive group."

"Well I like it. You forget which one of us is the Congressman?"

"Of course not, sir," DeLeet. "Let's just wait until Alex gets here to discuss this."

Then, as if on cue, Macro skidded into the office. "What's this craziness about calling on Clinton to resign?"

"Please, don't damn my idea with faint praise," Lattan said, trying to be funny. "Dismiss it outright."

"You're damn right I'm dismissing it outright!" Macro said. "We're not having this argument again. It's not a good campaign issue, even if Clinton's negatives are at an all-time high."

"Why not?" Lattan asked.

"Because if you do that, you end up in the same sentence with Dan Quayle and Oliver North. You need any other reason?"

"Come on," Lattan said. "There's gotta be a way to make political hay out of this."

"No one will take you seriously. You want to vent your rage at Clinton, Kentrell and I will listen. Think of us as your counseling group. But a press conference? No way!"

Lattan tapped his fingers on his desk, smudging the shine that had been buffed to a high polish by the cleaning crew. His cranium bubbled with visions of Clinton smiling smugly after his speech, thinking he got away with it once again, probably thinking to himself in that hillbilly drawl, *Ah fewled 'em agin', ha ha ha ...*

"I want a press conference, damn it!" Lattan pounded his fist on his desk. It nearly slid off. The side of his hand was covered with a shiny film of cleaning oil. He pulled a handkerchief out of his suit pocket and wiped.

"I'm telling you," Macro said, "There's nothing to gain with it. It's out. It's over as a campaign issue. All we can do is react to anything new, such as if Starr has Slick Willie testify again. And if you think you're going to make headlines out of this, forget it. I hate to burst your bubble, Congressman, but that little tantrum should have gotten you front page treatment, yet the state papers almost uniformly relegated it to the last paragraphs of their stories." Macro was speaking as if he was a doctor trying to sooth the family of a terminally ill cancer patient. "You can't make this work as a campaign issue."

"How can you be so sure?" Lattan asked childishly. "As Bob Dole used to say, 'Where's the outrage'?"

"I've been in this business a long time," Macro said, putting his thumbs on his chest under his suspenders. "You won't score by trying to demagogue this. You'll look desperate. It'll backfire and help Rich Cooper. Trust me. In a just world, it would work as a campaign issue. But it ain't. The public doesn't care as long as the economy doesn't go south. *Listen to my advice.* That's what I'm here to do for you."

Lattan stared straight ahead, hands on his desk, twiddling his thumbs at high speed. "So what's the plan for milking this issue? *Nothing*? What do I say about it when I'm out there pressing the flesh?"

"Just smile," Macro said, displaying a wooden smile and yellow teeth. "And if it's a reporter, just say that this issue should not detract from your message of fighting the french fry tax, protecting families, and creating jobs." He checked them off with his fat fingers.

Lattan nodded, mulling over his strategists' advice. Then, realizing all at once that he'd exhausted his arguments, he made a mental capitulation. He conceded they were right. How he hated when his staff was right ...

Chapter 12

Town Hall Pall

Lattan waited in the green room of the Spudsville Moose Lodge as the crowd of voters swelled into the building for his town hall meeting. How many of these had he done? Dozens ... hundreds, probably, answering questions about lost Social Security checks and what he was doing in Washington to make sure the Spudsville Main Street would be repaved. *God, what a joke!* It was as though the constituents flocked to these town stalls believing it was a revival meeting, as if they would come away with some antidote to their depression, some cure for their cases of burn-out and general weariness with life. Wasn't that what their Congressman was for?

Yes, he'd done more of these town hall meetings ... with their inane question and answer sessions, their little old ladies and their disillusioned potato farmers ... but at this moment, during this lull before the cacophony ... Lattan felt the feelings come on ... the feelings he always faced ... *The Doubts.*

They were charging through his brain ... the doubts! Always the doubts ... no matter how many silly meetings he'd presided over, no matter how many despairing constituents he'd inspired, no matter how many of Idaho's sullen and surly he'd uplifted ... at the very moment he was supposed to take the stage —

The doubts!

Just when he needed the sycophants from his staff to boost his spirits, they were out in the main room shaking hands and smiling, unfolding chairs, uncovering cellophane-wrapped trays of baked cookies, making sure the coolers full of soft drinks were packed with sufficient ice.

While he was in here stewing ... stewing! Into the vortex of self-doubt!

Who was he, really? What were his credentials? A few years as a plumber, a few years in the Idaho legislature, then one term in Congress. Attack him, they always did, they always would! The media, his opponent, Rich Cooper, if it wasn't for his opposition to the potato tax, it was for his calling on the president to resign ... Christ! He would probably get attacked tonight ... what would he do? How would he handle it?

Yet the voters were lining up. Maybe there would be 200 tonight.

Overburdened by the ennui of post-industrial America, emotionally spent from feeble exertion in mediocre jobs and passionless marriages, they were coming to have Congressman Charles Lattan tell them how he would improve their lives.

And tell them he would! *A vote for Charlie is a vote for change! A vote for me is a vote for your future!* God, the cliches were so bad, he wondered if anybody fell for them anymore ... and yet they were coming.

Why? They needed a pep talk. Someone to rouse their dormant enthusiasm for life. From him, Charles Lattan. If they only knew!

How much it was a struggle for him, how much he had to muzzle the voices of distress screaming inside his head, crowd the self-doubt out of his mind, force himself to act in spite of the omnipresent self-loathing ... put it all aside so he could muster enough free attention to offer his constituents a glimmer of hope for their wretched lives—

—the doubts! Who did he think he was? Serving a spicy broth of warmed over, *nay*, half-baked, government-is-on-your-side pablum to a spoiled, infantile public too self-absorbed to see that they wanted Washington to be their nanny just as much as they decried the instances when Congress acted in precisely such a manner.

Now Lattan was really sunk in it. His brain was feeding him all the negative thoughts, like a cue card holder flashing jokes to a late-night talk show host. His head was spinning, reeling, jouncing from one paranoid thought to the next—

The carping from his detractors in the media! Just last night, he'd reviewed the manila folder of newspaper clips compiled by his press guru, DeLeet, a file of stories criticizing his "reckless and feckless" call for the president's resignation ... those damn journalists, safely ensconced in their newsrooms, scoffing and sneering—

Oh, how easy it was to criticize in print! Questioning his motives, always harping on his status as a vulnerable incumbent. The phrases trundled across the newsreel in his mind ... *Charles Lattan, the ex-plumber who seems to revel in soaking up the Independent Counsel's leaks ... What does the advent of Congressman Charles Lattan say about the intelligence level of voters in Idaho ... Charles Lattan, the dud who defends the spud.*

Must stop the negative thoughts! Lattan inhaled deeply, tensed his atrophied muscles, clenched his nubbly fists. Then he exhaled, bursting forth with a huge gale from his lungs, attempting to zap the tension out from every pore in his body, fill the vacuum created by expelled anxiety with fresh confidence.

Here he stood, alone in the green room of the ... Spudsville Moose Lodge! Why had he let that fat bastard campaign manager talk him into this?

He had to get control. Just another town hall meeting. Just like in Potato Falls, Home Fries Hamlet, Cottage Fry Village. So many cities, one after the other, like a rock star on tour.

"Ready, Congressman?" Macro said, appearing suddenly in the doorway. How long had he been waiting, watching?

"Yes, of course!" Never let the staff see the doubts!

"I'll tell them to introduce you," Macro said, eyeing his boss as if he was checking the fit of a new suit in the mirror. "You look great."

He wanted to say, *I don't need an overpaid lackey to patronize me ...* But an extra kick of validation never hurt right before a performance. How could he not look great, in a Sears poly-wool blend off-the-rack suit, a fashionable lime green tie, and combover pasted perfectly on his head for such a natural full-head-of-hair look? He pinched the dimple in his tie, making sure it was still centered.

Then he followed Macro out of the prep room and up the stairs to greet the crowd, who ... applauded!

All the environmental stimuli provided by a roomful of clapping people, even if many of them did look silly in those goofy lodge hats, acted as positive reinforcement. ... The sheer *noise* of it all overloaded his mental synapses ...

the doubts were routed, forced back into the crevices of his cranium.

Here he goes! Congressman Charles Lattan! He's from the government, and he's here to help *you*!

The applause died down, and the audience seemed anticipatory. Lattan walked to the podium and smiled at the crowd, drinking it all in. Those silly hats. And nice old ladies. Thank god, not a pro-potato-tax protester in the house!

They looked normal enough, like the people whose pipes he'd unclogged during his days as a plumber. Many were clutching copies of his campaign literature that the efficient Macro had placed on every metal folding chair. Maybe he would be asked for some autographs after the show! Pose for pictures!

But then he looked more closely ... they seemed no more enlightened than the drudges he spoke to at any other town hall meeting. Except these voters didn't seem that enthusiastic after all ... actually, they looked kind of weak, their countenances heavy from the accumulated weight of life's little defeats.

Losers! He had an audience of losers! Not people like him, who were sanguine and prosperous by virtue of pulling themselves up by their bootstraps. ...

Oh ... who was he fooling? Not even himself anymore. The idea of a freshman Congressman driven by idealistic zeal now seemed silly, a relic from a bygone era, as faded and weather-beaten as the swingset in his backyard, rusting from lack of use, abandoned for the doleful realities of adulthood. Idealism. How quaint. How naive.

But he couldn't give into his cynicism now! Here he was ... *trusting the people* ... who were so ready to believe him. There must be something to what he says! Could the hundreds of people waiting to ask him questions about the machinations of government be wasting their time? Would the good people of Idaho allow themselves to be lassoed by some slick pitch from a snake-oil-peddling Congressman?

Nothing wrong with taking in a little adulation. It never went to his head. Christ, he spent enough time fighting the doubts, shouldn't he enjoy it when he was riding a crest of self-confidence? Why shouldn't he enjoy a little veneration from the people of Idaho? It wasn't as if he was some third-world despot presiding over a reign of terror. Or a preacher urging heavenly salvation through fealty to some unquantifiable entity. Or a cult leader practicing mind-control over his disciples. He was fighting for Idahoans in Washington, representing their interests. Him! Charles Lattan!

He adjusted the microphone. "Good evening ladies and gentlemen," Lattan began. "I am Congressman Charles Lattan, and I want to thank the good people of the Spudsville Moose Lodge for the opportunity to speak to you tonight." He then gave his standard stump speech, recounting his personal story of plumber-turned-Congressman, his commitment to the people of Idaho. He conspicuously avoided mention of the potato tax. He wanted to claim the high moral ground. He was convinced that the people of Spudsville were more concerned with what was happening on Main Street than what was happening on the banks of the Potomac River.

After about 20 minutes of speaking, he concluded and asked for questions. He stood motionless at the podium, and — dare he admit it to himself — eagerly awaited the first question!

But the room was silent. A few reporters flipped their notepads, clicked sides on their tape recorders. Audience members looked at each other, each too timid to ask the first question.

Macro looked at Lattan. *What now?* Surely the campaign staff had planted some softball pitchers in the crowd to ask the first questions, set a pro-Lattan tone to the proceedings. Certainly this was completely staged, every moment orchestrated ... wasn't it?

Lattan sensed the vacuum. And how nature, and Congressional Town Hall Meetings, abhorred a vacuum!

"Any questions?" Lattan repeated.

More silence.

"Any questions at all?" Lattan ventured again, his eyes desperately raking the room.

"Yes, I have one," said an elderly woman. "What is it you suppose the president and that little intern girl were doing smoking cigars together in the Oval Office? I thought Hillary made the White House a non-smoking building!"

Chapter 13
Punditholics Anonymous

The evening following his town hall meeting, Charles Lattan found himself standing behind the podium at a much different gathering. After introductions here, it was his turn to tell his story to the monthly meeting of Punditholics Anonymous.

"Good evening, friends," said the rangy, balding Lattan. "My name is Charles, and I'm a punditholic."

"Hi, Charles," the dozen in the room said enthusiastically, reciting the ritual response.

"It's good to see so many friendly faces to know that I am not alone in my struggle, to know that I have support from people who share my affliction," Lattan said, his eyes surveying the sparse crowd seated on folding chairs.

The timid crowd was silent, a few exchanging glances with each other. The usual discomfort at acknowledging one's addiction.

"I've been asked to tell you my story," Lattan said. "In many ways, I hope you can all identify with it in some way, because it's all of our stories. I know how we can all feel ashamed at times for being punditholics. I've found, as a member of this group, that hearing someone else's story can make us feel more at ease. It's important for all of us to remember at all times that we have a disease, and that it's not our fault we have it. It's easy to blame ourselves, but we now know that punditholism is a disease like alcoholism. The key is that we treat this disease with our 12-step program, modeled on other successful 12-step programs. All it takes for us to succeed is a genuine desire to give up our addiction to watching, listening to and reading pundits."

Lattan was speaking in a basement Sunday School classroom at a local church. He was a committed member of the group, which, like Gamblers Anonymous, Debtors Anonymous, and Overeaters Anonymous, was designed in the image of Alcoholics Anonymous. No last names, no judgmental comments, no strict membership criteria. Only a commitment to going cold turkey on pundits.

No MSNBC viewing, no *Washington Ledger* editorial reading, no talk show listening. You had to accept that you had a problem, make the decision to give it up, and stick to it in the face of constant temptation — made-for-TV "town hall meetings," Rush Limbaugh and Don Imus rants, ever-increasing web opinion journals.

Which was no easy feat, no easier than an alcoholic turning down booze at an open bar. For members of Congress especially, squandering attention on the punditocracy was an addiction as powerful as heroin. The pull to watch cable chat shows, to read op-eds, to return again and again to favorite web sites and hit "refresh," was at times overpowering.

Yet punditholism remained a taboo topic among the general public and especially elected officials. Much the way alcoholics could hide behind the veneer or social drinking, punditholics could hide under the veil of needing to know what the pundits were blathering about. But when that normal desire for information became an obsession, that's when it became punditholism, and that's when Lattan joined the group.

At first he was, like so many before, him, in denial. It was obscene to suggest that anyone could be *addicted* to pundits! To even suggest that a politician's desire to learn the very latest spin could be an *addiction* —

But Lattan knew from his own experience that an addiction was exactly what it was. When the social drinker began binge drinking, the punditholic began reading every op-ed by George F. Will. When the alcoholic went from the normal after-work cocktail to six after-work cocktails, the punditholic began taping every episode of "Hannity & Colmes" and "Hardball." When the "moderate" drinker was soon tippling before lunch "for medicinal purposes," the punditholic was spending every weekend channel surfing from chat show to chat show, filling out a scorecard on pundit appearances as if he were at a baseball game. The parallels were all too clear.

Lattan was careful to absolve himself of responsibility for his affliction. It was easy to understand why an elected official would want to know more. In politics, there was a proud tradition of slinging endless press releases to goose one's Nexis count. It was easy to hide under the gossamer of knowledge seeker, learned one, scholar. This tradition, coupled with an irrational, subconscious belief that in one of these CNN specials the punditholic would eventually hear the best spin ever recorded, teamed up to form a lethal cocktail of pundit addiction. Lattan knew he needed help.

The Punditholics Anonymous theory on treatment was simple: Give it all up. By the time anyone reads the *American Political Briefing*, he's ingested enough dross from the chattering class to last him all afternoon, even in the face of the inevitable counter-spin, ricochets and caroms it spawned in the dreaded journalistic echo-chamber. Continued pursuit of information was not a useful endeavor. There was nothing any pundit could say that would ever put the punditholic's mind at rest.

So give it all up. Admit that, through no fault of your own, but through cultural conditioning, you have an addiction to pundits. Then come to the meetings, tell your story, and rely on your network of sponsors and peers to talk you through it when you feel the urge to read the musings of Ellen Goodman, Matt Drudge, Maureen Dowd or Bill Press.

"I was raised in a normal working class household," Lattan said, beginning his story. "We didn't read the op-ed page. We read the sports page and the comics and the want ads. We never even watched the news that much, except for Walter Cronkite. But then."

He glanced around the room, making sure the audience was with him. To his satisfaction, the eight men and four women, ranging in age from early twenties to senior citizens, were giving him their complete attention. Their prurient interest in his story, he believed, mirrored their prurient interest in learning every possible detail about what the pundits were chattering about.

"Despite not being raised as a reader, I got lessons very early on about what it *meant* to be a news consumer, as far as my parents believed," Lattan continued. "My father couldn't care less about what was said in *The New Republic* or *National Review*. But from a very young age, he insisted on sharing with me everything he knew about what the self-appointed experts were telling the American public to think about the news. By the time I was in high school, I was watching the network news every night, searching in vain for an answer to my eternal question, 'Please, TV People, Tell Us What It Means.'"

The room was silent. They wanted to hear everything, they wanted corroboration that their disease was not a private struggle, so embarrassing that they couldn't even talk about it.

"I think my father wanted to protect me from the shrapnel of incoming spin," Lattan continued, his voice quavering. "That we were living in Idaho, a whole continent away from the epicenter of punditocracy in Washington, was of no concern to him. To my father, it was if Hugh Sidey, Jack Anderson and Mary McGrory were pontificating in his living room."

Lattan's eyes scanned the room, seeking validation. Like an alcoholic, a punditholic would never be cured, but forever in recovery, and forever concerned about how people, even other punditholics, would react to him.

"Needless to say, when I entered politics, I soon equated being a politician with being targeted by pundits," Lattan continued. "I soon had nightmares about Sam Donaldson, Cokie Roberts, Sander Vanocur, Garrick Utley, Howard Fineman, whomever, trying to explain things to me. Naturally, I wanted to know why — why these people felt so compelled to insult my intelligence. I saw *Broadcast News* 17 times in the theater, then bought my own copy as soon as it came out on video."

The audience seemed shocked by the severity of his addiction. But it was cathartic for him to come clean, and it helped to establish safety for others to share their stories later. They seemed to be enjoying his story, learning that perhaps someone had pundit fever worse than they did.

"When I finally realized I had a problem, and I joined this group, I'm happy to say that I threw away everything — the wonky books and magazines, the videos, everything. And I fight to stay clean every day. I occasionally slip, as we all will do, but I haven't watched 'The McLaughlin Group' or 'The O'Reilly Factor' for six months now."

Audience members nodded. Lattan then proceeded with his patented, crowd-pleasing finish.

"And I don't miss listening to Robert Novak one bit," he laughed, sparking chuckles from in everyone else. "Yes, I can honestly say that my life is better without Jonathan Alter." He chuckled again, and the audience joined with him. "Staying close to the people in this room, having someone to call when I feel the pull to watch Tim Russert or Brian Williams, has kept me clean. And the urge to read, the urge to watch, I'm pleased to report, is getting weaker every day. That's my story, and I thank you for listening."

The audience applauded. Lattan beamed. They were all looking to him for guidance. Their reaction reconfirmed his strength to overcome his addiction to pundits. Every time he told his story, it made him realize he had the willpower to give it up. Now he would take a seat while others shared their stories, and indulge his own morbid interest.

At the end of the meeting, Lattan hugged a few of his fellow punditholics and left. He drove home with an acute sense of well-being, listening to the sounds of smooth jazz instead of talk radio.

His car phone beeped. He hit the hands-free button. "Hello?"

"Charlie!" screamed the familiar voice of his Congressional chief of staff, Rachel Emmell. "You've got to come back to Washington early! The FAT executives want to have dinner with you at Planet Pundit ..."

From then on he didn't here a word she said. Dinner with the Federated Association of Taters? What did they want? Was he slacking in his fight against the proposed french fry tax? Were they going to threaten to yank their support from him? ... And the locale! He'd have to face his worst temptation while dining at ... Planet Pundit!

Chapter 14

Dining At Planet Pundit

Lattan arrived at Planet Pundit feeling tense ... both because he'd have to test his willpower in the face of the ultimate punditholic's temptation, and because he was meeting with Federated Association of Taters (FAT) executives for a reason yet to be revealed.

Lattan stood at the vacant maitre d' stand and waited to be acknowledged. He was wearing his finest pinstripe suit, sparkling wingtips, and a ferocious salsa-colored necktie. His white combover was plastered to his head with a thick coat of hair spray lacquer.

He wondered if he harmonized well with Planet Pundit's chattering class chic. There were no checkered, white-and-red vinyl table covers here. The linen tablecloths were only slightly less stiff and starched than the white shirts worn by the waiters. Crystal glasses, one for wine, one for designer water, others for cognac and cocktails, fanned around the place settings as if management expected to host a wine tasting. The menu boasted Legal Scholar Tort-ellini stuffed with red snapper and smoked lame duck. The only thing missing from the menu was the caveat *corporate expense accounts only, please*.

But the menu and table settings were nothing compared to the Planet Pundit decor. The walls were covered with pundit souvenirs and memorabilia, baubles and knick-knacks donated by talking heads to the first-ever theme restaurant established as an homage to their blather.

On the wall above the maitre d' stand was a glass-enclosed display of an authentic pair of Larry King's suspenders. Next to that was a mirror donated by Richard Cohen, taped to which was a hand-inscribed message that read, "My readers want to know my stream of consciousness thoughts today. People wait to read what I think!" Then there was Jack Germond's racing form, E.J. Dionne's autographed book of useless adverbs, George F. Will's autographed baseball, a first edition of Geraldo Rivera's autobiography "Exposing Myself" under glass, a giant poster of Tom Brokaw reading off of a teleprompter ... Bumper stickers and lapel pins from Lanny Davis' failed congressional campaigns, as well as unsold household cleaning products from his days as an Amway peddler ... a note from Jonathan Turley to his teaching assistant, which read "You gotta do Constitutional Law today, I'm on TV again!" ... Christ, this place was cheesy, Lattan thought ... don't come here if you're lactose intolerant.

On an opposite wall hung Lamar Alexander's plaid shirt from the '96 campaign ... Bill Schneider's first radio shack calculator, on which he once computed polling data ... a canceled check from Pat Buchanan to the Accused Nazi War Criminals Legal Defense Fund ... a photo of Howard Kurtz at home doing laundry, with the washing machine clearly on "rinse" ... Kellyanne Fitzpatrick Conway's Blueberry Princess costume ... Mary Matalin's high school yearbook, in which she's listed as "girl most likely to administer spin" ... Eleanor Clift's dog-eared copy of "It Takes A Village" ... piles and piles of complimentary copies of Bill Clinton's "Between Hope and History" and Newt Gingrich's "1945" stacked in each booth, but no one seemed to be taking them ... a copy of Ken Starr's speed dial list, with ABC's Jackie Judd penciled in at #1 ... it went on and on.

But, as much to his own surprise at it would have been to any other members of Punditholics Anonymous, Lattan was not feeling the urge to actually *examine* any of these displays as if he were in a museum of ancient artifacts. No, he was more disgusted at the phenomenon that those who were supposed to be reporting the news had now *become* the news themselves ... thinking they were movie stars ... accepting payment for their opinions ... how *tacky*.

Presently, a sultry hostess in a clingy diamante dress appeared and led Lattan toward a table in the rear of the restaurant. Lobbyists, lawyers, diplomats and other Members of Congress hobnobbed and burbled with drunken conversation as they dined and drank under the watchful gaze of a huge mural of "The McLaughlin Group."

Lattan sat and nursed a double Johnnie Walker Black, checking his watch between sips. He disliked waiting for lobbyists. Had they forgotten *he* was the Congressman?

Just then, FAT President Flip Screen swaggered in, sunglasses disguising his bloodshot eyes, cigarette dangling from his lips. Behind him was another FAT executive, John Tucancel, whom Lattan remembered from their Capitol Hill reception. Their eyes swept the restaurant like blind dates searching for each other in bars. Lattan caught Screen's gaze. Screen grinned, tapped Tucancel on the shoulder and nodded toward Lattan.

They walked toward Lattan, and upon arriving exchanged laconic, formal greetings.

"Thanks for the invite," Lattan said.

"The potato industry's pleasure," Screen said, taking his seat, along with Tucancel.

A waiter appeared to take their drink orders, then pivoted and headed toward the bar.

"Well, Congressman," Screen began tentatively, "you're probably wondering why we asked you to dinner so suddenly. I'm sure dinner with industry lobbyists isn't the first thing you thought you'd be doing upon your return to Washington."

Lattan braced himself... were they yanking their support?

"The thing is, Congressman, you've been a great friend to the potato industry, to potato farmers not just in Idaho but across the country."

"Why, thank you," Lattan said. Where was this going?

"In fact," Screen continued, "your service has impressed not only those of us who have had the pleasure of working with you personally against the french fry tax, but also our board of directors, who need look no further than your voting record to recognize what a good friend our industry has in Congressman Charles Lattan."

"Well, that's certainly kind to say ... I'm touched." What was also this buttering up for? They'd already maxed out the campaign contribution for the cycle.

"Congressman, sometimes the voters can't see what we see," Screen continued, with what were now appearing to be prepared remarks.

"Unfortunately, the people of Idaho's 17th district — some, not all, of course — don't know how hard you've been working for them."

"I'll say," Lattan chortled. "If only they were half as astute as you are!"

"We've just seen the latest poll numbers, and we don't have to tell you that Rich Cooper is more than just a fresh young face. You know as well as we do that he's a real threat."

Lattan sighed. "Yes, I'm afraid he is." The whippersnapper!

"Congressman, I don't want to assume the worst. But I want to let you know that there are options should the worst come to pass."

Lattan was stupefied. What on earth were they talking about?

"If, god forbid, we were to lose you as an advocate in Congress, it would be devastating not just to you and your family personally, but to our industry as well. We want to make sure that, in the absolute worst case scenario, that you are guaranteed security and we are guaranteed security. What I mean is, no matter what happens, we both end up winning despite what the election results are."

Lattan's brain was slowly computing. ...

"What we're prepared to offer is a starting salary of $500,000 — nearly twice as much as you'd ever make as a Congressman — expense account, no more worries about campaigning —"

"Now wait just a minute!" Lattan slammed his fist on the table.

Tucancel, who had been quiet until then, suddenly felt like a dinner party hostess who had to quell a marital spat erupting at her table. But he was at a loss for words.

"Now, I know none of us wants to assume the worst," Screen continued, undaunted, as though he'd rescued many a drowning Congressman on the trade association lifeboat before. "But think about it ... *corporate executive vice president for government affairs Charles Lattan* ... nine to five job ... no more town hall meetings, Rotary Club lunches, parades, constituent whining ... just a nice, cushy job where you talk to your own friends in Congress as an official advocate of the potato industry."

Lattan glowered at Screen, his jaw tightening. "I'm going to win this race, Flip!"

"We all want that, of course," Screen said, soothingly, nodding and winking to Tucancel, who nodded aggressively. "All we're saying is that if the worst —"

"Don't patronize me!" Lattan slammed his fist again on the table, nearly felling everyone's drinks.

"Congressman, with all due respect ... we wouldn't make this offer to just anyone."

That gave him pause. It *was* a nice offer ... a half mil to start ... easy hours ... expense account ... no more damn reporters to answer to, voters to answer to, special interest groups to answer to ...

Lattan sighed. "I'm sorry for losing my cool ... you don't know what it's like, having your career in the hands of the *voters*." He sneered on the word *voters*, as if describing an infectious disease.

"It's OK, Congressman," Tucancel said. "We understand the campaign pressure. Especially one like yours, where your hard work so often goes unappreciated. Frankly, if the voters of Idaho 17 don't understand that, then maybe they just don't deserve you."

"He's right, Congressman," Screen said. "Now, back to the offer. Of course, with these damn ethics rules, if you were to accept the job, we'd have you 'consult' for the first couple of years," he winked. "But then you'd be our go-to guy when it came to lobbying your former colleagues."

The phrase rattled around in Lattan's brain ... *former colleagues* ... was he cooked already, and everyone knew it but him? ... He was positively depressed by the whole thing, lucrative offer or not.

"I'll have to think about it," Lattan said clumsily. "But thanks for the offer. I'll let you know ... obviously, after November 7th."

"Of course," Screen said, exhaling a plume of smoke. "You'll let us know," he smiled, leaning back in his chair.

Suddenly Lattan lost his appetite. Why eat, anyway, when it was clear the business of this dinner had been completed?

"I've got to go," Lattan said, rising from his seat. "I'm probably already over the line with these damn ethics rules about wining and dining anyway. Thanks for the drink, and thanks for the offer."

"Always a pleasure," Screen said, standing and shaking his hand. Then Tucancel followed suit.

Lattan smiled the wooden campaign smile and turned to exit Planet Pundit. He raced through the restaurant, and realized how insignificant his pundit problem was in comparison to the panic that ensued when he really considered that he may soon no longer be a Congressman.

Chapter 15

Lattan Faces Intern Problems Of His Own

Lattan stormed out of the restaurant in a rage. The nerve of those trade association stuffed shirts! Assuming he was going to lose, having the gall to offer him a job as a consultant-cum-lobbyist. God, the indignity of it! As if he were already a defeated Congressman looking for a lifeboat to save him from having to go home to Idaho ... that godforsaken state.

Still ... it was a nice offer. ...

Oh, it was too much to think about ... Lattan needed to drink to drown the voices screaming in his skull.

He stumbled down Pennsylvania Avenue toward downtown ... then turned up 14th street ... no idea where he was going ... needed to find a nice quiet watering hole. ...

He came upon Gotham Glitterati, D.C.'s attempt to emulate New York nightlife. Outside, linebacker-sized bounces in banded-collar shirts demanded ten dollars cover, though it was a weekday. He tentatively handed a guy twice his size a crumpled ten-dollar bill.

Inside, women in black leather mini-skirts and tops blended with the black leather furniture and faux-marble sconce lights that illuminated the dance floor. Lattan moved toward the bar and ordered a double scotch, which he downed in one gulp. Then he ordered another and swayed toward the billiards room.

Two libertine women in black were standing at a table, one ready to break for eight-ball.

"If you loosen that tie, we'll let you play with us," said one.

Lattan fumbled for an answer. "I, uh, I'm not much of a pool player ... buy you ladies a drink?" He took their orders and returned in time to see the tall one, Jeannie, sink two balls on the break.

Lattan was satisfied to watch, continuing to slurp scotch. Jeannie, concentrating on striped balls, made small talk with him in between shots. Did he have a sign on his forehead that read, "Congressman Ready To Listen At All Times?"

She bleated about her divorce, her job search, selling her wedding ring to pay rent. But Lattan, now relaxing from a climbing blood alcohol level, was inclined to listen. It gave him an excuse to leer. Nothing wrong with a happily married man *looking*, for goodness sakes.

Her cheerleader face, draped in curly brown hair, emanated a schoolgirl innocence that belied the life story she was telling. When she glissaded past him to make a shot, she left behind a pocket of air redolent with heavy perfume.

After their game, Jeannie's friend, Paula, left to dance with a man with a pierced nose. Lattan and Jeannie retreated to a half-moon-shaped booth that made whoopie-cushion sounds when they slid into the seat. Jeannie continued talking as they both continued drinking.

Suddenly, Lattan had slid from pleasantly buzzed to dangerously drunk. He was fading fast. He begged her pardon and put his head on the table, feeling like a kid who'd spent too long on the merry-go-round. But the techno beat pounding through his chest reminded him he was not a nine-year-old at the park.

Presently, Paula returned, saying it had been fun but she had to work tomorrow, and would Charlie be nice enough to see them home.

"Sure," Lattan slurred, his enunciation as clear as someone fresh from root canal surgery.

The three piled into a cab, which Paula directed to her apartment. When she popped out, she scribbled her phone number on a gum wrapper and handed it to Lattan. "Give me a call sometime, *Congressman*," she winked.

Through his drunken haze, Lattan detected a tone of sarcasm ... did she think he was fabricating his vaunted stature to impress her?

Lattan listened to Jeannie's drunken directions to the cab driver — "left there," "make a right after that doohickey," "it's the next building, no *that* one" — and eventually they stopped in front of her building.

Lattan flashed her a sheepish grin: "It was nice meeting you."

"Would you like to come up for a minute?"

Lattan stumbled her into the old brick high-rise, one of countless apartment houses built in Northern Virginia after World War II to accommodate new Pentagon employees. He staggered behind his new friend, up three flights of stairs, banging his wingtips on the steps, ruining his shine.

"Make yourself comfy. I'll get us some drinks," she said, shutting the front door and disappearing into the kitchen.

Lattan stood with his hands clasped behind his back, looking around the living room like a prospective condominium buyer on rounds with a real estate agent. The battered cloth couch was clearly second-hand, possibly a hand-me-down from the parents. Bookshelves teemed with romance novels and baubles from tourist traps around the country. On top of her television, stacks of videotapes: *Buns of Steel, Legs of Steel, Abs of Steel.*

They sat on the couch like awkward kids on their first date. "So, what do you do?" Lattan asked.

"Oh, I don't really have a real job yet. Right now I'm an intern at the Department of Agriculture. But I'm hoping it will lead to something permanent. I know it's hard to get that first job in DC right out of school at 21."

Lattan winced ... 21 years old? The black leather, the make-up ... she looked at least 30 ... God, what was he doing here?

"Really?" he replied, trying to maintain his equilibrium. "Where are you from, originally?"

"Idaho. My father's a potato farmer. That's how I got to the Ag department. How about you?"

Idaho! Good lord! "Well, ah ... that's quite a coincidence, actually ... you see, er, I represent a portion of Idaho myself ..." A potato farmer's daughter! Might even be one of his contributors!

"So you really are a Congressman, huh?" she giggled. "Prove it."

Lattan groped for his wallet, and produced his electronic voting card.

"Wow — you are a Congressman! I thought you were just trying to impress us! Hey — if you're from Idaho, you must know my father ..."

Lattan already had more information than he wanted. He had to get out now!

"Well, it was nice meeting you, Jeannie," Lattan said. "Good luck with everything. I've got to be going."

"Not so fast," she purred, lunging at him and kissing him. Lattan felt himself stiffening. Then he pulled away.

"Young lady!" Lattan said, stupefied. "I'm flattered, but I'm old enough to be your father!"

"Oh, come on, *Congressman*, I know how this town works ... you can help me get a job, and I can help you feel like a young spud again."

She leaned over and kissed him again, then stuck her tongue in his ear, exhaling hot, boozy breath. Lattan felt a rush of heat to his face.

"Please!" Lattan said, pulling back and standing up. "I'm a happily married man! This is not proper!"

"Oh, come on ... don't you want to play 'Bill and Monica'?" she said, pulling his tie.

"No ... I'm sorry, I'm just not that kind of politician," Lattan said, stumbling backwards toward the door. On his way out, he noticed her last name on the door—*Jeannie Fisher*—and tried to remember it so he could look it up to make sure her father wasn't a Friend of Charles Lattan, an esteemed donor to the Re-Elect Committee.

Moments later, safely in a cab, he began drifting in and out of consciousness. Back home in his Capitol Hill apartment, he slumped on his bed. Though drunk and exhausted, he was unable to fall asleep. He stared blankly at the ceiling, trying to piece together an evening of adventitious events that led him to be lying here wondering whether he was about to be engulfed in his own intern scandal.

Who was her father? Would she tell anybody about tonight? Embellish her story? Would his fingerprints in her apartment be his physical evidence, like that Hillbilly's stain on the dress? Oh, God, the very thought of it!

Chapter 16

The Remorse Of The Morning After

Lattan sat at his Cannon House Office Building desk shortly before noon, ignoring MSNBC on the TV. His morning-after self-recriminations were in full throttle, and Lattan was livid at himself for the previous evening's behavior.

What was he thinking? Going up to that young lady's apartment ... him, a married man, descending into the squalor of infidelity ... with a potato farmer's daughter!

He knew he was a bad drunk. But this was way beyond the normal booze-induced lapse in mental faculty.

Who was she? He couldn't even remember her name ... no way of knowing if her father was a donor, a Chamber of Commerce member, a Farm Bureau official.

God, what would happen if this got out? Dare he consider ... Those bastards in the media would just love it!

He knew he was getting paranoid. Truth was, he wasn't important enough to warrant a sex scandal.

How pathetic. His saving grace was his lack of consequence in the politics of personal destruction consuming Washington.

And he hadn't even done anything! He was a loyal husband, always had been ... Even in his drunken fog, he'd had the rectitude to do the right thing and get the hell out of there.

Well, why were you in there in the first place, Congressman?

A good question. To talk farm policy? That was laughable. *And a follow-*

up, if I may ... in light of the recent climate in Washington, don't you think the voters have justification to question your judgment?

Oh, this was a pointless exercise. There was nothing he could do, no one he could tell. Hell, anyone he *would* tell would probably chide him for not reciprocating to the young lady's overtures.

He tried to focus on business. He grabbed the remote and clicked to C-SPAN. The House had just gone into session, and Members were doing "One Minutes." God, what a silly exercise that was ... unless you were like that character from Ohio, what's-his-name.

Lattan didn't speak often in front of the House. He wasn't telegenic, his words didn't rouse. But with the race tightening, he knew he could use the face time. Talking in front of the House was cheaper than buying more commercials.

Maybe he should ask his chief of staff, Rachel, to prepare one for tomorrow—something nice and nebulous. Avoid specifics that could hurt in the campaign.

But—what if *she* watched C-SPAN and recognized him—and fingered him as her potential paramour?

No, couldn't take the chance ... had to keep low until he was sure there would be no fallout. He'd have to grit his teeth at Rotary Club dinners, town hall meetings and rubber chicken church lunches for fear of her "outing" him.

"The gentleman from Ohio is recognized for one minute," the fat Speaker announced. Lattan watched the Member march to the podium and adjust the microphone.

"Thank you, Mr. Speaker." The gentleman from Ohio looked sideways in both directions. "Mr. Speaker, what constitutes perjury? To find out, we don't need constitutional surgery. To me, it's as clear as the rule of 12 people per jury. We don't need legal liturgy, or White House urgery, to know that perjury is impeachable. Now, maybe the president's lawyers aren't exactly reachable. Maybe they're not teachable. But they better be breachable through all of those legal defenses if we're going to avoid a crisis whose affect on our nation is leachable. Mr. Speaker, let's stop the legal hair-splitting, the attempt at constitutional retrofitting, being incorporated now to keep this president's status as one who's 'sitting.' Let's stop the spinning, pledge a new beginning, and get on with our duty to make sure that, in the end, it's the

American people who are the ones winning. Thank you, Mr. Speaker, and I yield back the balance of my time."

Lattan tendered a smile and nod of approval. He was entertaining, this fellow from Ohio, even if his hair was funny and his ties too thin.

"Good morning, Charlie," Emmell said, appearing in his open doorway.

"Mornin,'" Lattan said, taking a long glance at his chief of staff. She would stick by him if this erupted, wouldn't she?

Lattan was always amazed at how Emmell overcompensated for being a woman. Not many female chiefs of staff on the Hill. Had to prove herself not only as a top aide, but as a female in a traditionally male job. So she repressed her femininity, acted like a man. Squared her shoulders, used expletives with the impunity of a locker room brute. Inside her slender, 38-year-old body was a paunchy, martini-swilling political logroller trying to get out. Lattan would tell her so if he could think of a way to phrase it as a compliment.

Not an unattractive woman ... preternaturally thin from high-metabolic political intensity ... sharp dresser ... but that nervous tick of playing with the pearls on her necklace — it would almost be better if she bit her nails.

"Ready for the staff meeting?" she asked.

Staff meeting?

"Oh, yes, of course," Lattan replied. What on earth for? "Round up the troops," he said, chuckling nervously.

Lattan braced himself for the managerial fire drill. Emmell was prone to overreaction, but ... what if this was a meeting to discuss damage control to what's-her-name's claims?

Now Lattan was bracing for the worst. But why would she announce it to the staff before talking it over with him first?

It couldn't be! It had to be just another one of Emmell's pointless staff meetings, didn't it? He was now inured enough to know that she overreacted to everything, from less-than-laudatory news stories to voter barbs at town meetings. Lattan clung to the wistful hope that this meeting would be characteristic Emmell. Call everyone in, relay a constituent complaint about not having her letter answered quickly, then re-emphasize the need to execute every duty with an idea of how it will help re-elect the Honorable Charles Lattan.

First in was senior legislative assistant Don Root, U.S. Congress scratch pad in one hand and U.S. Congress pen in the other. He sat in the large leather chair, the most comfortable in the room, across from the Congressman's desk.

Then the rest of the staff meandered in. Legislative director, legislative assistants, scheduler, receptionist. It looked more like the early moments of a fraternity-sorority mixer than a Congressional staff meeting. Low pay attracted only the young and idealistic, who were willing to sacrifice decent salaries to be able to say, "I work for a member of Congress."

"I appreciate everyone dropping everything for an unscheduled meeting," Emmell said. She sat on the couch caddy-corner to the Congressman's desk, facing the staff. "I know everyone's busy, but I wouldn't pull you away if I didn't think this was critical."

"This discussion must stay in this room," Emmell continued. "This is not official Congressional business. It's campaign related. I know federal election law prohibits us from working on the campaign before we've put in our 40 hours for the government, so let's just assume that we're all going to work more than 40 hours this week anyway, and that this meeting is taking place on our free time. We may be bending the rules, but everyone does it. As long as we keep it quiet, what those prigs at the Federal Election Commission don't know won't hurt us. Agreed?"

Silent nods, a few wrinkled noses. Resentment that she assumed everyone cared about campaign matters as much as she did, was willing to contribute to the cause. As if the legislative staff was immune from the voters' wrath! As if their jobs weren't on the line too!

Such apathy! It was as if they believed the walls of the Cannon Building protected them from the voters' verdict, and the campaign was a war fought in a far-off land, waged by others on their behalf.

"I've just read a copy of today's *Daily Political Briefing*," she said, holding up the web printout in her hand. "It contains an unflattering piece that some joker over there believes qualifies as comedy. It reads, and I quote, Rep. Charles Lattan, who opposes the french-fry tax, has called on Clinton to resign. Given Clinton's well-known fondness for the greasy snack, wouldn't that hurt potato farmers in his district?'"

Lattan's face tightened. First shock, then fury, then relief, then confusion. What did this have to do with that farmer's daughter?

"I didn't know about this until a few moments ago, until I got my e-mail alert," she said. "Apparently, they think they're real cutesy over there. This is what gets me ... *Real* scandal, *real* dirt, *real* negative information, that I can handle. Coordinating effective damage control is one of the purest joys of politics. But this kind of crap — "

"You mean that's it?" Lattan asked hopefully.

"Yes, Charlie, *that's it*," his chief of staff said sharply. "Well, I suppose we should all be glad *you're* not unnerved by it." She shook her head. "But I don't know what we're going to do about this, if anything."

Lattan's mind was sprinting victory laps around the track ... the sheer absurdity of getting apoplectic about a little snide attack in the press! And of his being paranoid about the Idaho intern ... when he hadn't even done anything!

"I think we're losing focus here," said Don. "Let's focus more on attacking Rich Cooper. You win campaigns by pummeling your opponent, not by painting your guy as Mr. Wonderful. Let's not worry so much about *containing* our negatives as we do about *driving up* Cooper's negatives. The secret to winning is making your opponent's negatives higher than yours. You don't win by being loved more than your opponent, but by being hated less. Am I right?"

"I appreciate your input," Emmell said dismissively. "But until we have that opportunity, assuming we can find dirt on Cooper, I want everyone in this room to be extra-careful about everything they do." She struck the armrest with a karate-chop. "That means every letter you write, every phone call you take, every vote you recommend, must be done with the thought of how that single action will contribute to victory. Clear?" A final karate-chop for emphasis.

Don piped in again. "Why don't we save ourselves some time and just start tying the guy to Clinton? That's the easiest way to drive up his negatives."

"Point well taken," Emmell replied, proceeding to go into a treatise on campaign theory that Don, among other young and impressionable staff members, was eager to absorb. Made them feel like kingmakers, handlers, spinmeisters.

But Lattan was no longer listening ... he was laughing inside, laughing at himself for getting so exercised about nothing, laughing at his staff for being so concerned about a little jab from a political newsletter. *Yes, by all means, let's make my opponent as inseparable from Bill Clinton as Monica's name ...*

New campaign ads ... challenges for Cooper to condemn Clinton, make him distance himself from the party leader ...

Yes, Charles Lattan was once again confident about this election! The french fry tax, his votes on issues, his media image were less important to his chances than whether Clinton would cause a Democrat bloodbath at the polls. So what if meant winning ugly? It was still winning. Oh yes, right after this meeting, Lattan would call his media guru, Kentrell "Alt" DeLeet, and tell him to get the media buy going. By the time DeLeet was done, the voters would think Rich Cooper was Clinton's clone.

Chapter 17

The Infomercial

"Cut," the producer said, thinly disguising his eroding patience. "Congressman, we need you to be more, how shall I say it, *warm*, for the camera. Television is a cool medium, yes, but not a cold medium. You have to sell yourself to the voter as if you were a new diet plan or get-rich quick scheme."

Congressman Charles Lattan sighed and slumped back into his chair. He knew he wasn't telegenic. It wasn't just the bad combover, which contrasted horribly with Democratic nominee Rich Cooper's Kennedyesque looks. No, it was that damn GOP disposition — cold, stern, uptight.

Lattan realized that the sooner he warmed up for the cameras, the sooner they could finish taping what was to be only an obligatory cameo appearance. But he was weary with the banalities of taping a 30-minute infomercial to run on cable TV stations throughout Idaho in the midnight-to-6 a.m. "sellovision" slots. He was sick of this exercise, and he could sense that his normally unflappable media guru, Kentrell "Alt" DeLeet, was getting flapped.

The make-up girl, as if sensing an opportunity, took advantage of the break in the action to dash onto the set and blot Lattan's balding pate with a giant powder puff.

Perhaps he was upset by the sudden change in strategy. The original plan had been to go negative. But then they scrapped the idea, deciding at the last possible moment to go warm and fuzzy — Hi, I'm Mr. Wonderful, Congressman Charles Lattan, back from Washington to help *you*.

Lattan had agreed with DeLeet and the producers that it best if he were on the show as little as possible ... no matter how hard he tried, he always spluttered through a series of "ahs," "ums," and "you knows." He wasn't so inured to reality that he didn't realize he was too old, rumpled, and inarticulate to do half an hour of self-aggrandizing campaign video.

So they concluded the rest should be hosted by a washed up movie or sports star they could get on the cheap, with testimonials from happy potato farmers peppered throughout. Lattan would have a total of maybe two minutes face time, and even then only to respond to the host's probing "*So why are you such a great Congressman*" questions. The campaign and production teams would take care of the rest, with direction from DeLeet.

But this two-minute segment was proving to be the hardest part, and carried the added significance of being the last part they taped.

The host was Bob "The Bomber" Bonner, an aging quarterback from the '70s who'd gone on to an illustrious post-athletic career as a B-movie shoot-em-up tough guy. Over the last few years, however, the Hollywood roles had shrunk in direct proportion to the direct expansion of his waistline; his fame had receded as steadily as his hairline. So he fit the host profile they wanted perfectly: household name, bargain price, amenable to saying whatever they wanted about the Congressman.

And what a great shill he was! The infomercial opened with a grabber line from a newly svelte and tan Bonner, back in fighting trim, asking viewers from a poolside perch, "Have you given up on Washington? Do you think being cynical about your elected officials is an inevitable part about surrendering your silly notions about good government? I'm former NFL quarterback Bob Bonner, and I'm here to tell you about a Congressman who's not your regular corrupt politician on the take." Cut to file footage of the sleek quarterback throwing an 80-yard touchdown pass. Then cut back to live shot, with Bonner hamming it up for Congressman Lattan, looking credible in polo shirt and khakis.

Bonner's spiel was standard infomercial boilerplate:

"Over the next few minutes" — never tell the viewer you're going to browbeat them for half an hour! — "I'll be talking to you about the difference Congressman Charles Lattan has made in Idaho, and we'll hear from average Idahoans, like yourselves" — don't let them think only celebrities can be TV shills! — "who have benefited from the yeoman work Charles

Lattan has done for us in that cesspool known as Washington D.C."

The arguments over how much to highlight Lattan had been intense, with DeLeet leading the charge for maximum face time. But the cooler heads in production had prevailed, arguing that the goal was not public love for Lattan but to earn fifty percent plus one votes. And they would earn votes based on the viewing public's desire for one thing only: to stop the inanity on the beaches of the Potomac River.

So it was agreed that, for the purposes of infiltrating the world of psychic friends networks, stop smoking tapes and get-rich-quick schemes, *The Charles Lattan Story* would be marketed like a rotisserie barbecue or a Chia Pet, with as little presence from Lattan as possible.

Bob Bonner would be the huckster, satisfied spud peddlers the testimonial-givers, and the opponent mentioned only in passing.

Yet how would you market Charles Lattan as the solution to the problems in Washington when he was incumbent member of the political governing class? The questions had consternated the campaign folks.

But campaign manager Alex Macro had a riposte. Bonner would "interview" the "man from Spudsville" only briefly, and only when they were twenty-two minutes into the show, to make sure the viewer/voter was already hooked and wouldn't change his mind.

So here they were, slogging through this two-minute Lattan cameo, the other twenty-eight minutes done. It was a good ad, Lattan had to admit, as the director coached him on warming up before the next take. Lattan tried to reassure himself that this slick infomercial would convince scads of nocturnal viewers plowing through bags of chips on the sofas of their double-wides that Lattan could make their lives better.

"Can you smile a little more?" the director asked Lattan. "It's only two minutes. Please, sir, it will help you sell yourself."

The director seemed as unfazed about *The Charles Lattan Story* as he was about the psychic connection or the amazing juice diet. To him, it was just another late-night pitch, another job to do. He, and the rest of the camera crew and staff, probably weren't the least bit interested in politics, but only in how much longer they'd have to prostitute themselves this way until they'd get their big breaks that would allow them to pursue their dreams of making movies, of being artists.

And Bonner didn't seem to care either. Then again, he was just a dumb jock with a smooth delivery. And an aging one at that. He seemed genuinely enthused about this drill, riding a wave of renewed self-esteem resulting from being back in front of the cameras. He was too happy with his rekindled success to give a damn.

"I'll try," Lattan said. "I'll smile more."

"OK, let's take it from the top one more time," the director said, backing away and waving his arm in a semi-circle to signal everyone on the set to get ready for action. When everyone was in place, the director nodded at the cameraman, who began rolling, and then gave a thumbs up to Bonner.

"Remember, folks, operators on our toll-free number are standing by, waiting for your call," Bonnor said. "That number is on the bottom of your screens, so call in to get your free voter's guide now!"

Bonner turned away from the camera and then toward Lattan, seated across from him in a deck chair.

"Now we're going to talk to the man who's done so much for Idaho, Congressman Charles Lattan, for his insights. Congressman, thank you for joining us today."

"My pleasure," Lattan said, forcing a weak smile.

"We understand that you have been leading the charge in Washington against this repressive french fry tax."

"Yes, that's correct," Lattan said, crossing his legs. "Many people think a french fry tax is a victimless tax. So I took it upon myself to figure out how to explain to them the suffering such a tax would inflict on the salt-of-the-earth people in Idaho ..." Lattan finished with a few more bromides, then shut up and let Bonner close out the segment.

DeLeet looked pleased, as though a sanguine Lattan was answering the questions according to the prepared script.

Bonner nodded pensively. "Thank you for some insight into what's going on in Washington," Bonner said, turning away from Lattan and back toward the camera. "Well, there you have it, folks. Straight from the Congressman. So what are you undecided for? Remember to vote for Idaho — vote for Charles Lattan in November!"

Bonner continued to stare into the camera with a smile plastered on his face.

"OK, that's a wrap," said the director, waving his arm downward to signal the camera crew to stop rolling. "Well done, gentlemen. That'll do it."

Lattan was relieved. Dare he entertain the possibility that the video could bolster his sagging poll numbers?

But at that very same moment, back in Washington, a potato farmer's daughter named Jeannie Fisher was plowing through the *Almanac of American Politics* to see if she recognized a photo of this guy named Charles Lattan. ...

Chapter 18

The Confrontation

Lattan sat in a booth inside downtown DC's Wild West Grille, listening to his media guru, Kentrell "Alt" DeLeet, try to spin the lousy ratings for his campaign infomercial, *The Charles Lattan Story*.

Lattan pretended to listen, but he was distracted by the denizens of legal assistants, executive secretaries and government consultants hovered over the bar, sipping lime-garnished beers and crunching tortilla chips and salsa. Southwestern decor, with fake cattle skulls, Mexican blankets and cactus paintings, covered the stucco walls.

"You've got to put things in perspective," DeLeet said, ever the counselor. "Much as I hate to say it, you and I both know the economy and dot bombs are going to have more to do with the outcome of the race than anything we do."

Lattan felt as weary as an aging cattle rustler. "Come on, Kentrell. Don't spin me like you spin the media. You promised me big numbers. You promised me this would swing momentum back in my favor." His voice was as prickly as a cactus.

DeLeet took the lime wedge from his Corona and flung it into an ashtray. "You think my job is easy? You think the press is a public relations firm?"

Lattan's thoughts galloped away ... if only DeLeet knew! Lattan pictured himself returning to the plumber's life ... holding a plunger, wearing rubber gloves, assuring some bloated middle-aged housewife, *"It's just too much toilet paper, ma'am."* Can't let that happen!

"But you're the one who's always saying that when a race is this tight, every little thing counts. Any one thing that could sway a chunk of votes could make or break us."

"You think some civic group in Spudsville or Cottage Fries Falls is gonna no longer support you because of a stupid infomercial? Of course not."

Lattan shook his head, scratched the paint off of a Corona bottle with his fingernail. "I guess you're right." He stood to leave. "Thanks for the drinks and spin."

He trudged toward the subway station, and resolved to expel the issue from his mind. But as he stood in front of the Farragut North terminal, his spirits dampened again, albeit for a different reason. Once more, he was going home to a lifeless apartment.

Sleeping alone in Washington had been getting old. His wife was back in Idaho. And he'd always remained loyal. But where had it gotten him? With lower poll numbers than ever!

Halfway down the stairs of an idle Metro escalator, he reconsidered his destination. He turned around and trotted up the steps, drawing frigid glares from overworked commuters clumping downward. He headed West on L Street, toward Roxanne's Club Room.

Inside Roxanne's, patrons crowded around the stained wood bar. Stooped businessmen in puckered suits hunched over their drinks, refusing to concede the end of happy hour. Near the back, a deejay sorted stacks of compact discs. At the edge of the dance floor, young women fidgeted, sipping draft beer from plastic cups, waiting for the music to start.

Lattan planted himself on the first available barstool. He remained silent through six Heinekens. Young women soon secured stools vacated by departing businessmen. He didn't make eye contact.

After consuming a series of shooters with her friends, the woman next to him pivoted to face him. Chipping, if not breaking, the ice.

"Nice to see you again, Congressman!"

It was her! Again with the black leather miniskirt and too much make-up! Jeannie! The potato farmer's daughter! He was speechless.

"So, buy me a drink?" She blew smoke out of the side of her mouth.

What to do?! Think! ... Had to play along! ... He flagged down the bartender and ordered.

"So, how's the campaign going?" she asked.

Eager for attention, judgment blurred from too much drink, Lattan started. And he went on. He kept buying her drinks, for he knew that if he stopped buying, she would stop listening. And he kept buying for himself, to avoid looking like the lightweight he knew he was. Fortunately, she seemed dazzled by his stories of Capitol Hill.

"It must be exciting being a Congressman. Is it like being a movie star?"

"You get used to it after awhile," Lattan said, waving his hand drunkenly. "We're just people like everyone else. You'd be surprised at how human we are."

"But you make the laws and everything. You have to get elected by zillions of people. There must be something special about it. Isn't that what attracted you to politics in the first place?"

"Yeah, I guess," Lattan said plaintively. "I used to be impressed with all the pomp and circumstance. But now that I've seen everything behind the scenes, I'm not that impressed anymore."

"But you must still believe in what you do for a living, or you wouldn't do it."

"I guess I do," he said, realizing too late that he'd talked his way out of impressing her with his job. How drink absconded with discretion.

Worried he'd dominated the conversation, he tried to draw her out. Fortunately she talked. And talked. He'd berated himself for saying so much earlier, but now he was confident he was following the constituent service manual. Play Congressman, be fascinated with whatever she says.

Jeannie's friends returned from the dance floor. She excused herself to caucus with them for a moment, then turned back toward Lattan.

"We have to get up early for work, so we're going now," she said, holding her hand out to shake his. "It was nice seeing you again. Thanks for the drinks."

Lattan held out his hand. She shook it, limp. He stood silent, expressionless, stupefied. Then, inhibitions blunted, drunken anger acute, he ceded control of his mouth to his emotions.

"After all the drinks I bought, you should be coming home with *me*."

Her polite goodnight smile disappeared, replaced with a crimp.

"Boy, you had me fooled. I thought you were a nice guy, different from most of the political drones I meet in this town." She shook her head, *tsk tsk*

tsk. "But you're not. You're like all the rest of the Congressmen." Then she turned to catch up with her friends.

"Why? Just because I expect a return on my investment?" he caterwauled, liberated by defeat. "What happened to your offer to play 'Bill and Monica'?"

She froze. Then she turned around and marched toward him. Her mouth constricted, her eyes narrow, she stopped only inches from his face.

"You know something? You are incredibly rude! Would you say that in front of my father? He's a big shot in the farm bureau, you know."

Patrons stared. Lattan felt his face getting as red as hot sauce. He folded his arms in front of him, defiant. Fortress Lattan. But nothing to say.

"Yeah, I thought so," she said, nodding, voice low. She turned around again, and then walked out.

Lattan stood for a moment, then realized people were still staring.

"Show's over, folks. Nothing to see here. Keep moving," he said, doddering to the bar to pay his tab. Ninety-five dollars.

He waited until she was out of range. Then he staggered out of Roxanne's toward the subway station. He boarded the empty train, and wondered what he'd done wrong. How could her mood have shifted as abruptly as his polling numbers? He felt a twinge of regret.

The train lurched in the tunnel. Lattan sat with his arms over his stomach, leaning his head forward, fighting an urge to vomit. He stumbled out at the Capitol South station, then plodded up the escalator to the deserted street. He wrapped his arm around the first available lamppost and leaned over. Foamy beer froth and stomach acid blasted out of his mouth with the velocity of a firehose. He hung on the lamppost to catch his breath. Then he exploded again. Another brief rest, then a final purge. Sweat dripped off of his face into the puddle of vomit.

His condition improving, he navigated the two blocks to the aging high-rise behemoth in which he lived. A rusted metal sign greeted him. CONGRESSIONAL TOWERS. Inside, peeling paint, moaning elevators, lobby furniture from a yard sale. He managed a drunken wave to the night desk attendant.

To his cold, dark, empty hovel: "Honey, I'm home." A forced laugh. He collapsed on his torn futon, too exhausted to remove his vomit-crusted clothes. He picked up the remote control, clicked on the television. Before he could switch to the late rerun of "Special Report With Brit Hume," he passed out.

At five-thirty a.m., Lattan's head thudded like the music vibrating from a speaker on a nightclub dance floor. His tongue was dry, coarse, bitter.

He didn't have to rise for another two hours, but he couldn't get back to sleep. New positions did not help. Burying his head in the pillow did not diminish the pain.

The mental and physical energy he was expending to get back to sleep had the opposite effect. He tried so hard to achieve unconsciousness that it roused him. Turning the pillow over, then back to the first side, pulling the covers over him, then throwing them off, and burying his head under the pillow all failed to elicit relief.

Head throbbing, stomach gyrating. The physical pain was bad. But the mental anguish was much worse. Self-recrimination, the hangover's unavoidable by-product. He cringed at the memories. The embarrassment of a whole bar witnessing his humiliation.

A sudden urge propelled him into the bathroom. He leaned over the toilet. His entire midsection contracted and expanded, expelling nothing through his oral cavity but air and loud groans. Then a moment of peace, as he clutched the seat with his face hanging over the bowl, panting, sweating. Then another heave, then another, then the urge passed. He stumbled back into bed and buried his head in the pillow, the headache still grinding.

He vowed to stick to solitary, homebound drinking as a method of damage control against his inevitably shoddy drunken behavior. Then he realized that would only amplify his loneliness. He thought of waking up next to his wife at home in Spudsville, talking about what to have for breakfast.

He got up, shambled toward the door to retrieve *The Washington Past*, stubbing his toe on his ripped recliner. Walking reconfirmed how awful he felt, adding dizziness and lethargy to the list of symptoms.

He toddled toward the kitchenette to get his first Mountain Dew of the day. He sat at his metal table with his soda and scanned the front page.

He felt better once the caffeine kicked in, and he plowed through the national, world, and business sections. Then, as he read the Style section's

"Reliable Poacher," a small item caught his bleary eye: "We hear radio grump-jock Don Imus called Congressman Charles Lattan's office yesterday to set up a guest appearance, but Lattan did not return phone calls to Imus or to us."

He wanted to scream. But all he could muster from a fitful sleep was a guttural "God dammit," pathetic and feeble, a cry serving as a perfect encapsulation of how pathetic and feeble his political career had become.

Chapter 19

Don Imus Rants

"Where the hell is Lisa Myers, you fat bastard?" Lisa Myers being the NBC anchor supposed to file a story on MSNBC, the fat bastard being "Imus In The Morning" producer Terry Irving, the progenitor of the angry question being Don Imus, the original radio shock jock.

"Well, if you can't find her, get that no-name Congressman on here then, you weasel."

The no-name Congressman was Idaho Representative Charles Lattan, who cowered in the MSNBC/WFAN green room as he watched his host let fly with one of his patented rants.

What had caused the rant wasn't clear. It could have been the toddler keeping him up all night. It could have been more angry reaction to his flip-flopping on the political issue of the day. Or it could have been the futile, wanton anger of the recovering drunk incensed that he can no longer douse his flaming inferno of rage with a fifth of bourbon.

But that didn't really matter. All that mattered was that Lattan was about to walk into the crossfire.

Oh, the idea of being a guest on "Imus in the Morning" had seemed good at the time. And Lattan's media guru, Kentrell "Alt" DeLeet, had talked him into it as easily as he talked reporters into printing his press releases verbatim. Get some national exposure, look Congressional on national television (though how "national" MSNBC was was an issue itself), make that young whippersnapper Rich Cooper look like the neophyte that he was.

But now, in the wake of Imus' rancor, it didn't seem like such a good idea.

"Congressman, we're ready for you," said dapper producer Terry Irving, resplendent in pinstripe suit, crisp tab-collar shirt and blue repp tie.

"I'm ready," Lattan said tentatively, as he stood to follow Irving into Imus' lair during a commercial break.

Lattan sat across from the I-Man, hoping this would be no more taxing than sitting in radio booth in Spudsville, taking calls on a local radio show.

"Joining us now is Congressman Charles Lattan of Idaho," Imus said. "Now, Congressman, I don't mean to put you on the spot here, but what the hell distinguishes you from those other 434 weasels spending our tax dollars down in Washington?"

Lattan took a moment to size up his host ... he looked every day of his 59 years — the same age as himself! — but somehow didn't seem to wear it as well. Now, Lattan admitted to himself his bald spot, but other than that — why, he looked much better than Don Imus! That weary, weather-beaten skin, leathery like the wild-west theme he seemed trying to evoke with that silly cowboy hat. The bolo tie, the eyebrows pitched in the permanent scowl of the drunk who knows he can never touch another drop of booze ... such a sight!

AWell, Mr. Imus, I've been a leading advocate of—"

"Leading advocate? What kind of Washington phony language is that? My foppish producer Terry Irving was kind enough to inform me that your claim to fame is opposition to some proposed french fry tax. Is that right?"

"That's right," Lattan said, beaming. "I've been—"

"Well, lemme tell you something, Charlie. Anyone who listens to this show knows I'm foursquare against letting those fat bureaucrats in Washington get their hands on any more of any American's hard-earned money. But, on this one, I gotta tell ya, Charlie, I get one look at that lying, cheating, good-for-nothing fat bastard president, and I think, maybe I support this tax."

"Well, some people think this is a victimless tax. I don't blame you a bit, but—"

"I mean, plenty of those fat phonies, like Newt Gingrich, Jerrold Nadler, Henry Hyde and J. D. Hayworth could benefit from a fat tax. All these fat bastards packing away the french fries."

"Well, the fact is that —"

"Let me tell you, Congressman ..."

Lattan was now second-guessing his decision to do this interview. Yet he remained composed in appearance, listening attentively as Imus inveighed against fatties. Though he had every right to erupt in anger, he kept a cork on his ire.

But it was all he could do not to explode at his host. It was scenes such as this that made him rethink a career as a Congressman. It was all an act, and he had a more difficult time every day keeping it up. The chorus of self-reproach had become part of his daily routine.

As a freshman taking the oath only two years ago, Lattan was imbued with the fire and passion that propelled people into public service. But now, Lattan sat across from the original grump-jock ... Dare he admit it to himself? The political romanticism of public service was just so much window dressing.

Until he'd entered public service, Lattan had been content to drive himself to exhaustion unclogging toilets, spend his off-hours jockeying for position in the plumbing business rat race, drinking with pipe-fitters, and devoting whatever time was leftover to Ariel, she of the cliche, The Long-Suffering Wife.

It was the drive. The middle-class, second generation American, must do better than my parents, upward mobility as a means of security drive. Family, friends, hobbies were all subordinate to the obsession of Pursuing the American Dream.

Yet settling down as a family man — husband, father, small business owner, had ignited in him the question: Is this all there is?

It was a phrase. Settling. Down. How naive his idea of public service fulfilling his unquantifiable inner emptiness now seemed. The idealistic Idaho state legislator had, in a few short years, become a cynic. The hope of doing meaningful work had been replaced by the reality of insufferable constituents, chronic lobbyist fatigue, and the assorted feelings of despair. His ardor was almost completely gone. The zeal that once drove him to work early and stay late now seemed so quaint, so much folly.

He became more inclined to go through the motions of life. He'd fought it valiantly with a combination of denial and self-delusion. But somehow, sitting across from Don Imus, trying to get a word in edgewise as the I-man cut loose with one of his trademark attacks on weasels, phonies and fat bastards, the resignation set in for good, replacing the dreams that had departed.

Then there was his receding hairline, expanding waistline. ...

"— Christ, people die every day from obesity. Aren't you a little bit ashamed that your claim to fame is giving me more people to refer to as 'fat bastards'?"

"No, of course not," Lattan spluttered.

"Hold that thought, we have to go to commercial, but I promise you a response when we return." Imus paused. "We'll be right back after this commercial break."

Lattan's thoughts again began drifting ... the MSNBC background music was so mesmerizing ... it was as though he wasn't even there in the studio with the I-man, but watching himself in the third person. His thoughts again returned to his midlife crisis that propelled him into public service from life as a plumber. He remembered it well ... he'd been at a psychiatrist, trying to assess what was causing this feeling of inner emptiness ...

"I just don't understand it, Dr. Tonerlowe," he'd found himself admitting to his psychiatrist during one of their weekly sessions. He didn't know why, but Lattan was able to admit to Dr. Tonerlowe things he scarcely admitted to himself. "I just don't feel fulfilled in my life as a plumber."

Dr. Tonerlowe stroked his long grey beard, then tugged at his eyepiece. He nodded pensively.

"Vell, Charles, have you considered that your career choices might be the cause of these problems?"

"Of course, I think about that all the time," Lattan responded. "But plumbing is a noble profession."

"Let's go back to your childhood," Dr. Tonerlowe said. "Tell me what it was like when you were growing up."

Lattan sighed heavily and sank into the plush couch of his therapist's office. "I don't like to think about it. It was so painful. I'd rather focus on the problems I'm facing now."

"Well, sometimes we must look at the past to understand the present," Dr. Tonerlowe said.

Lattan sighed again ruefully. "People made fun of me."

"Aha!" Tonerlowe said. "Zere is a clue. Go on."

"It was so humiliating. I tried so hard to get people to like me."

"Yes, yes, it's coming clear." Dr. Tonerlowe stroked his beard and nodded.

"I've always felt I needed to prove myself more, show everyone that I'm not some clown they can ridicule."

"Yes, this is a classic response to such feelings," Dr. Tonerlowe said. "You feel like you must get back at those people in your childhood who caused you pain, so now you displace your anger at them by acting as though you must prove that you should be taken seriously. Hence your propensity to talk loudly and attempt to draw attention to yourself."

"Uh, er," Lattan sputtered. "Is it, that, uh . . . you seem convinced."

"It's classic," Dr. Tonerlowe said.

"So you're saying that people might respect me if I didn't try so hard?"

"Vell, that is part of it."

"And what's the other part?"

Dr. Tonerlowe hesitated. Honesty might cost the doctor his best customer. Psychiatric patients didn't pay to hear the truth, or to have their neuroses cured. They paid to be validated, to have the doctor tell them the world was against them, that they were right and that everyone else was wrong. But he knew he had to tell Lattan the truth.

"The other part is that you feel inadequate because you feel in your heart that you are not a good plumber, and it's tearing you up inside, despite your rationalizations to the contrary."

"You are clearly desperate to crawl out of your own skin and shed this part of your identity," Dr. Tonerlowe continued. "You hope that by showing how much you hate your working class identity, you will somehow be able to get rid of it. And all the while, you are paranoid that your efforts are transparent to everyone, and that everyone else knows what you are trying to do except you. But you are lying to yourself, and you are fooling yourself, if you think you can do anything to change what you are, and will always be, no matter what you do."

Lattan had flinched and sat up from the couch, his eyes ablaze with panic. What if the doctor was right? And was it that obvious to everyone around him?

"So what do I do?" Lattan shouted.

"Simple," Tonerlowe said. "The only solution for people who need to be constantly validated, for people who constantly need attention to overcome their chronic feelings of inadequacy, is to go into politics."

And that had been Charles Lattan's epiphany ... the reason he had chosen to go into public service. The turning point in his life that had led him to be sitting across from Don Imus, trying to explain why he opposed raising taxes on french fries.

Chapter 20

George Magazine Lauds Lattan

Lattan sat in his Pocatello campaign office, beaming — positively luminous! — as he read the latest issue of *George* magazine. Just as he'd been on the verge of despairing over his re-election prospects, the glossy political magazine had included *him* on its list of the season's best political quotes!

Here, as he drank in the printed words on page 116, savoring every *letter*, reading it again and *again*, he was beside himself with glee.

Rapture! How he'd proved the conventional wisdom watchers wrong! How he'd proved his own campaign strategists wrong! How he'd triumphed in spite of his own sometimes crushing self-doubt!

He knew he was acting a little too much like the kid on Christmas morning. But he'd had so much to be depressed about lately, why not bask in some good news for a change? Why not show that he was as capable of reaching the highest highs as we was of plummeting into the depths of dolor?

On one side of his chair stood his stoic media guru, Kentrell "Alt" DeLeet; the other his campaign manager, Alex Macro. They flanked him like flagstands. How DeLeet must have been silently *fuming* that this public relations coup wasn't the result of *his* press releases or spinning exercises or news conferences! No, this undeniable slice of creampuff press was the result of Congressman Charles Lattan's own brilliance!

The rest of the staff started filing in, having been summoned to share the magical moment. Lattan used the presence of new underlings in the room to read the piece again aloud for those who hadn't yet heard it.

"So the headline on page 116 of the November 1998 issue of *George* reads, 'They Said What?'" Lattan began, smiling smugly. "And it reads, and I quote, 'What with all the Washington scandals, it's been a rough year for politicians. Maybe that's why it's been a great season for political quotations.' Close quote."

"Go on," Macro urged.

Lattan looked up at his staff and smiled broadly. Then he returned his gaze to the glossy magazine splayed open on his desk, its shiny pages gleaming in the reflection of the grey tube lighting above.

"Well," Lattan continued, trying desperately to affect a matter-of-fact one, "The list includes two Senators and a former White House flack," he said. "Then, in bold face type," he paused and glanced quickly to make sure all eyes were upon him, "I'm quoted as saying, 'You make it sound like it's our fault that crooked bastard couldn't keep his hands off his interns! I can't understand why I can't score any political points by attacking the scoundrel!' And the tagline is, 'Idaho Congressman Charles Lattan, after an aide advised him to refrain from criticizing President Clinton."

"Outstanding, sir!" Macro said. The assembled staff and volunteers, as if responding to the cathode-ray gleam of a game-show APPLAUSE sign, erupted with loud clapping.

"Good thing I didn't listen to *you* guys," Lattan said in an *aw shucks* tone, winking and smiling at DeLeet, then Macro. Couldn't resist the gentle dig! Make sure they remember who's the Congressman around here!

"Wow. *George* magazine!" said a young female volunteer, whose name Lattan couldn't remember.

"Well done, Congressman," ventured Dot Com, an elderly phone bank volunteer.

"Very impressive," said Doug Click, another young volunteer.

"Thank you for indulging me," Lattan said to the staff, trying to feign modesty. "Now, if you'll excuse us, Alex, Kentrell and I are going to figure out how to milk this coup as much as possible. Though their advice has been wrong in the past," he said, chuckling, "I'm going to give them a chance to redeem themselves."

"OK, folks, back to work," Macro commanded. "Still got a campaign to wage."

The staff gamboled out of the office, their boosted morale evidenced by their lightness of gait. After the last one closed the door behind her, DeLeet turned toward Lattan and began:

"Congressman, you know I am just as happy about this as you. And I admit my poor judgment in this case, advising you against trying to use Clinton's general venality as a campaign issue." He paused. "But this thing with *George* is just gravy. We can't exploit this. No one in Idaho reads *George*! Maybe if you'd been quoted in *Soldier of Fortune* or *The Potato Press* we could do something. But this is one that helps only on the Potomac. It'll be great for your dinner party invitation prospects in D.C. for the next Congress. But you have to get re-elected to that next Congress first."

Lattan was at an utter loss for words. The insolence! His own media guru trying to pooh-pooh this golden moment merely because it resulted from him, Lattan, going against staff advice!

"You're kidding, right?" Lattan said, attempting to keep the tone light. "This is the best thing that's happened to my campaign in months!"

"I hate to be the bearer of a reality check, Congressman, but he's right," Macro said. "This is great for invitations to receptions and Fox News Channel interviews. But it doesn't do anything for us in our effort to beat Rich Cooper."

"You're crazy," Lattan sputtered. "We should put out a press release saying, 'Lattan Recognized As Thoughtful Critic Of Clinton,' or whatever, I dunno, you work on the precise wording and spin, and this will put me over the top."

"Not likely," DeLeet said, shaking his head slowly. "Rich Cooper will say, 'This is further proof that Lattan has contracted Potomac Fever, has joined the Inside-The-Beltway crowd, is part of the problem in Washington, and out-of-touch with the average citizen of Idaho.'"

"The hell he will!" Lattan said, pounding his fist on his desk. "This is my moment of glory! I should get all kinds of good press on this, and Rich Cooper shouldn't even be heard from."

"I'm afraid that's not realistic," Macro said. "I'm sure Cooper will have plenty to say, regardless of whether we try to flog the *George* thing or not."

"What makes you confident you're so right?" Lattan asked. "You guys were wrong about this in the *first place*. How can I be sure you're dispensing sound advice *now*?"

"It doesn't matter what *we* think, Congressman," Macro said evenly. He paused. "Don't tell me you've forgotten!"

"Forgotten what?" Lattan asked.

"You're debating Cooper at the League of Women Voters next week!"

Chapter 21

Barbs Fly At Debate

Lattan sat in the back seat of his campaign Buick, pretending to listen as campaign manager Alex Macro briefed him on the way to his first and only debate with Rich Cooper. For Lattan, this exercise was only for show. His spirits still buoyed by the quote in *George* magazine, he wasn't the least bit interested in such a petty nuisance as a debate. He saw a lively exchange with his opponent as no more necessary than faxing campaign reports to the Federal Election Commission.

But Macro insisted that Cooper's past few weeks of stage drama — debating an empty chair — was having some resonance (with the media, at least, if not the electorate). So here he was, on his way to a debate at the Idaho Falls Town Hall.

They turned onto Main Street toward the event ... and he saw the crowd. Waving placards, marching around, chanting. Supporters! For Congressman Lattan! Wow! Macro had turned out the troops!

But as they got closer, he saw the signs: JUST SAY NO TO "BOY GEORGE" LATTAN. LATTAN IS A SELL-OUT. LATTAN'S GONE WASHINGTON, BY GEORGE. CURIOUS? GEORGE IS, BUT IDAHO'S NOT. WE'RE NOT IMPRESSED, GEORGIE BOY.

Protesters! Controversy! Controversy meant media coverage — and more exposure for Rich Cooper!

The anger on their faces! He could see it as the car crept closer ... placards and bullhorns and chants ... TV cameras swarming like bees on a honeypot

... Christ! Could it be? Was it even metaphysically possible? — That the notoriety from *George* was backfiring?

"Don't worry, Congressman," Macro said, as if sensing the candidate's anguish. "This means more media coverage. We've been running out of ad money anyway. This is great for us!"

Oh, the campaign manager was spinning away, but Lattan wouldn't buy any of it. He was too incensed with the crowd. The *chutzpah*! How dare they! Accuse Charles Lattan, *a plumber*, for chrissakes, of selling out!

But deep in his abdomen he felt it ... the class anger engendered by his attempt to flog a favorable bite ... oh, they'd seen the quote in *George* magazine ... on that glossy page ... amid ads for perfumes and fancy clothes and designer baubles and expensive knick-knacks ... and they'd obviously concluded Lattan is no longer one of *us*!

Macro was yammering away, something about the need for cooler heads to prevail and the need to focus on issues and our children's future and the work for the people of Idaho and stopping the madness in Washington ... all the points he was supposed to make during the debate ... but all he could see was *the anger on their faces* ... the contorted look caused by the indignation that *our Congressman has been quoted among Ralph Lauren ads!*

Lattan stewed silently, pensively, trying to make sense of it. Sure, he'd faced angry denunciations from waitress moms, college students, radio talk show callers. But this — before a debate! It would play right into Cooper's hands!

The media would feast on it! The irony! Mr. Big-Time-Quoted-In-*George*-Comes-Back-To-Idaho-To-Be-Among-The- Little-People! The ex-plumber-turned-Washington-elitist! It was despicable!

Lattan could see the police escort containing the throng. Another waved Lattan's car toward the entrance. The driver, silent the whole way, guided the sedan in gingerly, his greatest concern apparently limited to the potential for scratched paint.

"Take a look around," Macro said, stretching a flabby arm sheathed in polyester toward the window. "There's enough police here to keep it under control. It's just a media circus. Embrace the attention. It means more votes!"

Lattan craned his neck around, surveying the visage of blue uniforms restraining the mob behind wooden horses draped in neon orange tape declaiming POLICE LINE DO NOT CROSS. There must have been 200 protesters, shouting, raging, pumping their fists in the air, waving their placards ... over a quote in *George*!

The police cleared a narrow path through the crowd, cordoning off a trail with the wooden horses. A young officer opened the car door. Lattan took a deep breath, buttoned his suit coat, and stepped onto the pavement.

Immediately the jeers: "Fancy Boy!" "Media Whore!" He tried to look stoic against the barbs, attempting to affect the countenance of an avuncular statesman. Camera crews recorded every gesture, holding fuzzy microphones in front of the demonstrators for maximum sound quality.

The police created a gauntlet, led by beefy brutes in blue, and whisked him and Macro inside.

"This ain't as fun as bein' in *George* magazine, is it?" he heard a woman shout as the door closed behind them.

Then it was a blur of introductions and hand-shaking and thanks-for-coming and right-this-way-Congressman and Macro's *remember-to-stay-on-message* ... and Lattan found himself standing behind a podium in front of a huge audience of the League of Women Voters ... distracted as the moderator explained the format.

"Mr. Cooper, your opening statement."

And Lattan found himself staring at his opponent for the first time. This young whippersnapper, Cooper, looked even more youthful and — he had to admit — even more Kennedyesque in person than he did on his campaign commercials. Coal-black hair plastered to his head ... bookish eyeglasses ... ruddy good looks ... fashionable three-button suit ... like the kind advertised on the glossy pages of *George*! Well, I'll be damned if this kid shows me up!

"Congressman Lattan, your opening statement."

"Thank you, and I thank the League ..." and he recited the text as Macro had written it.

"Thank you, Congressman," the matronly woman said. "First question to you, Mr. Lattan. You voted for the presidential impeachment inquiry. Do you think Bill Clinton should be impeached?"

"Well, I want to make clear that I voted in favor of an inquiry to get all the facts ..." he began, and instantly could sense the crowd tuning out. They'd had enough! No one cared! Scandal ennui! *They'd had enough!*

Got to turn it around!

"... but that is not what I came here to talk about tonight, which is—"

"Time's up," the moderator interjected. "Mr. Cooper, rebuttal?"

"Thank you, madam chairman," Cooper said, tugging on his eyeglass frame. "Congressman Lattan's vote for an impeachment inquiry is just one of the many indications about how out-of-touch he is with the people of Idaho. A president's extra-marital affair, and his lying about it in a civil case, is not a high crime. But I'll tell you what is a high crime: Mr. Lattan's disregard for the problems of Idaho ..."

Lattan felt his body tensing ... this kid was smooth ... reading right from the Democratic Campaign Committee script ... and the crowd was eating it up! Hell, they were mainlining it!

"... And while I may not say anything colorful enough to be printed in some flashy political magazines, you can bet I'll do the right thing for Idaho," Cooper concluded.

The audience burst into applause. Lattan was apoplectic. Savages! Idiots! Falling for such cheap rhetoric!

The moderator interjected. "I'll remind the audience to please refrain from applause, which only takes away time from your candidate ..."

But Lattan was only too happy to have some help in crowd control. Oh, please, let them clap if they must! Anything to get Cooper to shut up!

"Mr. Cooper, next question is for you," the moderator said. "What is your position on the proposed french fry tax?"

"I've made no secret that I agree with my opponent on this issue," Cooper began. "The tax is a bad idea, it's bad for Idaho, and I commend Mr. Lattan for his work to fight it. But it is not the only issue important to Idaho. Unfortunately, Mr. Lattan has ignored ..."

Lattan tried to hide what he knew was an expression of utter shock on his face. Cooper opposed the french fry tax? It was news to him! Why hadn't he been briefed on this little morsel?

But then he remembered: Macro had said something about it in the car on the way over, right before he saw the protesters.

But what did it even matter now? Even if he had known? Cooper had not merely neutralized it as an issue in the debate, he'd actually managed to turn it against him ... Now he was *Charles Lattan, the Johnny one-note on the spud tax*. And though he frequently misjudged things, Charles Lattan at that moment had utter clarity that there was no recovering from this bombshell.

Cooper had already won the crowd, won the issue, won the debate. The rest would be perfunctory. Lattan was already on to the next campaign event, clinging to that old campaign nostrum about how *debates don't change anyone's mind anyway.*

Chapter 22

Lights Out In Idaho On Election Night

Ka-*thrrraaaaaaaakkkkkkkkk*!

A great crash of thunder made Charles Lattan's rib cage vibrate as he huddled with supporters in his campaign office. The rain was raging outside this election night, pelting and then streaking down the windows, each thunderclap closer than the last.

And seconds following this latest blast—

The lights flickered.

And went out.

And everyone found themselves in the dark, both literally and figuratively. Even now, shortly after midnight, the race with his opponent, Rich Cooper, was too close to call. And the televisions to which they'd been tethered were now big, black, silent boxes, telling them nothing.

"Everyone stay calm," said campaign manager Alex Macro. "We'll try and get some candles and flashlights until the power goes back on. In the meantime, everyone please keep enjoying the complimentary open bar. Because I guarantee you we will soon have confirmation that this is a victory party!"

Oh, save the spin, Lattan thought, sick of the *waiting, waiting, waiting, waiting* for the results. And now this.

Powerless. How symbolic.

Macro dispatched some of the volunteers to find temporary light, then attempted to resume working the phones to find some information. Everyone —from the Chamber of Commerce to the Farm Bureau to the state GOP

— seemed to be caught in the blackout, held hostage to the slow machinations of the Idaho Gas & Electric Company repair crew.

Which meant ... *more* waiting.

Lattan took advantage of the darkness to stop smiling, stop shaking hands, stop saying "Thanks for coming." He navigated through the nervous throng to the bar and grabbed a scotch.

He took a long pull from his drink, then retreated to his private office, where he sat and drank in the darkness, listening to the rain slap the windows, the thunder rattle the glass.

A lanky silhouette soon appeared in his doorway, closing the door behind him.

"Thought I might find you here, Congressman. It's me, Kentrell."

"Come on in," Lattan said, his voice now even from the surge of alcohol in his bloodstream, calming his nerves.

His media guru, Kentrell "Alt" DeLeet, toddled over to the chair across from Lattan's desk and plopped down. He gripped a bottle of beer with a moist napkin stuck to the bottom.

After a long moment of silence, Lattan finally spoke.

"Is this it?" he asked, like a seven-year-old asking his parent if God exists.

"Honestly?" DeLeet said, with a hint of a slur. "I think you're gonna pull it off."

"What makes you so confident?"

"Bad weather," DeLeet said. "It suppresses turnout, particularly among undecideds. They usually vote for Democrats."

Lattan winced. So this is what he was clinging to. Campaign help from an Idaho thunderstorm.

"I'd like to think there are other reasons I could be re-elected."

"Sorry, boss," DeLeet said. "Don't mind my cynicism. Media relations does that to its practitioners. When you get your spinning license, you have to trade in your idealism for cynicism."

"What is that supposed to mean?" Lattan asked. "You mean you've always been jaded?"

"No, of course not," DeLeet said. "There was a time when I used to respect how I made my living. But with all due respect, Congressman, when you work behind the scenes, and you see the actors without their makeup, costumes and scripts, you realize you're getting paid to help put the charade on stage. You're faced with a choice: make your peace with it or get out. As long as I'm always honest about the ruse, I can live with it. Sure, gaining that wisdom meant giving up a few silly notions. But it was a fair trade."

Lattan had no response. He didn't know whether to be disgusted with the pretense of politics or grateful for DeLeet's candor.

"I'm gonna get a refill," DeLeet said. "You want another?"

Lattan shook his head, and DeLeet rose and left.

Lattan stared at the lifeless TV screen on his credenza. Moments before, outside among the partisans, he and everyone else had remained rigid in front of the dozen tubes, compelled to watch every detail by a combination of prurient fascination and the hope that the next return from commercial break would bring news that things were swinging their way.

His eyes followed the line of signs and posters on the floor, the picked over deli trays laying in silent testimony to the hordes who tried to stuff their tension with ham and turkey sandwiches. Then, as if in a trance, he gazed once more at the television, clicking at it feebly with the remote control.

Powerless.

The inevitable chorus of "where did I go wrongs" began clamoring in his skull. Soon he was reviewing every campaign miscue, every weak answer to a reporter's question, every bungled decision, over and over in his mind, until they were as vivid as videotapes he popped into his VCR.

What if each successive blow in the White House scandal hadn't lost its impact to shock the public, scandalize and damage the Democrats? Sure, to Lattan and the rest of those who had played cameos in this drama, it was great stage fare. But most of the audience — the American people — had long since left the theater, bored by a vaudeville act that was no longer even remotely entertaining.

Oh, it was futile, this exercise in second-guessing. Had to move on, adjust to life as a former Member of Congress, to losing the appurtenances of elected office. His staff, his stature, the attention of the media ... even if it was negative ... at least it was attention.

But now — life again as a plumber! The humiliation! What a mighty fall! Maybe he could get a job as a lobbyist, the common career move for newly defeated Congressmen. ... But to walk the corridors as the representative of an industry, lobbying members of a body he failed to win re-admission to, on behalf of some cartel seeking a tax break ... No! For shame.

Holding any job in Washington but Congressman would be unbearable. Every day he'd go to work, as a visiting fellow or resident scholar or special envoy or commission head or whatever, and be reminded of his failure to reach his own career aspirations. His heart wouldn't be in any of those consolation jobs they give to has-been former Congressmen. He'd think everyone viewed him through the prism of failed politician.

Suddenly the lights flickered and then blazed on. The TV glared to life with a buzz and a whirl.

He frantically fumbled for the remote and began surfing ... looking for a channel with the Congressional results running on the bottom of the screen like sports scores on CNN Headline News.

He found a Fox or CNBC or C-SPAN or some such channel ... they were talking Senate and governor races, and had the usual political analysts offering commentary and insight and spin and the meaning of it all ... everyone talking about this bald-headed fellow in Minnesota ... a wrestler, for godsakes, was elected governor ... surfing, surfing ... finally, a station with the House race results running at the bottom of the screen.

Florida ... Georgia ... then Hawaii 1, Hawaii 2 ... then Idaho 1, Idaho 2, Idaho 3, Idaho 4 ... all of his colleagues were winning with 56 and 58 and 63 percent of the vote ... 100 percent of precincts now reporting ...

His heart was clanging away in his chest ... It was humiliating, waiting for his political *coup de grace*. His mental synapses were flailing around like severed power lines, sparkling and sizzling but not connecting. He felt an acrid taste in his dry mouth. His heart beat faster and faster ... his forehead was spangled with sweat. The entire campaign headquarters was silent ... everyone was holding their breaths collectively.

Idaho 15, Idaho 16, Idaho 17 ... Lattan (R) 50.4%, Cooper (D) 49.6%, 100% of precincts reporting . ...

Could it be?

He looked at the numbers again, before they vanished from the screen: *Lattan (R) 50.4, Cooper (D) 49.6, 100% of precincts reporting ....*

And then he heard the whoop, which confirmed he wasn't hallucinating. Macro's whoop. Again whooping. More. Then several whoops. Cheers.

Then Macro flung open the door, slamming it against the wall, his fat face puffed into a smile.

"Hot damn! You did it, Charlie, you did it!"

Then they all rushed in, Kentrell and Rachel Emmell and Dot Com and Flip Screen and Ariel and Dr. Tonerlowe and Don Root and John Tucancel. . . . and the volunteers and the phone bankers and the yard signers and the bumper sticker slappers ... whooping, cheering, drunk from victory and an open bar ...

And Lattan was utterly speechless ... in complete disbelief ... humbled, even ... more so than when he had first been elected ... his faith in the common sense of the average Idahoan restored ... amazed at his own capacity for histrionics when things don't seem to be going his way. ... into each life some rain must fall ... and he was glad the rain in his life this day had kept the undecideds at home.

Chapter 23

Watch It!

Though the campaign was over and he had been re-elected, the discussion taking place in the office of Congressman Charles Lattan made it hard to tell. As they had so many times before, Lattan's aides were trying to talk him out of pursuing what he *knew* was a great idea.

"Congressman, you're not going to go to Iowa to 'test the waters,'" campaign manager Alex Macro scolded. "You're not running for president. Period. With all due respect, it's a laughable concept."

Lattan was incredulous that his aides had instantly dismissed his idea of exploring a White House bid. No discussion, no debate, only scoffing. But if a wrestler could get elected governor, if a president facing impeachment could outlast a House speaker from the opposition party, what was so crazy about a newly re-elected Congressman running for president?

"I beg to differ," Lattan said. "A common man, a decent man, might be just what America wants after this exhausting year of scandals."

"Maybe," said his media guru, Kentrell "Alt" DeLeet. "But you have other problems far more serious than the usual political considerations."

"And what's that?" Lattan asked sarcastically.

"For starters, you have an image problem that even the biggest PR firms might not be able to solve," DeLeet said. "Your major obstacle is that people think you're a fictional character."

"What?" Lattan cried. "How do you mean?"

"I'm afraid it's true," Macro said, his flabby arms folded across his chest, standing across from Lattan's desk. "People don't believe that you actually exist."

"What on earth are you talking about?" Lattan caterwauled, pounding his fist on his armrest. "I'm the Congressman from Idaho's 17th district, and—"

"Just watch," DeLeet said, pointing the remote control to the VCR on the credenza, then clicking PLAY.

The screen flared to life, and on it appeared the blond talking head of MSNBC's Laura Ingraham, bouncing and bobbing against the backdrop of "Watch It!" In her guest chairs were two young men identified as "The Pundit Boys."

"Listen, Congressman," DeLeet said.

Ingraham began: "OK, now, you guys sometimes catch magazines, pundits like me, in big, big flub-ups. And I want to read something that we have a graphic of, this is from the *American Political Briefing*. This is quoted in *George* magazine: 'You make it sound like it's our fault that the crooked bastard couldn't keep his hands off his interns. I can't understand why I can't score any political points by attacking the scoundrel.' That was, supposedly, Representative Charles Lattan, *George* magazine in November. Whoops, what's that all about?" Ingraham asked her guests.

"Supposedly?" Lattan said. "Of course I said that! This is an outrage!"

"Keep watching," DeLeet said.

Lattan looked back at the TV, which now featured a young man from the Briefing: "Well, Charles Lattan is the fictional representative from Idaho 17, the congressional District 17 in Idaho which doesn't exist. On our web site we run a serialized account watching him go through his election, kind of mirroring what's happening in real life. *George* magazine picked up that quote in the November issue, where it ran what people are saying about the scandal."

Ingraham: "You guys basically made up this totally bogus soap opera, and *George* magazine editors are like: 'We've got stuff to fill, we have some empty pages here. Let's go through *the American Political Briefing*, what are they writing? Oh, my God, this is a great quote from Charles Lattan.'"

"Where's my congressional book?" Ingraham asked. She then riffled through a *Congressional Directory*. "I looked up Charles Lattan, all the faces in this congressional book—you see all the faces of current Members —Charles Lattan isn't in here, *George* magazine!"

DeLeet clicked off the TV and folded his arms across his chest. "That's what I call an image problem."

Lattan was speechless. *Totally bogus soap opera*, she said. The nerve! Why, sure, he had his share of misadventures, but to say he was the star of a *totally bogus soap opera* ... the insolence!

"So, you see, Charlie, there are some basics we need to work on before you start spending time in Iowa," Macro said. "And we've got other things, real life things, we need to work on. So if you'll excuse us, we're going to finish filling out your FEC reports."

Macro and DeLeet left Lattan alone in his office. Did he detect a note of ... *derision* ... in their attitude about all of this? Well, if they weren't interested in taking on this image problem, and then serving on his presidential exploratory committee, he'd find people who would! And he would start by calling up this Laura Ingraham and booking himself on her show to prove that he was a real person!

The next morning, Lattan sat in the MSNBC green room, watching on the monitor the blond host who was about to interview him. With one irate phone call yesterday, he had booked himself as the guest, ready to set the record straight about who was bogus and who wasn't.

But the sense that he was fictional wasn't nearly as troubling as the sense that he was .... getting older. Or did these MSNBC news people seem to be getting younger? This Laura Ingraham — host of her own political chat show — was young enough to be his daughter. And she wasn't even the youngest of them. This fledgling cable network, MSNBC, was nurturing plenty of its own young birds, raising them to be full-fledged members of the pundit flock. These young birds were hatching all over, chirping and nesting on the weekend chat shows ... making a 59-year-old Congressman feel positively old!

"Coming up after the break, we'll be joined by a Congressman who makes other politicians' PR problems look mild — Charles Lattan of Idaho, who has to fight just to make people believe he's a real person," said Ingraham, staring into the MSNBC camera. "Stay tuned to Watch It!"

"Congressman, will you follow me, please?" asked a young woman appearing in the doorway ... all smiles, this one, they all seemed to have that

TV smile, even if they weren't on-air people ... how old was she?

Lattan tried to divert his eyes from her derriere as he followed her onto the set. ... Quite an exquisite tail feather on this bird ... nothing wrong with looking, right? It wasn't as if he was pawing her in a windowless corridor, like *some* politicians. No, this Congressman was proud to still be a boy scout!

The crew seated him and hooked up the mike and did the usual *testing testing testing please say something* and he watched this Laura Ingraham look over her notes ... quite a looker, she was ... blond page-boy hairdo ... penetrating eyes ... nicely sculpted jawline ... sharp dresser ... lissome, even ... packaged seductively in a navy skirt, white silk blouse and navy blazer. Too bad that voice nearly spoiled it ... it was like a blender on frappe.

"Thanks for coming on such short notice," she finally said. "When I heard that you were demanding to be on my show, I bumped my whole guest list."

"Pretty bold move on behalf of a bogus soap opera star," Lattan said.

"Ha ha ha ha," she tittered ... blender on frappe ... he couldn't get it out of his mind.

"Thanks for having me."

"My pleasure," she said. "You know, I try to look balanced, but I'm always partial to my Republican guests," she said, winking awkwardly.

Lattan thought better of saying, "As anyone who watches your show knows."

"Ten seconds," the cameraman said, then counted down.

"Welcome back to Watch It!" Ingraham said, staring back into the camera. "We're joined now by Congressman Charles Lattan of Idaho, who is here to prove that he is not a fictional character. Congressman," she said, turning toward him, "thanks for being here."

"My pleasure," Lattan said.

"So, tell me, what is it like having to fight the perception that you don't exist? Must be tough."

Someone who understood! A sympathetic ear! An ally! Ready to let him tell the world! Or at least MSNBC's audience of shut-ins, unemployed and militia members.

"It's quite absurd," Lattan began. "Here I am, fresh from being re-elected, exploring the possibility of—"

"Congressman, I'm sorry to cut you off, but I've just been informed ... are you sure? ... Right now? OK ..."

Who on earth was she talking to?

Ingraham put her hand on her earpiece, nodded, then turned away from him and toward the camera.

"I've just been informed that we're going to go live to the White House, where President Clinton is going to apologize once again to the nation and talk about his continuing journey of atonement and spiritual redemption. Apparently we're just seconds away, and MSNBC will go live to the Oval Office as soon as White House staff is able to locate a Bible and place it in front of the president."

And just like that, the interview was over, Lattan's moment on national TV snatched away by that ... that ... *cipher* in the White House ... that *pretend* president ... that *imposter*!

"Congressman, I apologize," Ingraham said, as the crew removed his mike. "Decision made, as they say, above my pay grade."

"Not your fault," Lattan said, finding it impossible to feel any animosity to this young pundette who seemed to understand it all.

And within moments, he found himself waiting in the lobby at 400 North Capitol Street, wondering where the Lincoln Town Car was that would take him back to the other side of Capitol Hill. His brief stint as MSNBC guest had now been an utter waste because the Oprah Guest In Chief had decided once again to brazenly showcase his 12-step program on national television. God, the fellow truly had no sense of shame.

Where was the justice? An intern-fondling liar was president of the United States, and he, an honest, decent, hard-working Congressman, was a back bench nobody from Idaho who was barely able to get re-elected. ...

Oh, Lattan felt it in his gut ... this nation was ready for a boy scout after this embarrassing national drama ... hell, if the failed governor of a small state could be president, why not a mediocre Congressman from a small state? At least he owed it to himself to *explore* the possibility ... with or without his campaign handlers.

Chapter 24

Secret Meeting At Bardo Rodeo

Lattan stepped out of a taxi in front of Bardo Rodeo in Arlington, eager to meet the reporter to whom he was going to provide an exclusive on his plans to run for president.

Bardo was a typical dive, with pugnacious bartenders and sour swill brewed on premise. Except that it was billeted in a converted automobile dealership.

An old Plymouth was planted halfway through the showroom window, the glass cut around it, sealed with putty. Front end inside, rear end jutting onto the sidewalk. The front seat was gutted to house a jukebox. Patrons made selections by pressing a keypad installed in the driver's side door.

Bardo also boasted the area's only totem pole, a ghastly wooden monument towering over the entrance. And it offered patio seating in its "beer garden" shaded by a silo.

Inside, showroom walls were overlaid with savage neon murals resembling kindergarten finger paintings. Former selling floors were covered with pool tables and kitschy furniture that looked as if it had been swiped from college dormitory rooms. Chairs that didn't match coupled with tables that wobbled because of legs with different lengths. It was a miracle everybody didn't spill their drinks.

Lattan shuffled toward the entrance, timorous about whether to feel excited or disgusted: excited because he was meeting a journalist who could propel him to national stature; disgusted because he didn't think he should have to resort to meeting second-tier reporters in smoky dives.

When he'd decided to give a lucky reporter an "exclusive" about his presidential campaign plans, he thought the George Wills and Bob Novaks and Bill Kristols and Fred Barneses of the punditocracy would all jump at the chance.

But instead of hungry reporters lining up for an off-beat story about a back bencher's quixotic quest for the GOP nomination, he'd received a series of polite rejections from newsprint-stained misanthropes bitter that their careers had stalled along someone else's campaign trail.

So he moved to the second-tier political scribes. That was why tonight he walked into Bardo to meet Westley Prune of *The Washington Star-Bulletin*, author of "Pruning on Politics." Prune suggested the locale to be sure he wouldn't be spotted by any members of the chattercrat class. Apparently, he had just as many reservations about Lattan as the others, but was driven by a primordial urge to pursue anything that could help him scoop *The Washington Past*.

Lattan and Prune had agreed to meet by the Plymouth in the window at eight o'clock. Just the two of them, no aides, like a hostage taker collecting his ransom.

Lattan was early. A hulking black man sat on a barstool inside the doorway, ready to check IDs. A youthful barback wiped linoleum tables. A scrawny waitress tapped a keg. A pony-tailed bartender counted money at the cash register. The only patrons were a few bike messengers drinking pitchers of Bardo Beer. They smoked clove cigarettes, emanating a floral scent.

Lattan scanned the bar, poked his head into the back room, then peeked in the beer garden. No sign of Prune. He commandeered a barstool and ordered a beer.

He looked at his watch. Three minutes before eight. He took out a 3" x 5" card on which Kentrell "Alt" DeLeet had written down talking points on Prune. Next to his phone number, DeLeet had listed salient information: "Works for Moo-moos, but not member of Unilateral Church. Frequently cribs original reporting runs it as his own column without giving proper attribution. Hard-right."

Lattan continued watching people wander in. All couples or groups. No sighting of a short, stocky man toting a laptop. But then, at about ten after eight, he spotted Prune. ... and Lattan was ... instantly in a panic!

What if this would be a hatchet job? What if Prune would mock him in his column, as he mocked so many liberals? What if he was about to be hung with his own words in the (admittedly unread) pages of *The Washington Star-Bulletin*?

Must leave — now!

He hopped off of the barstool and darted toward the pay phone by the restrooms. He retrieved two quarters, and the briefing paper, from his jacket. He punched in Prune's number. Four rings, and Prune's voice mail picked up.

"Hi, Mr. Prune," he began, feigning his best mea culpa tone. "Oh, gosh, I guess I just missed you. I was hoping I could get you before you left, but . . . anyway, listen, something came up, and I'm going to have to cancel for tonight. You'll never believe it, but this . . . uh, constituent . . . who blew into town tonight, needs to be shown the sights . . . you know these constituents, believing their Congressman should conform to their itineraries . . . Anyway, I hope I haven't inconvenienced you too much. And I hope you call in for messages. Couldn't be helped, totally unexpected. Let's try and reschedule. Take care."

Lattan placed the phone in its cradle. He strode out through the beer garden and started hiking up Wilson Boulevard to the Metro.

Back in his apartment, Lattan tried to distract himself by playing computer chess. He hunched his bony shoulders over the table, a stony expression on his face. He brooded over his next move. The apartment was silent, save the faint laugh track filtering through the wall from his neighbor's television. Lattan envisioned them laughing at him.

Knight to Rook five? Bishop to King four? Should I castle? I've got to get my Queen in play ... Lattan pondered the possibilities.

Lattan took his eyes off of the chessboard for a moment, reaching for the open can of refried beans on the table. He picked it up and reached for the spoon. He scooped out a dense mass of its clay-colored contents and, careful not to cut his hand on the jagged lid, brought the spoonful into his mouth and ate. Washed it down with a gulp from a two-liter bottle of soda.

"Queen to your rook five." Lattan picked up the piece and moved it to its new position. "I'll mate your ass in three." He felt confident his long losing streak was about to end.

He pushed the button on the board to register his move. Lattan's opponent announced its move in an electronic monotone: "King's . . . Knight . . . to . . . Bish-op . . . six . . . check . . . mate."

Lattan blinked with incredulity, saying nothing. He looked at the board, convinced there had to be a way out. Never trusted the computer. But after a few moments of searching for possible escape routes, he acceded.

"How did I miss that?"

Still eager to anesthetize his frayed nerves, he made himself a scotch and lit a cigar, then sank into his black leather sofa, remote control in hand. After a few drinks, he felt like a giant jellyfish, with no skeleton to support his sinews. He slumped into the couch and watched the hazy cigar smoke float up, illuminated only by the light of the muted television. A grey mist hovered near the ceiling, the odor of smoldering tobacco leaves permeating the entire room. The only sound for a long while was that of ice cubes clinking together as they melted in his glass.

The phone rang, and he considered ignoring it, abhorring the thought of having to engage his cerebral muscles. They had gone flaccid for the evening. But his curiosity got the best of him. He lifted his heavy arm toward the phone.

"Charlie, is that you? It's Kentrell. Were you sleeping?"

"No, I'm jes washin' a lil' TV." The words came out in slow-motion.

"You sound tired. Are you OK?"

"Fine." He straightened himself on the sofa.

"So how did the meeting go? Pruning on Politics gonna write a nice fluffball piece about the earnest campaign of Charles Lattan?"

"No. Didn't work out."

"Whaddaya mean?"

"No show," he lied.

"Sheesh," DeLeet said. "Stood up by second-string hacks. Well, look at it this way. Until your campaign is recognized by the media, it doesn't really exist. Which means we don't have to worry about stuffing and licking envelopes just yet."

Though handicapped by a drunken, medicated haze, Lattan achieved the instant clarity of an epiphany. "That's it!"

"What's it?" DeLeet asked.

"That's our slogan."

"What's our slogan?"

"That thing about licking envelopes. That's our appeal — I'm so boring that I worry about licking envelopes, which means I can't possibly be groping interns."

"A little too long for a bumper sticker, Charlie."

"OK, how about this. You ready?"

"Go," DeLeet said, exasperated.

"Charles Lattan For President. His Interns Lick Envelopes."

DeLeet was silent.

"Didn't think I had it in me, did you? Think you media guys are the only ones who can come up with those catchy slogans."

"I'm pleasantly surprised," DeLeet said. "A press conference announcing that theme as your campaign mantra might just generate some interest."

"Well, what are we waiting for?"

Chapter 25

The Bonfire Of The Lattan-ities

Lattan jostled with harried journalists as they rushed out of an elevator in the National Press Club. Lattan was there to stage a press conference, the journalists ostensibly to cover it.

Lattan's pinstripe suit, fresh from the cleaner that morning, hugged his wan physique. A screaming pumpkin-colored necktie, punctuated by bile green polka dots, was knotted around his neck with a perfect half-windsor dimple. His white combover was plastered to his head. His mind swelled in anticipation of using his brilliant slogan for his nascent presidential campaign: *Charles Lattan For President. His Interns Lick Envelopes.* ... God, it truly was a stroke of genius.

His campaign manager, Alex Macro, and his media guru, Kentrell "Alt" DeLeet, followed two steps behind him. DeLeet toted a calfskin portfolio zipped tight with press releases and fact sheets he'd written and photocopied minutes before.

Today's mission was a little announcement that he, Congressman Charles Lattan, was running for the Republican nomination for president. After much hand-wringing over whether to announce his intentions in Idaho or in Washington, the Lattan braintrust, such as it was, decided that they'd get more attention by adhering to that old real estate rule of location, location, location. The National Press Club, ensconced on the thirteenth floor of the National Press Building in downtown D.C., was a favorite stage for politicians looking to earn newspaper ink or television face time. Its ornate furnishings, large conference rooms and high standing in the minds of reporters conferred instant status on those who held events there. It offered validity a back bench member such as Lattan could never earn from inviting the media to Idaho.

And a Press Club event guaranteed a full room. On the twelve floors below, the Press Building housed dozens of trade newsletters, wire services and capital bureaus of newspapers from across the country. Hundreds of reporters were only an elevator ride away.

Lattan's task was to foist his message on those reporters. He, Macro and DeLeet knew that attempting to get long profiles by the top political reporters was futile. But attempting to get coverage by virtue of being the *first* candidate to announce—the novelty of it!—was slightly less futile, ranking a couple steps short of hopeless. So Lattan steeled himself and ventured toward the conference room.

Lattan wanted to seem nonchalant. Slip into the room without any fanfare, subtly meander to the podium, make his announcement, then drop that bombshell—my interns lick envelopes!—and let the media proceed with questions.

The journalists trundled past him, not even recognizing the man they were here to cover. But who could blame them? Aside from a brief MSNBC appearance, Lattan was relatively unknown.

Lattan and his retinue of advisers crept toward the entrance. Standing by the registration table checking credentials was a gritty young woman. Press club intern, Lattan figured, as he sauntered in as if he owned the place.

"Excuse me, are you members?" the hoyden asked.

Lattan's chest instantly inflated with a blast of hubris, as if an airbag had detonated in his sternum.

"No, I'm Congressman Charles Lattan, and I'm here to make an announcement," Lattan replied haughtily.

"You're here to do what?"

"It's all legit, young lady," Macro said, stepping in between Lattan and the Press Club's self-appointed sentry. "We've booked this room, paid in advance, we've got the Congressman right here, my colleague has his press releases, and, as you can see, reporters are filling the room in anticipation of The Congressman's arrival and subsequent announcement of *national* importance," he said, waving a flabby arm toward the room like a carnival barker enticing customers at the state fair.

As if on cue, DeLeet unzipped his portfolio and grabbed a stack of press releases.

The woman didn't budge.

A brief pause then ensued, signaling —

— that this —

— had become —

— a standoff.

Seconds later, but which seemed like an eternity, a middle-aged woman, frizzy black hair streaked with gray, outfitted in a floral sack dress, excused herself from a conversation four feet away to intervene.

"Excuse me, I'm executive director of the Press Club. And you are?"

"This is Congressman Charles Lattan of the 17th District of Idaho," Macro said, his tone and inflection as if he was scolding a first grader. "I'm his campaign manager, this gentleman to my left is his media adviser, those good people in that room are reporters, and we're here to make an announcement which they are patiently waiting to hear. Now, if you'll check your manifest, you will see that we have booked this room, paid the Press Club's fee in advance, and signed and delivered all of the proper materials. So if you'll excuse us, my good lady, we will now enter this room and conduct our business. I'm sure The Congressman will forgive your lapse —"

"I'm sorry," the woman said, "but I couldn't help notice your placards on the wall and the content of the materials your colleague seems ready to distribute. You are aware, of course, that it is against Club policy to conduct any kind of campaign related event here, are you not?"

Lattan sensed a shift in momentum. Macro looked feverish. His eyes ballooned in panic, darted toward DeLeet, back to the woman, then to Lattan, then back to DeLeet.

"We, uh ... we ... uh," Macro stammered. "We have paid for this room."

DeLeet jumped in: "Are you telling me a Member of the United States Congress is prohibited from using these facilities to —"

"We have a strict policy about political events," the woman said, emboldened by the Rule Of Law.

Macro responded: "Are you telling me you won't make an exception for a man who may be the next —"

"No, we cannot! I'm flabbergasted you have the nerve to even ask. Now, with all due respect to the Congressman, I will have to ask you to show evidence that you do not intend to use this event for political campaign purposes. Otherwise, you'll have to leave. I'm sorry. Policy."

The aging hippie stood victorious with her hands on her hips.

Macro was speechless. DeLeet was pathetically riffling through the contract, as if searching for a miraculous loophole, some escape clause, that would let them go in there and make their announcement for president. And Lattan stood there helpless, torn between pulling the "I'm the Congressman, that's why" routine and risking an embarrassing news story guaranteed to dog him along the campaign trail.

DeLeet finished rummaging through the contract, then glanced up at Macro and shook his head helplessly, his mouth sloping downward at an awkward angle.

Finally Macro capitulated. "I'm sorry you feel that way. Thank you. Good afternoon." He turned and left, with DeLeet behind him. Lattan scurried to catch up, like the little kid chasing after playmates on the ball field yelling "wait up!" There was no "Hail To The Chief" playing in his head.

Lattan, Macro and DeLeet shuffled through the revolving door of the Cannon House Office Building, past a blowzy police officer who looked more like a bank guard than a sentry to the world's greatest deliberative body. DeLeet now toted an empty portfolio, having in a fit of rage discarded the campaign literature in a trash receptacle on his way out of the Press Club.

They paused to look at the latest art display in the rotunda. It didn't look like art, but the three men seemed to prefer it to conversation. If you walked in and didn't see *Cannon House Office Building, United States House Of Representatives* in big letters on a plaque outside, you'd think it was another Smithsonian museum. It was as though Congress made an effort to look cultured, rotating these various art displays which, until today, none of the three had ever paused to study.

Back in his office, Lattan smiled at the receptionist, who interrupted her game of computer solitaire long enough to return the gesture. Then the three walked into his office and clamped the door. Lattan sat behind his big oak Congressman's desk. At least he had these digs for another two years.

"Congressman, I apologize. I'll have to take the blame for this one," Macro finally said.

"Yeah, the both of us. We screwed up," said DeLeet.

Lattan was enjoying this little act of staff contrition. It was all too rare an occurrence, almost making up for the fiasco.

"I guess we go back to Idaho and do it. Or rent a hotel ballroom," Macro said.

"What will we tell those reporters?" Lattan said. "Won't they write sarcastic stories about this screw-up?"

"Actually, that might be the good news in all of this," DeLeet said, his voice warbly. "None of the heavy hitters we anticipated showed up, from what I could see. So we only lost the B-listers — FOX, MSNBC, *The Potato Press*. Maybe this all worked out for the best. Maybe we should wait until the beginning of the year. Take some time to strategize and raise some money, get some organization in place."

Suddenly Lattan was enraged that his staff hadn't gotten at least somebody from the national media. "Or maybe I just need a new media guru," Lattan grumbled. "I've got a proposal here from USA Media Communications that looks pretty good. Maybe I should replace you two with Nick Thimmesch and Bill Napier."

"Congressman, please, let's not be rash," DeLeet said. "Just give us some time to put together a campaign plan, raise some money, like I said, and let's do this thing right. Maybe if we hadn't been so rushed with all of this, we would have realized that rule the Press Club had, and none of this would have happened today, and ..."

And at that point Lattan tuned out. Whatever DeLeet was yammering about was certainly beside the point. Hell, it was more likely three steps behind the point.

Maybe he should take a break for the holidays, get some rest and get in shape before a presidential race. It was clear this political operation wasn't even ready yet to put the patient under anesthesia.

Chapter 26

Ambush At The U.S. Department Of Journalism

Lattan ripped open the cardboard package before the UPS delivery man was even out the door of his campaign headquarters. Like a kid on Christmas morning, Lattan tore through the wrapping in anticipation of the goodies inside.

He reached in and pulled out a stack of gleaming blue-and-white bumper stickers, and inhaled the chemical smell of cheap vinyl as though it was the most redolent perfume on earth. There they were, in his hand—confirmation that the journey had begun. Bumper stickers bearing the slogan CHARLES LATTAN FOR PRESIDENT. *HIS* INTERNS LICK ENVELOPES.

Too bad his campaign manager and his media consultant weren't there to share the moment. But he didn't mind their absence, because they were back in Washington laying the groundwork for his White House campaign.

At that moment in a newspaper newsroom nearly 3,000 miles east of Idaho, a young copy aide named Webster Link cursed another day as a drone in the distended bowels of the *Washington Past*. Link was transcribing voice mail messages of a comics page columnist who earned his keep at the *Past* by using those transcriptions as the basis for his daily column.

"Hi, Bob," a caller began. "I was just wondering. Is it me, or does the scaffolding on the Washington Monument look like a prophylactic on a phallic symbol?"

"Idiots," Web murmured under his breath. "I make my living listening to idiots, I make my living writing down what the idiots say, and I make my living helping idiots comment on the other idiots."

Web had been tethered to his computer all morning, using cappucino-induced mental clarity to execute the mundane tasks for his superiors. After he finished the voice mail, he would write a list of cliches and tired metaphors for which the same columnist seemed to have a quota every day.

Web's glassy brown eyes surveyed the newsroom. Other editors sat at their terminals, trying to make sense of jumbled news copy. Reporters scribbled quotes delivered from sources over the phone. Interns trawled documents from fax machines, scanning cover pages to determine who got what.

At twenty-two, Web Link was already cynical about journalism. He'd been with the *Past* nearly a year since college. Before that, he'd worked a few months as copy editor for a small paper in rural Nebraska, until he was fired for rewriting the daily horoscopes with malicious intent.

Which had at the time had seemed great for his career. His temerity was a mismatch for that sleepy, small town newsroom. He reveled in the fervor of the *Past*, and the dizzy roar of its newsroom more closely mirrored his visions of becoming a star political journalist at the premier newspaper in the nation's capital.

But starting as an entry-level scribe had been difficult. Each day he hoped he would be discovered, that his new employers would be impressed with his lean prose, his ability to write and edit on deadline, and his political insights. But it never seemed to happen. ...

The phone next to his terminal chirped. He picked up the receiver without taking his eyes off of the computer.

"I'm on deadline, so this better be good." Eyes fixed on the screen.

"What if I had been a subscriber?" asked Mike Rosoft, the chief copy editor.

"Then you'd know not to call so close to deadline."

"You never know who's going to be on the other end of the phone, so at least try to act courteous, even if you don't feel like it."

Web ground his teeth. "I've got reads to do and heads to write if you want this baby out on time. If it's late again, you'll really see what happens when our subscribers get pissed."

"They're already pissed, and you get to see them right now."

"Come again?" Web cracked his knuckles.

"A couple of political hacks are in the lobby. Seems they're dissatisfied with our coverage of their boy, who they claim is a serious presidential contender. I've got to finish editing our lead story if we're gonna roll on time. So they're all yours."

"I don't have time to humor any campaign hacks," Web said. "Tell them to write an angry letter or make death threats, like everyone else."

"No good. They're here and they aren't leaving," Rosoft said.

"What about the political reporters?"

"They're all out. Iowa, New Hampshire, wherever people are announcing their candidacies. So you get 'em."

"Who are these guys?"

"Work for a nobody Congressman from Idaho, some chump named Lattan. Now go smooth over those egos."

Web sighed. "Where?"

"I'll go to another computer so you can use my office. I'll tell the front desk to send them there."

Web hung up the phone. He stood and buttoned the top of his chambray shirt, straightened his cotton tie and threw on his sport coat. He picked up his notepad, lit a cigarette and rushed to the editor's office, a rare location where the newsroom sounds were muffled by walls.

Web had no time to listen to political operatives whine about the *Past*'s failure to paint tableaus about their candidate. What was he, the complaint department? But he nevertheless rushed through the newsroom, past the sports columnists penning relentless stories in defense of the town's hapless football team; past the gossip columnists cribbing items from the wire services; past the op-ed writers doing brain dumps of exactly eight hundred words each.

He smiled superciliously and sauntered into the editor's office. Cigarette secured between his lips, he shook hands with the two standing amid the clutter, thinking they looked like Laurel and Hardy.

"Alex Macro, campaign manager," said the fat one, drawling. His jacket puckered over his bulging stomach, the button poised to fly at any moment.

"Kentrell 'Alt' DeLeet, media consultant," said the thin one. Blond bangs, damp from perspiration, stuck to his forehead. A ratty, oversized black sports coat hung on his spindly frame.

"Please feel free to clear yourself a space and sit."

Web maneuvered behind the old metal desk and sat in the torn, mustard-colored vinyl swivel chair. His guests removed stacks of paper from two folding metal chairs and sat. Macro made a great effort to cross one of his blubbery legs over the other. DeLeet sat erect, a garden vegetable propped up by a stake.

"We know you're busy, so we'll make this short," Macro said. "Our campaign is a professional organization, and we treat the media with respect. All we ask is that you treat us with the same respect we treat you."

"Fair enough," Web said, his voice raspy from smoking. He searched for an ashtray amid the mounds of debris on the desk — coffee cups, beer and soft drink cans, food wrappers, newspapers, magazines, faxes, copies, press releases, layout sheets. No time to clean on deadline. For fear of losing something vital, the janitor was forbidden from touching the mess, so it just grew. Web grabbed an empty can and tapped his ash in it.

"We're running a serious campaign for the GOP nomination, and frankly we think you ought to be covering it," Macro continued. "You know how the media can affect people's perceptions of candidates and campaigns. Everyone involved in politics reads the *Past*, and if we're not covered, it's as if Charles Lattan doesn't exist. Then we can't raise any money, and it all becomes a vicious cycle."

"You mean vicious circle."

"I do? I never know which one it is."

"I'm pretty sure it's circle."

"You're the writer," Macro chortled.

"Yeah, well, anyway, I think you overestimate our impact," Web said, though enjoying the attempt to suck up.

"I don't think I am," Macro said, gnawing a cuticle. "We're running a campaign based on ideas, and all you're reporting is the horse race aspect — as long as you're not a dark horse!"

Web had dragged himself away from his deadline duties to listen to this pap? He waited before responding, reminding himself to be diplomatic.

"I appreciate your concern. And I can assure you that Mr. —"

"*Congressman* Lattan!"

"—Congressman Lattan will get every drop of ink he deserves. But first he has to show that he deserves that ink."

Macro's doughy face deflated with a sigh. "What does he have to do, ambush your top political reporter at his vacation home in Michigan?"

Link placed his cigarette on the edge of the can and watched the smoke float up. He pulled gently on his left ear. Why must he suffer interruptions on deadline? Why must he listen to more campaign goons who didn't get it? Who thought the purpose of political reportage was to reprint their press releases? He blew out the last puff of his cigarette and dropped it to fizzle in the bottom of the can.

"We're not here to make your campaign happy, or to make your opponent's campaign happy, or to promote this candidate, or to degrade that candidate," Web said. "I couldn't care less if you win or lose. And don't think you're the first ones who've complained. We get it from both sides, all the time. Around here, we tell ourselves that if both sides in a story get angry at us, we've done our job. Everybody complains. No one's ever happy. That's why reporters are so cynical."

Macro raised his eyebrows, gave DeLeet a bemused look, then looked back at Web. Web knew his temper was flaring. He took a breath before continuing.

"We mean no offense to you or anyone in your campaign, or Mr. Lattan, who I'm sure is an upstanding citizen. But for you to believe that we're plotting ways to ignore your guy is ridiculous. We don't care enough about him, or anyone else running for office, to even try to make him look bad. And even if we did care, we wouldn't have time to conspire against him. Don't flatter yourselves. We don't care about anyone on either side. We're just looking for a good story. That's what makes us objective and impartial."

Macro's mouth contracted. He leaned forward, placing his hands on his pudgy thighs, summoning energy to hoist himself from the chair. "It seems we have nothing left to discuss," he said, wheezing.

Web watched them file out of the office. Macro, his polyester suit jacket straining over the fleshy lobes of his stomach, shimmering as he waddled. DeLeet, underarms drenched through his blazer, blond hair pasted to his forehead. Web leaned back in the editor's chair, put his feet on the desk. He lit another Camel and took a long drag, blowing smoke rings with remarkable precision. Ah, the euphoria. Validation from angry readers. The only satisfaction he ever got out of this lousy job.

"Oh, Christ." He dropped his feet to the floor and tore out of the office. He'd almost forgotten he was still on deadline.

Chapter 27

Impeach Cobbler

"The gentleman from Idaho is recognized," said the Speaker, tapping the gavel.

And with that official recognition, Congressman Charles Lattan, clutching in his sweaty fist remarks prepared by his staff, marched into the well of the House and adjusted the microphone.

"Thank you, Mr. Speaker," Lattan said, spreading out his unread speech on the podium, then clearing his throat.

"Mr. Speaker, today we vote on an historic issue, one that will define this institution and us as legislators and representatives for decades to come," Lattan began reading. "Indeed, let us first not lose sight of the miracle of democracy that even allows us to deliberate such an issue."

That he was here on the floor speaking at all was Lattan's own miracle. All week, the campaign staff and the official staff had argued back and forth over whether Lattan should participate in the debate, or whether it was best if he avoided the possibility of embarrassing himself on national TV. They'd argued as if they were his parents, with the campaign staff (mommy) pleading for a wedge to help them jump-start the already stalled presidential effort; the official staff (daddy) adducing that there was no way to score political points on the vote; and Lattan (the child) remaining silent until the parents decided what to do.

So here he was, a pawn of his staff once again, speaking on the House floor and on national television only on the condition that he not waver from a carefully prepared text.

And how they'd edited it and refined it and crossed out lines and written another iteration and printed it out again and *let's see it one more time ...* so many changes, so many drafts, that he hadn't had a chance to read it after the final version squirted out of the printer and his chief of staff, Rachel Emmell, had placed it in his hand on his way to rush to the House floor.

Luckily, the Speaker had agreed to squeeze him into the line-up right at the end for just a minute, right before the respective party leaders gave final speeches immediately preceding the vote.

"— and we are indeed fortunate that, as a democracy, we have the power to act to remove a president if the situation warrants," Lattan spoke emotionlessly. The words were as fresh to him as to those allegedly listening. "For we are not a dictatorship ruled by the will of a strongman, or a monarchy ruled by the divine right of a king, but a republic with checks and balances to keep all branches of government accountable."

Lattan found himself thinking he sounded pretty good ... how adept he had been at hiring staff!

"Our solemn duty today is to exercise that check and balance, Mr. Speaker," Lattan continued automatically. "We have a chief executive who has committed what can only be described as impeachable offenses. Yes, *impeachable* offenses. For while my distinguished colleagues on the other side of the aisle have argued all week that lying about adultery is not a high crime under the Constitution, they have ignored the Constitution's other criteria for impeachment: misdemeanors."

"I'm willing to concede the point that covering up an affair is not a high crime," Lattan said, grinding away at the text. "It is true that the president's conduct, however sordid, did not imperil the state or our national security. But the Constitution says high crimes *and misdemeanors*. Certainly, if one were to follow the logic of the president's defenders, this whole tawdry episode qualifies as a misdemeanor, does it not? Does it not stand to reason, therefore, that we should vote to impeach the president for his misdemeanors?"

"When the average American commits a misdemeanor, he is not absolved from punishment simply because of the relatively minor severity of, say, jaywalking or speeding. No, he must pay a fine, possibly appear in court, even perhaps lose his driver's license if he speeds too many times. Therefore, it is our solemn duty today to revoke the president's driver's license, and to impeach him, so that he no longer terrorizes the highways and, yes, even side streets, of America's public life. Thank you, and I yield back the balance of my time."

With that, Lattan pushed the microphone aside triumphantly and marched back up from the well of the House, utterly satisfied with himself. Yes, yes, the driver's license bit was the pure genius of someone on his staff. Put it in terms the average American can understand!

He returned to his seat and watched absently as the rest of the members, then leaders, on each side gave their speeches. Then the Speaker banged the gavel and ordered the vote, to be taken by electronic device. The bells and buzzes started blaring away, and Lattan reached into his coat pocket for his electronic voting card.

Which wasn't there.

Maybe the other pocket ... no, not there either ... all of a sudden he was madly frisking himself, right here on the House floor, while the other four hundred thirty-four members inserted their cards to vote.

Back pants pocket, front pants pocket, shirt pocket ... frisking himself for his voting card ... then he opened his wallet, tore through his credit cards and driver's license—reminding him of the speech he'd just given—where was his voting card? Not in the wallet either ....

He looked at the vote clock: Time remaining 12:43. Time for someone to rifle through the office and run it down to the floor.

He rushed into the Cloakroom to call ... ringing, ringing, goddamn constituents tying up the lines ... ringing, ringing ... finally an answer ... Emmell saying hold on we'll check ... holding, holding ... time remaining 10:47.

Finally she returned to the phone.

"Charlie, are you sure you don't have it?" Emmell said frantically.

"No, I told you!" Lattan screamed. "Did you check my desk?"

"It's not there!"

"Under the thingie in the drawer?"

"The thingie?"

"Nevermind! In the time it takes to tell you where to look I could find it myself! I'm on my way back!"

He slammed the phone down and tore out of the House chamber, glancing again at the clock: Time remaining 8:22. Running through the Capitol ... faster in the tunnels or outside? Outside!

And he dashed out of the side of the Capitol and across the pavement and up the steps of the Cannon Building ... goddamn revolving door ... up the stairs to the fifth floor, down the hall. ...

And into the office, his shirt wet and stuck to his torso, his combover flopping to the side of his head, his face aflame and drenched with sweat ... god, what a mess he must look.

To the receptionist: "Find it yet?"

She shook her head nervously.

"Damn it!" He rushed into his office, where everyone else on staff was turning everything upside down, flipping sofa cushions, opening and slamming desk drawers. ...

"Charlie!" Emmell said. "Are you absolutely sure —"

"Yes, I'm sure! I don't have it!" He glanced at the TV locked on C-SPAN ... that insipid music playing as the vote was tallied ... time remaining 4:19. ...

Emmell looked at the clock. "Charlie! There's no time! You've got to get back to the floor and ask the Speaker to find some way for you to vote!"

"Christ!" She was right. He bounded back out of the office, down the hall, down the stairs, out the door of Cannon and on to the street —

Red light.

He waited for traffic to subside. Waiting, waiting, no opportunity to cross.

Then finally the light changed and he darted across the street, back into the side door of the Capitol, back on to the House floor, where —

The time remaining clock read 0:00.

The Speaker was announcing the vote count, the yeas and nays, the numbers of which he couldn't hear—

But then he clearly heard:

"With one member not voting."

He stood there, panting, his heart throbbing in his chest, sweat pouring down his face. And the only thought going through his mind was the likely third paragraph of the AP story that he knew would go over the wire in mere minutes: *The single member not voting was Charles Lattan of Idaho, whose 'no vote' was all the more baffling given that minutes before he'd spoken so forcefully in favor of impeachment.*

Oh, now he'd get his coveted national press coverage, all right.

Chapter 28

Las Vegas Campaign Finance Jackpot

Lattan sat in the back seat of his campaign Buick, gazing in disbelief at the neon lights of the strip while campaign manager Macro lurched forward in the traffic on Las Vegas Boulevard. Against his always questionable better judgment, Lattan was on his way to beg presidential campaign financing from Mark Text, the guru of Las Vegas' latest, most meretricious and utterly tasteless edifice: Stalin's Hotel Resort and Casino.

He knew the old claptrap about the danger of accepting tainted gaming money. But for Lattan, *any* money in the sunken campaign war chest would be a welcome implant for its pectorals.

Vegas ... always open, always busy. Best of all, it offered, apart from its drifters and pensioners weaving in and out of some forty casinos on the strip alone, the opportunity to milk gaming bovines looking to rise above the herd of blackjack croupiers and slot machine change attendants to gain access and influence in Washington. That Lattan's chances of winning were about as good as hitting a royal flush on video poker was of scant concern.

Macro guided the car past the various gaming parlors — Stratosphere, Pioneer, Stardust, Circus Circus — working his way south, slithering in and out of traffic ... further down the strip ... past the Imperial Palace, Barbary Coast, Treasure Island, The Mirage, Bally's, Tropicana, Monte Carlo, MGM Grand, New York New York, The Excalibur, The Bellagio and Caesars.

How did they come up with such silly themes? Caesars, with its talking Roman statues and cocktail waitresses dressed as members of an old Roman empire. The Frontier, designed to resemble an old wild West gaming town. The Luxor, a replica of an ancient Egyptian pyramid. ... What market research went into casino theme development? Did some number cruncher specializing in consumer preferences announce to a board of directors that, "Our research clearly indicates that the gaming public is hungry for a casino with an Old West theme?" How could anyone possibly produce any research to demonstrate that?

But Pioneer and New York New York were nothing compared to the warped craniums that produced Caesars. There it was, with its faux-marble facade, statues, walkways and columns designed to remind the serious gambler of ancient Rome. Lattan couldn't envision how such an edifice could entice someone into losing his money: "Honey, all this ambience has made me feel as invincible as an ancient gladiator. Nothing can stop me tonight! A thousand on red, and let the roulette wheel spin!"

Wasn't Caesar an unsavory character? Lattan wasn't sure. He'd never paid attention in his Roman history classes. Obviously, it didn't seem to matter. No one seemed to be avoiding the casino out of moral indignation. *Nearly two thousand years after the fall of Rome, I, Claudius, double down on 11. Et Tu?*

But who was *he* to question? Congressman Charles Lattan, Republican presidential candidate, was on his way to ... *Stalin's Hotel Resort and Casino!* A real, identifiable historical theme that would resonate with the gambling public. ...

Macro pulled into the horseshoe driveway and got out, whereupon a hammer-and-sickle-clad valet parker replaced him behind the wheel. Then a communist dictator casino greeter opened the back door and welcomed Lattan, drawing him in like a carnival barker, though he, too, was also dressed in KGB uniform. "Welcome to Uncle Joe's," he said, grinning and waving them into the casino. "Won't you please follow me to Mr. Text's office?"

Lattan followed Macro behind the KGB impersonator into the casino. Lattan snickered at the scene. ... Vanguard Video Poker ... all-you-can-eat borscht buffet ... Russian Roulette Room, where they dare you to purge the bank ... Uncle Joe's Loosest Slots On The Strip ... cocktail waitresses adorned in revealing babushka attire. A hammer-and-sickle on every blackjack chip. Face cards modeled on old proletariat recruiting posters, featuring brave warriors, Queens and Jacks resplendent in party uniform. ... the Useful Idiots High Stakes Room, Sandinista Slots O' Plenty, Ruble's Bar & Grille ... back, back through the casino. It was easy to see how people lost themselves in the mesmerizing glow, the mellifluous bells and whirs, the stale tobacco aroma of a video poker machine.

Upstairs, in the executive suites, Lattan and Macro were seated outside Mark Text's office while the pit boss completed a meeting. Lattan tried to practice his sales pitch, but was unable to concentrate as Text's secretary carried on a phone conversation with her friends about the burning topic of where to meet for happy hour.

The secretary — Susie Lou Rubella, according to her nameplate — was a bottle blonde of indeterminate age, an apparent career receptionist whose greatest ambition in life seemed to be finding the bar with the best happy hour specials. Her caked-on makeup and adolescent wardrobe disguised her true age well enough, but a closer glimpse revealed the unavoidable facial lines and expanding rump attendant to middle age.

"Well, we can meet at the bar at five, and then go to dinner afterwards," Rubella said. "Or, we could go to dinner and then meet for drinks . . . wait, I'll meet you outside the bar, and then we'll have one drink here, and the next drink there ... no, let's go to the restaurant first, then have a cocktail, and then go to another bar, and then have another drink, and then take a cab to a club, and ..."

Waiting, waiting ... How low had he sunk?! Waiting to beg for campaign money from the owner of an establishment called Stalin's Hotel Resort & Casino! Oh, for some scotch to cut through the tension!

"Mr. Text will see you now," Rubella said, jolting Lattan out of his downward mental spiral. At once he stood up and followed her and Macro into the gaudy office of the casino president.

"Howdya' do, Congressman," said Text, gripping Lattan's hand in both of his and shaking with a ferocity so intense it had to be fake.

Lattan took in his host ... Blond hair, perfectly coifed; wardrobe from Brooks Brothers, J. Crew, J. Press or similar blue-blood clothiers; an athletic build that emanated the intimidating air of big egomaniac on campus ... carrying himself with the authority of a fraternity president who just got done having his way with the homecoming queen in the backseat of her daddy's Oldsmobile. How Mark Text had ever ascended the casino boss hierarchy Lattan couldn't understand. Perhaps one could ascribe his ascendancy to such a lofty position at the tender age of forty to having his nasal protuberance inserted into the gludial cleft of what remained of the Vegas mob. Lattan didn't know whether to blanch at his phoniness or admire his panache.

"So, where's the plan?" Text asked, his tone suggesting that Lattan and Macro should have had *the plan*, whatever it was, ready for his perusal.

Lattan avoided the natural instinct to flail himself for not understanding what his sponsor wanted.

Macro gave Lattan a look of *hell if I friggin' know.*

"And what plan is that?" Macro replied, looking back at Text.

"You know, the plan for the campaign you want me to finance," Text replied, as if Macro had just uttered the most ludicrous question ever uttered in this ludicrous town. "You can't expect me to finance a presidential campaign without looking at a strategy plan first, can you?"

Lattan rifled through his mental files. Had Text asked for such a plan before, communicated his expectations, clarified what he wanted delivered on this date, at this meeting?

No.

"Refresh my memory, please," Macro said, sweat spangling his brow.

Text snorted derisively, as though Macro and Lattan were idiots for not knowing what was expected.

"Come on, the plan," Text said superciliously. "I'd think you'd be especially eager to have a sharp plan, given your dubious status on the impeachment vote."

Lattan felt a sucker punch to the solar plexus ... the first of what he feared would be several derisive references to his voting card fiasco.

"With all dues respect, sir, you never mentioned that you expected to see a detailed campaign plan at this meeting," Macro said, his voice quavering. "We can't read your mind. You have to tell us what you expect."

"Oh, so you're complaining that you can't read my mind, eh?" Text sneered. "Don't you know I expect all of my candidates to be able to predict my expectations?"

The impudence! Forget this! Lattan was ready to bolt—

"We, uh, don't remember that," Macro said obsequiously. "You're making it sound as if it's our fault for not knowing we're supposed to read your mind."

"It is. And if you could read my mind, like you're supposed to, you would know that."

Lattan was dizzy from this collapse in linear logic. But Macro kept sparring.

"But *how are we supposed to know* that we're supposed to know to read your mind?"

"By having that skill."

"But—"

"So, now that you're supposed to be able to read my mind, predict my unpredictability and sense my senselessness, where's the plan?" Text asked.

And all at once it hit Lattan ... this guy ... this town ... was like a science fiction movie ... where the time-space continuum buckled under the weight of its special effects ... erupting volcanoes and pirate ship battles and talking statues ... nothing here was real, from the silly themes, to the perpetually open bars and casinos, to the windowless gaming parlors, to the lack of clocks, to the never-ending cacophony of bells, buzzes, dings and whirs ... to the lights flickering and flashing ... it turned your brain into mush, where you could no longer tell fantasy from reality. And this fellow was the ultimate product of it—a success within the confines of Vegas, but unable to discern reality otherwise.

Now the only question that mattered was: how to exit gracefully and cut their losses—time, travel expense—without losing anything else in this town of casinos.

Chapter 29

Big Game Hunting

Lattan reclined on a soft velvet cushion, sipping a scotch as he took in the view of the D.C. monuments from the bar atop the Hotel Washington. He enjoyed the warm rush from his second drink as he waited to meet Sharon Silver, a lobbyist from the Leisure Games Of Chance Association, the Washington arm of gambling interests.

And to think — only three days ago, upon returning from the botched meeting with a casino magnate in Las Vegas, he was panic-stricken over the notion that he'd fecklessly fumbled the chance to use gambling money to finance his presidential campaign.

Now he had the chance to recover. ... In his Tumi attaché he had a campaign plan drafted by his campaign manager including a media plan drafted by his media guru — the lack of which had doomed his trip to Vegas.

He instinctively smoothed his tie, checked to make sure the knot was still straight. Christ, the goddamn cleaners kept shrinking his shirt collars! In anticipation of his presidential campaign, he'd spent a hundred bucks apiece on custom made, tab-collared Sea Island Cotton dress shirts, and his dry cleaner kept shrinking the collars on him. Or maybe he had put on a few pounds recently.

He glanced down his shirt front, noticing the perceptible arc of his Italian silk tie over his stomach. His suit jacket, also custom made, was getting harder to button, and his trousers were tighter, pinching the emerging lobes of his midsection, the gabardine wool chafing against his inner thighs when he walked.

Maybe it was finally time to try a damn diet, get into proper fighting trim for the big national campaign.

Lattan smoothed his white hair ... at least he wasn't completely bald; at least he could get away with a combover. Then he cupped his chin, and let his hand slide down his neck. The beginnings of a double chin!

He tried to douse his uncomfortable physical sensations with an elixir of liquor, downing the drink and motioning to the waiter for another. ... Hopefully this lobbyist would be impressed with his campaign plan ...

Oh, who was he kidding? It was absolutely delusional! Anyone who goes through the ordeal of being a lobbyist, giving money to candidates who will, once elected, represent their interests as loyal lackeys, obviously wants to give money only to the exclusive fraternity of the Brotherhood Of The Electable. Surely one of the greatest pleasures of spreading filthy campaign lucre around is acquisition of the right to *scoff* at the also-rans. Certainly this lobbyist would revel in the opportunity to sneer at someone still wallowing the muck of dark-horsedom. And clearly one of the principle reasons — nay, *the* principle reason — one gives money to candidates is the reflected glory engendered by proximity to the holder of elected office. Practical business reasons are a distant second.

Lattan had now thoroughly demoralized himself. It was one thing to be a back bench Congressman. That was hard enough. But to be a hopeless presidential candidate? The lovely Sharon Silver would get one look at him and either burst into laughter or turn around and scamper to the nearest exit.

He checked his watch.

"Are you Congressman Lattan?"

Out of nowhere, she now stood before him. She was stunning. Dirty blonde hair framed a cherubic face. Her eyes were the color of faded denim, her nose sleek and tiny, her lips thin yet as juicy as strawberries. She wore a tight dress obviously selected to highlight the tautness of her physique. That it was sleeveless and cut above the knee served to accentuate muscular limbs. His only thought was: there was no way this girl would give him money.

"Yes — Sharon? Please, sit down."

He rose with an unintentional heave that only served to remind him of the contrast of age and beauty. As she arranged herself in the chair, he searched her face for signs of revulsion at his countenance. Discerning none, his spirits buoyed.

"Great view, huh?" he asked, gazing at the Washington monument, sheathed in scaffolding, now bathed in the early winter sunset, casting a long shadow over the National Mall's grass fields.

"Incredible," she replied. She looked for a long moment at the scenery, and Lattan looked for a long moment at her. Abruptly she turned back toward him, catching him leering.

"Thanks for meeting me," he said. "I hope you agree that this beats sitting in an office."

"Oh, absolutely."

The waiter appeared.

"Diet Coke for me," she said.

"Another one of these, please," Lattan said to the waiter, then turned toward her. "Sure I can't interest you in anything stronger?"

"I need to avoid empty calories," she said.

"I need to avoid them myself," Lattan said, embarrassed.

"Good for you," she said, with the encouragement of a parent boosting a child's decision to try out for the math club, and without any hint of condescension.

"You're an inspiration," he said, reaching for his briefcase. "As I mentioned on the phone, I have a campaign plan that I think you'd be interested in. It includes complete compliance with the gambling interests' agenda. Hell, if you give me enough, I'll say I support video poker machines in DC bars."

He handed her the 12-page, legal-sized document, single-spaced. "Don't worry about all the campaign mumbo-jumbo. I assure you it's all formalities. Just look at page four, paragraph two, subhead 'Charles Lattan on the issues — responsible gaming.' I think you'll be pleased."

Sharon riffled to the right page. "Wow," she said, he eyes ballooning.

"I thought you'd be pleased. I'm not usually so principled on an issue. But, hey, as they say, if I can't be bought, I can be *rented*."

"I don't know what to say," she stammered, flipping back and forth among the various pages. "I suppose we need to read this all very carefully, and have a lawyer look at it to make sure we're not getting ourselves into something messy."

"Don't worry about that," he said, waving his hand dismissively. "I assure you it's all kosher."

She stared at him blankly for a moment, as if trying to decide whether he was a snake-oil-peddling charlatan or a genuine businessman.

"What do we have to do, specifically? It seems like it would take days to figure that out from reading this."

"It's all very standard stuff," Lattan said, taking a long pull from his cocktail. "Just show me the money, honey, and I'll do the rest."

"Well, I'll show this to our government relations team, and we'll let you know, Congressman." She fidgeted in her seat.

"The sooner you sign on the dotted line, the sooner we can get started, and the sooner I can get to Iowa."

"We really do need to take a few days to think about it."

"That's fine. I understand completely. And feel free to call me with any questions. I'll put you on with one of my campaign guys if you want some of the gibberish explained. But I can tell you it's all on the level."

She continued looking at the document, flipping the pages, but it was obvious she was too confused to read any of it. And he knew he would have to give her time. Then he remembered one other thing he had to ask.

"Oh, by the way — you don't have a problem with my, uh ... how shall I phrase it ... *status* ... on the impeachment vote, do you?"

"Status?"

"You know, my, er, ... distinction ... from my colleagues."

She looked bemused. Instantly he regretted having asked her. But he'd been required to do it. The goddamn Macro had insisted. And surely, at some point, she'd be asked. So he'd better know now how much re-education he'd have to do, assuming she even agreed to be re-educated.

"Actually, I do have something else I need to ask you about," she spluttered.

He felt his lungs collapsing. This was going to sink the deal.

"What's that?" he asked, his voice quavering.

"Why haven't you ever pushed for casinos in Idaho?"

Chapter 30

Iowanna Go Home

"Hey handsome, buy me a drink?"

The request, from an unknown female now seated on the barstool beside him, snapped Lattan out of his drunken torpor. He'd been quietly contemplating the adventitious journey that landed him here, in Hog Heaven Bar & Grille, a local Cedar Rapids, Iowa, watering hole in which he'd sought solace following his debacle of a press conference moments before.

He'd said he wanted to be alone — meaning his campaign manager, his media relations guru, and his wife, who'd made the first foray to the first caucus state with him, were back in their rooms at the Comfort Inn, undoubtedly channel surfing and seeking inspirations in HBO reruns of "Primary Colors."

He pivoted in slow motion, his dexterity slowed by the half-dozen scotches he'd slurped down in the past hour.

"I'm Joleen," she said, snapping her gum. "Whatchyer name?"

He took in the visage of this specimen before him ... Christ, she looked scarcely old enough to drink, let alone have an interest in a 59-year old Congressman ... sleek and svelte. Glommed-on makeup ... penetrating black eyes framed by more black goop ... hair teased from here to Des Moines ... the apertures of her figure hugged by tight denim pants, fringed vest and cowboy boots.

"Why lookin' so glum, hon?"

"Oh, you doan wann no." Lattan slurred.

"Shore I do, darlin! You don't look like you're from these parts, and I'd hate to think we Iowans have been slackin' in the hospitality department."

"I'm not from around here," Lattan said. "I'm from Idaho. I'm a Congressman, ashally, represennin' the seveneeth dissrick."

"Never heard of it."

"I'm not surprised," Lattan said. "Mose peeple don' theen it exisss."

"So what brings you here?"

"I'm running for prezzzdent," Lattan said. "Ha-HA! Makes me laugh jus' sayin it."

"You don't say," she said, smirking. "So how's the campaign going?"

"You wanna know? I've got one word for you: Squeeeeeeeeeee!"

"Squee?"

"Like a stuck pig," Lattan said. "I came here to examine the plight of Iowa's hog farmers and their porkers."

"You don't have to tell me. We've got problems—"

"You've got eighteen thousand hog farmers, four hunnerd eighty thousand hogs in this state ... enough for a whole Congressional dissrick."

"Sounds like you know your stuff."

"Aw, it's just on this sheet," Lattan said, plucking a list of talking points from his coat pocket and throwing it on the bar. "My media guy wrote it up for me so I'd look good talking to reporters at a hog farm."

"And did you?"

"I did until Al Gore showed up, that stiff phony bastard."

"Al Gore, as in the vice president?"

"The Vice Pretender," Lattan said, sneering. "St. Albans boy, grew up in Washington, rich punk. Probably never been on a farm in his life. Wouldn't know a pig if he saw a strip of bacon on his breakfast plate."

"So what happened?"

"I was going about my business, examining this squealing pig at this hog farm, when, like in a scene from *The Candidate*, ol' Al Gore parachutes down in his helicopter and all the media just swarm around him, because they know the phony is going to announce government grants for Iowa pork farmers."

"Is that right?"

"Yeah," Lattan said, his mind drifting back to the events of mere hours ago ... He'd been allowing the press corps to follow him around a hog farm as he inspected the plight of the besieged Iowa hog farmer, and even before Gore came on to the scene, he was literally being drowned out by squealing pigs!

The idea had been the genius of communications director, DeLeet: a prop to make a good visual for the television cameras. Turning live pigs into a political event would certainly signify seriousness, wouldn't it? So there Lattan had been, surrounded by bucking, squealing pigs, ruining his Allen Edmonds brogues by stepping through pig dung, *ha-ha-ha*-ing through it like it was the funniest thing ever, this Congressman ruining his wing-tips by stepping in pig poop ...

But the swines were having none of his rally. As though the little porkers *knew* they were part of a stage set and resented it. And the reporters had laughed when one little porker interrupted Lattan's speech with squeals! He'd had a good mind to give the beast to his wife afterward to make a nice Sunday dinner of pork chops. ...

Then there had been the protesters ... chanting, "Don't you think using a pig for political purposes constitutes animal cruelty?"

And then Gore dropped in and commandeered the attention of the cameras and the reporters, and no one even noticed when Lattan slipped away ... that St. Albans phony, with his feigned Tennessee accent! Didn't anybody see through it?

So Lattan sought refuge in the bar, with an obvious regular on the barstool to his left ... his great rolls of fat spilling on top of the counter. An immense man in his fifties, with a bulbous chin and one large eyebrow that ran across his face. A brown striped polyester dress shirt stretched over his huge torso. It was opened down the front of his chest; he couldn't have buttoned the top of it to wrap on a tie if he'd wanted to. A tuft of hair stuck out over the dingy T-shirt underneath. ... and this new woman friend to his right.

"Maybe I need to get a copy of a book, *Presidential Campaigning For Dummies*," Lattan chuckled, trying to make light of the situation and not depress his new friend.

"The nerve," she said. "Why don't you let me make it better for you ..."

It was all very contrived, too forced, too fake, this woman's interest in him, this laughable presidential candidate. But the liquor was in control, and he felt an indescribable primal need to be coddled, cuddled and pampered.

So he let her lead him away from his barstool and out the door ...

Lattan woke the net morning pinned under the sleeping woman. For the first time in his life, he sensed something truly catastrophic had taken place. Her head was on his chest, her arms around his torso. "Excuse me." She didn't budge. "Ah, miss." Nudging her a little. "Excu — I need to go to the bathroom." Still no acknowledgment. He looked at the clock. Shortly after nine.

He waited a few moments. Then he lifted her left arm and placed it at her side. Next the right arm. Slipped out from under her nude body. He gently lowered her on the bed, her face in the pillow. Still asleep.

He gathered his clothes from the floor and surveyed the debris. Empty wine bottles, accompanied by two empty wine glasses. Her clothes, which had clung to her like cellophane, in a pile on the floor. Torn condom wrappers next to the sofa!

Lattan shuttered at the sight. He looked around for clues, hoping to find something to contradict the sucker punch to his solar plexus.

He started yammering in a early morning, hung over baritone. "Jesus H. Christ! How Could I? Not possible! Holy .. ! She was still out.

He retrieved his clothes in a mound by the side of her bed and struggled to get dressed, all the while wanting to scream but fearing he'd wake her. "God damn it! Goddam it! Goddammmitt!!"

"Well, good morning, Congressman," she said, stretching. "You weren't planning on sneaking out of here without buying a girl breakfast, were you? I thought you were a gentleman."

"I, uh, I'm terribly sorry, miss ... I uh, there's been a serious mistake here ... not that you weren't very nice ... but, uh, did we."

"Oh, Congressman, you were wonderful!"

"Oh, Jesus!" He couldn't even remember ...

"What's wrong," she giggled, her hair matted against her head.

A pang of guilt. His wife ... back at the Comfort Inn ...

She sat up, the sheets crunching underneath her. She put her arms around his neck. Smiling at him, "So, where are you taking me for brunch?"

"I'm sorry ... I must go. Take care, thanks for everything."

And with that he rushed toward the door, bracing to fend off her attempts to make him stay. But the weirdest thing ... she just sat on the bed, smiling and waving *buh-bye* ... making no attempt to stop him.

Then, as he unlocked the deadbolt, a curious object on the telephone stand next to the door caught his eye ... he leaned over to inspect it ... it was a business form of some sort ... a payroll check perhaps ... made out to his new friend ... from ... from ... the personal account of Larry Flynt! And then the *coup de grace* ... in the little notation section FOR .... *seducing Congressman Charles Lattan*! And while he screamed inside, he could hear nothing but her giggling as she rolled on the bed ...

Chapter 31

When Larry Flynt Is The Least Of Your Problems

Larry Flynt sat at his desk reviewing the latest reports on the infidelities of Members of Congress when the phone erupted with a call from Joleen, the assigned seductress of Charles Lattan.

"Get anything for me?" Flynt asked urgently.

"Nada."

"Nothing?" The tone of a kid jilted by the tooth fairy.

"Sorry, the guy passed out on me before I could get him to do the nasty," Joleen said. "I left some empty condom wrappers on the floor and undressed him just for a laugh — you should have seen the look on his face when he woke up — but he's still technically a boy scout."

"Damn," Flynt muttered. "I'm supposed to out this guy on O'Reilly tonight, and you're telling me I got nothin'."

"Sorry. He's a lightweight — in every sense of the word," she said. "You're wasting your time. He isn't even worth the effort. Can't hold his liquor, much less his end of the deal, so to speak. No way that guy will ever be president."

"Damn it to hell," Flynt said. "Well, I'll still go on Geraldo just for the hell of it. People are used to him hyping something that turns out to be a farce. He always comes up looking bad, but I'm guaranteed a few more wire stories, at least."

At the same moment, in the makeshift Iowa campaign headquarters he and his staff had erected at the Cedar Rapids Comfort Inn, Lattan sat and stewed as volunteers jerked papers from the fax machine. Staff whisked in and out of the conference suite, phones jingled, people yelled at each other across the room. He was oblivious to it all.

His wife, campaign manager and media guru had bought the story that he'd spent the night walking ... *contemplating* ... *ruminating* ... about this business of running for president ... *walking* ... all over the deserted streets of Cedar Rapids, Iowa, asking himself, *Who am I?* ...

And he didn't even know what he'd done with that ... that ... odalisque! When was Larry Flynt planning to expose Charles Lattan as the next Republican to be ashamed of his own sexual improprieties? Lattan twiddled his thumbs ... the waiting was unbearable ... had to do something ... pre-empt it somehow ...

He called information for the number to *Hustler* magazine. And then, after convincing several secretaries and receptionists he wasn't a crank caller —

"Mr. Flynt? Congressman Charles Lattan. I wondered if I could ask you some questions."

Flynt smirked. "Before you say what I think you're going to say, Mr. Lattan, lemme tell you that this is your lucky day. I may be a porn peddler, but I ain't a liar."

"I'm not sure I follow you."

"I got nothin' on ya'," Flynt conceded. "My ... *associate* ... told me you fell asleep before you committed anything ... *incriminatin'*. So stop yer worryin.' Flynt sighed. "I guess I'm gonna hafta find another Repullican to trap."

Lattan curtailed a sardonic smile. He was still a boy scout! "I appreciate your honesty," he said. "I didn't expect it from —"

"A guy who prints nudie magazines?"

"You said it, not me."

"Thanks for calling, Congressman," Flynt said.

Lattan hung up the phone and smiled. Then he noticed the figure in the door.

"Charlie," said DeLeet, with quavering voice. He tugged at his shirt collar. "We got a problem."

A what? Lattan was incredulous! Why, he'd just gotten off the phone with that pornographer —

"I received a call this morning from Web Link of the *Washington Past*," DeLeet continued. "Seems he's writing a story based on review of your FEC reports, which caused him to do a Nexis search that revealed that one your donors, Al Tavista, invested in a Russian matchmaking service called 'Glasnost Girls,' which coupled desperate Russian girls with desperate American men. He asked if we had any comment."

"A Russian matchmaking service?" Lattan asked, hoping he'd heard incorrectly.

"So it seems," DeLeet said, swallowing hard. "Link wanted Mr. Tavista's number. But I didn't give it to him. Then I called Mr. Tavista, asked him for the facts, and told him to keep quiet until we decided how to handle it."

"And what did you find out?" Lattan asked.

DeLeet riffled through his notes, his hands trembling.

"Mr. Tavista confirmed that he invested in Glasnost Girls in ninety-two. He wasn't directly involved in the operation. He was more of a silent partner. He's been losing money on it. Several times, he considered selling his interest, but the guy who runs it promised eventual profits if he stayed in. He was surprised that anyone considered his old investments news. I agreed, but you know journalists." Looking up, he added, "It's all legal."

Lattan rubbed his temples. "What have you done so far to diffuse this?"

DeLeet stiffened. His forehead moistened with perspiration. "I, er—"

"So far, you've probably made it worse by telling Mr. Tavista to keep quiet," said campaign manager Alex Macro, appearing in the doorway, glowering at his press guru. "Look at it from Link's perspective. Link calls you, you say you know nothing and you'll get back to him. Then he calls Tavista, who doesn't talk because you told him to clam up. Get inside Link's conspiratorial mind. If you were Web Link, what would you think?"

DeLeet looked at Lattan's withered face. "That the campaign is looking into it and will get back to me."

"Wrong!" Macro slammed his chubby fist into his open hand. "He's going to think cover-up. That we've got something to hide. Even if this is a non-story, it looks bad if we're telling people to keep quiet. The best way to make this disappear fast is to be open, show we've got nothing to be ashamed of. Because we don't. But now, you've helped to make it a story, when we had a chance to kill it if we'd handled it correctly."

DeLeet chewed his lip. "Link is intent on making it a story no matter what."

"Let's assume he was — when you talked to him," Macro said. "But if Tavista had talked to him, been candid and friendly, Link might have thought, 'If these guys are acting like it isn't a big deal, maybe it isn't.' You think a successful businessman such as Al Tavista needs advice on how to handle the press?"

DeLeet swallowed again. "I thought it would be better if he heard it from me first, rather than have Link blindside him."

"Al Tavista could have chosen to talk to Link, or he could have chosen not to talk to Link, and called us first. But now, you've created a situation where we're embarrassed because it looks like our campaign is run by amateurs, and Link thinks he's got himself a big-time story."

"I'm sorry," DeLeet said, spluttering. "I just thought I was doing the best for the campaign."

Lattan wasn't focusing ... His thoughts were stuck on a topic his aide had covered only briefly, as if who botched what was more important than ... than ... a Russian matchmaking service? Who cares? How were they planning to stop it from affecting the campaign? Lattan's face hardened. He leaned forward to speak.

"So we're looking at a story implying that, because one of my donors invested in an overseas bridal service business years ago, an investment I don't know about, and I don't care about, I'm suspect as a social conservative?"

"That seems to be the gist," DeLeet said, voice cracking.

"No goddamn comment!" Lattan said, pounding his fist on the desk. "Where Al Tavista puts his money is not my concern. If he wasn't a shrewd businessman, he wouldn't have given me as much as he has. This is absurd."

"I know," DeLeet said, gnawing a cuticle, trying to reclaim role as media guru. "But if we don't comment, you'll look like a hypocrite. We have to talk. No comment will look bad. We can't ignore this, much as I'd like to. Let's appease Link, let him have his story, and it'll go away."

"It better," Lattan growled. "I don't have time for these distractions." He leaned back in his chair. His chin sank into his chest. DeLeet stared, waiting for his decision. Then Lattan leaned forward again and hit the speaker button on his phone. He punched in a number.

"Mr. Tavista's office," a middle-aged female voice said.

"Charles Lattan calling. Is he available?"

"One moment, Congressman."

Lattan drummed his fingers on his desk.

"I had a feeling I'd be hearing from you," Tavista said.

"Sorry to interrupt you with such a piddling irritation," Lattan said. "But there's a reporter with a burr up his ass doing a story on one of your investments. I don't care about it, nor do I know why he cares. But we need to say something."

"He called here not half an hour ago," Tavista said. "I didn't take his call because I wanted to talk to you first."

DeLeet's facial muscles loosened.

"I want to make sure we know everything so we can clear this up and get back to the campaign," Lattan said. "I hate to ask you, but do you mind telling us, so we can figure out our spin and get on with things?"

"Not at all," Tavista began, and proceeded to tell Lattan the same story he'd told to DeLeet moments before. "I still haven't seen any profits."

Lattan looked down and shook his head. "Why does anyone care?"

"So far, only Link seems to care," DeLeet said.

"Any idea why?" Tavista asked.

"Who knows?" Lattan ventured. "Reporters spend a lot of time looking for skeletons to exhume."

"Reporters," Tavista said derisively. "Maybe if they had more going on in their own lives, they wouldn't worry so much about everyone else's." He chuckled.

"OK," Lattan sighed. "Thanks" He clicked off the speaker. "So it's nothing. What do we tell this reporter?"

"We'll tell him what we just heard," DeLeet said. "It's a legal investment, he lost money on it, it has nothing to do with the real issues of the Lattan campaign — that your interns lick envelopes."

"Sounds good," Lattan said. "Should I call him?"

DeLeet thought for a moment. "No, I'll do it. If you call, it becomes a bigger story. If I call, it shows them we're not concerned, that this is routine."

Moments later, at a secluded cubicle, DeLeet called Link. "I'm told you have some questions regarding an investment made by one of our campaign donors."

"That's correct," Link said. "I understand Mr. Al Tavista put some money into a Russian made-to-order bride business."

A pause. "Mr. Tavista is a well-respected member of the business community in Idaho. Among many investments he has made is the one you mentioned. It also happens to be one on which he has lost money. I'm sorry there isn't more of a story there for you."

"Really?" Link asked, tapping DeLeet's words on the keyboard, watching them become real on the screen. "How much?"

"I don't have the numbers, and I don't think it's important," DeLeet snapped. "The important thing is that we will not allow this to divert attention from our message that Charles Lattan's interns lick envelopes."

"Right," Link said, rapping the keyboard. "That's all I need. Thank you for your time."

Link knew he needed an opposing quote to offset Lattan's flack. One-source stories lacked credibility. After five minutes of rumination, Link snapped his fingers and jumped from his chair. His eyes enlarged. A crafty smile came over his face. He flipped through his Rolodex for the number of Women for Family Values, then phoned the group and requested the spokeswoman.

"This is Rhea Rhodes, may I help you?" He pictured a plump old lady in an apron and reading glasses sitting by the phone.

"This is Web Link from the *Washington Past*. We're doing a story on the Charles Lattan presidential campaign, and I wonder if I may ask you a few questions."

"Who?" she said.

"Charles Lattan, Idaho Congressman, running for president."

"Never heard of him."

"Well, if you had heard of him, what would you think of him if you knew one of his major donors was an investor in a moneymaking scheme to bring Russian ladies to the U.S. to marry American men?"

"Excuse me?" As if Link had uttered an obscenity at her dinner table.

"Al Tavista, a big donor of Lattan's campaign, is a major investor in Glasnost Girls, which exports Russian women to the U.S. for betrothal. Any comment?" Link leaned back in his chair.

"If that's true ... good heavens ... it's outrageous! I could never imagine such a thing. That goes against all of our principles. ... I never heard such a thing ... oh, my."

Link lunged forward to type her quotes into his computer. He pressed. "Would this cause you to take a position *against* Mr. Lattan?"

"Well, we certainly believe the only basis for marriage is love. Making it a business transaction would be against everything we stand for," she said, like a second-grade teacher explaining manners to her pupils. "I suppose that yes, if what you said is true, we will have to take a stand. But this is the first I've heard of it. I'm sure ... I hope ... there's an explanation for this, or it's just a misunderstanding. Oh, dear."

"Thank you for your time." Link hung up.

With the FEC report on his magnetic clipboard, and the quotes from DeLeet and the spokeswoman on the screen, Link wrote the story. On the front page of the next day's *Washington Past:*

LATTAN FINANCIER'S INVESTMENT IN BRIDAL IMPORT BUSINESS OUTRAGES WOMEN

A Charles Lattan donor's investment in a business that brings Russian women to the United States to marry American men has outraged a major women's group, the *Washington Past* has learned.

Idaho businessman Al Tavista invested an undisclosed amount of money in Glasnost Girls, which began matching Russian women with American bachelors in 1992 following the break-up of the Soviet Union. Rep. Lattan (R) is running for the GOP presidential nomination.

Tavista did not respond to inquiries about his investment. But Lattan campaign spokesperson Kentrell Alt DeLeet dismissed the revelation as unimportant.

"There is no reason to believe that the voters will be concerned about this," DeLeet said. But a spokesperson for the state chapter of Women for Family Values, a conservative group, called the investment "outrageous."

Chapter 32

Lanny Dearthofwits, Pundit For Hire

Lattan was finally getting some press — but the kind he didn't want.

The morning that *The Washington Past* published its story linking him — guilt by association! — with the Glasnost Girls matchmaking service, he was forced to postpone his first campaign event that day: shaking hands at a hog processing center in Waterloo, Iowa. He wanted a meeting with Alex Macro, Kentrell "Alt" DeLeet, and Al Tavista to decide how to handle the burgeoning scandal.

"Is Tavista ready on the conference call?" Lattan asked DeLeet and Macro.

"Couldn't get in touch with him directly," Macro answered. "Left messages at his office, home and cell."

"God dammit, how can we have a meeting without the principal?" Lattan pounded his fist on his bed.

"As long as we tell him what we decide in this meeting, we don't need him. He's told us everything we need to know about this situation. All we have to do today is decide what we're gonna say if anyone else picks up the story and asks any new questions," Macro said. "There's no reason to press the panic button."

"How can you be so sure?" asked Lattan.

"I've been in this business a long time," Macro said. "The attention span of the press is shorter than the average viewer of FOX. When they see there ain't nothing there, they'll move on."

Meanwhile, in the *Washington Past* newsroom a thousand miles to the East, Web Link stood next to the fax machine, reading the missive it had just squirted out ... he couldn't believe his eyes ... a fax of *another* news story sent to his attention anonymously ... from some newsletter he'd never heard of ... so obscure it wasn't part of the permanent archive of Nexis ... explaining why he hadn't seen it during his thorough search into the history of Congressman Charles Lattan.

He began reading with the headline—"'GLASNOST GIRLS': OFTEN YOUNG, OFTEN FORCED" ... and then the body copy ... "An American company that brings Russian women to the United States to wed American men often trades in underage girls forced to leave their native land against their will.

"Glasnost Girls, launched as one of the many businesses seeking to profit from a newly free Russian economy, touted itself as providing an international matchmaking service. Russian women, weary of living in a country known for its repressive weather and equally repressive government, would be able to emigrate to the United States and pursue the American dream: marrying a rugged American male, living a comfortable life.

"But Glasnost Girls wasn't all that its brochures cracked it up to be, according to several young Russian women who said they were coerced into joining the company as 'clients.' They spoke of their ordeals in exclusive interviews with *Overseas Investment News* in Moscow.

"'The men who ran this company were former communist party leaders in my neighborhood,' Svetlana, a pretty, diffident 16-year-old, said through a translator. 'They told me that they had jobs in America, that I could help my family. But I didn't want to go. I wanted to stay here with my friends. They threatened me, saying it would be very bad for me, that my father could lose his job if I didn't go.'

"Many young Russian women corroborated Svetlana's story, offering their own version of similar experiences."

Link kept reading. The president of Glasnost Girls denied everything, but backpedaled when questioned about the ethics of his Russian partners. Al Tavista was mentioned only at the end of the story, as one of the many investors to whom *Overseas Investment News* had placed phone calls, and who did not call back with comment.

Link was immediately drunk with the thrill of discovery, the delirium of having a piece of furtive information you're about to spring on the world.

Why hadn't the story mushroomed? Uncorroborated charges from Russian minors, made through interpreters ... And the story disappeared. ...

How could Al Tavista have been be so stupid? Communists or fledgling capitalists, you could never trust the Russians. Not with arms control, not with mail-order wives. What would be his excuse? That for every underage killjoy, ten concupiscent consorts were happily married, shopping at outlet malls, taking language lessons to lose their accents?

He decided to go to the source first. The secretary said Mr. Tavista was unavailable. All press inquiries should go through the Lattan campaign. He called the campaign, asked for Alex Macro. Unavailable for comment. How about Kentrell Alt DeLeet? Also unavailable. Left a message.

He began to write, hoping an idea of whom to call would reveal itself as the news copy unfolded:

"A top donor to the Charles Lattan campaign was a major partner in a Russian operation that forced underage women to emigrate to the United States against their will to marry American men, the *Washington Past* has learned.

"Al Tavista, top donor for U.S. Rep. Charles Lattan's (R-Idaho) presidential bid, is a primary investor in Glasnost Girls, a firm that acted as conduit for American lonely hearts and former Soviet women interested in becoming Western wives.

"According to an article in *Overseas Investment News*, Glasnost Girls frequently employed former communist party bosses who threatened the women to join the group or face dire consequences. Both did not return phone calls seeking comment.

"*The Past* reported earlier that Tavista was an investor in the business. The Lattan campaign downplayed the significance of the revelation, saying there was nothing illegal about the investment."

Link didn't know where to go next. Needed quotes to give the story life. His eyes lit up. He snapped his fingers.

He flipped through his Rolodex for the number of pundit Lanny Dearthofwits, a fixture on the political talk shows and in the papers. Dearthofwits was one of those people famous because he was famous.

Though his credentials as a political expert were suspect — he'd been an Amway salesman, failed Congressional candidate and lawyer for accused killers — he'd appeared on enough programs, been quoted in enough papers, that political journalists routinely called him for instant analysis on a breaking situation. Even his most picayune observations would often become conventional wisdom, if for no other reason than he was the first talking head to offer a sound bite.

Dearthofwits' image as political sage worked because he was the antithesis of the blow-dried, dapper network news anchor. This paunchy, disheveled, middle-aged nerd certainly looked the part of "expert," so he must know what he's talking about.

"I was wondering if we could borrow a kernel of your insight for a story," Link said.

"You're far too kind. What can I do for you?"

"I don't know if you've been following the story we've been doing on Charles Lattan's campaign aide who invested in a Russian bridal import business—"

"Yes, of course I've been following it. I read you every day."

"We've just found out that the business trafficked in women under eighteen, and attempted to coerce them to leave their families to marry in the United States."

"That right? Where'd you get that?"

"Sources."

"*Rea*lly."

"Yeah. So gimme some punditry."

"What has the campaign said?"

"Won't return my calls. You're my go-to guy, if you're interested."

"I'm flattered. You're sure about this?"

"Absolutely. I've got the article in front of me in black and white," Link said.

Dearthofwits cleared his throat. "It's unclear at this point what the impact will be. What is clear is that the Lattan campaign isn't doing itself any favors by keeping silent. It only adds to the perception that they're hunkering down, rather than facing this and dealing with it."

Link typed furiously. "Hang on a sec," he said, rapping the keyboard.

Then, when he caught up, "So, do you think this will prompt calls for Lattan to drop out of the race?"

"You may see that ... maybe some vocal opposition."

Link finished typing. "A pleasure, Mr. Dearthofwits. Thanks for your time."

Link wrote the story and marched it into the office of his editor, Mike Rosoft. Rosoft read it and handed the story back to Link.

"What do you think?" Link asked. "Lead story?"

"Not without Tavista or Lattan or both."

"But they won't talk. I tried." Practically whining.

"We can't run a story saying a guy bought and sold Russian teeny-boppers, based on an article from some newsletter."

Link slumped into a chair. "So you're spiking the story?"

"Until you get quotes from the Lattan camp, youbetcha." Rosoft turned to resume editing at his terminal.

Link sighed, then stood up. "I'll work on it." He slouched out.

"Attaboy." Rosoft didn't look up.

Back at his computer, Link dialed Tavista and Lattan again. Still unavailable. Eyes lit up again, the same as when he thought of calling Dearthofwits. He snapped his fingers.

He grabbed the story and walked to the fax. He took a fax cover sheet out of the tray above the machine and filled it out. To: Lattan campaign. From: Webster Link, *The Washington Past*. Then date, time, fax number. Message: "We are doing a story on this for tomorrow's issue. If you would like to comment, please call. Thanks."

Lattan was sitting on a bed in his Comfort Inn Suite, talking damage control with Macro, when came a knock at the door.

"We're in a meeting," Macro said.

"It's important," came the warbling voice of DeLeet.

"It's gonna hafta wait," Macro said.

"I don't think it can," came the voice through the door.

Macro sighed. "This better be good."

DeLeet entered, sweating as always. Perspiration dampened the papers in his hand. He closed the door gently and walked toward them.

"What's so important?" Macro asked impatiently.

"This." He held out the crinkled fax.

"We don't have time to read it. Whazzit say?"

DeLeet's eyes darted between candidate and campaign manager. Voice faltering, he said, "Mr. Tavista's business forced underage Russian girls to work for them. Link's doing a story on it. Wants our comment."

Macro grabbed the papers. He stood silently and read. Lattan waited for an indication that DeLeet was somehow mistaken.

"Oh, good lord!" Macro said.

"What does it say?" Lattan bellowed.

Macro handed him the fax. "See for yourself."

Lattan read the fax. Glasnost girls ... coerced ... underage ... former communist party officials ... Al Tavista! Please God, this can't be true. This can't be happening!

"God dammit!" He crumbled the papers and threw them across the room. DeLeet retrieved and straightened them. Lattan glared at Macro. "I thought the worst was over!"

"How was I supposed to know about this?" Macro pleaded.

"It's your job to know, dammit!"

Lattan's head sunk into his chest. ... Let's handle this calmly ... He hit the speakerphone button, punched in the number. Ringing reverberated around the room. He ran his fingers through his hair, then leaned back in his chair.

"Charles Lattan for Al Tavista."

"One moment, Congressman."

"What's up?" asked Tavista, oblivious.

"We've got another problem with your Glasnost Girls," Lattan said. "That reporter's got a story from some newsletter saying young girls were forced into action."

A moment of silence. "Oh, Jesus."

"I assume you know what I'm referring to." Lattan looked at Macro and DeLeet like a doctor announcing that a cancer patient's chemotherapy was failing.

"I thought I'd seen the last of that story," Tavista said. "None of it was ever proved. It was trumped up by women we rejected because they were too young for the program. They got bitter, felt they were being denied the

American dream, so they dished up this wild tale to that newsletter."

"Is this the last of it?" Macro asked, playing detective, pacing. "Nothing new going to come out next week, no Chinese water torture, nothing to get reporters writing trend stories?"

"No," Tavista said, his voice disembodied through the speaker. "Jesus, I can't believe anyone would see it as a legitimate story."

Lattan rubbed his eyes. "I want you to tell me what we're going to do to mitigate any potential effect on the campaign." A purple vein throbbed in his temple. "Suggestions?"

"How about a press conference?" DeLeet asked.

"Oh, for God's sake." Macro threw up his hands. "That's all we need. Get this on every network, and played over and over on C-SPAN."

"You got something better?" Lattan demanded.

"We're talking about a newsletter story that's full of lies," Macro said. "We're probably overreacting. All we need to do is say this is another attempt to divert attention from the campaign, and it's unfair to the voters. Charlie, you'll talk to Link. You talking instead of me means we'll get our side higher up in the story."

Lattan nodded slowly ... what he'd like to tell that bastard reporter! "What do I say?"

"A story full of baseless charges against a company in which one of your donors was involved has no pertinence," Macro said.

"Get that reporter on the line," Lattan said. "Al, we'll let you go."

DeLeet rushed to the phone. He read the number on the crumpled fax paper, then punched it in.

"Washington Past," said a youthful voice on the speakerphone.

"Congressman Lattan for Web Link." He said the name as if describing an infectious disease.

"Thank you for getting back to me so quickly," Link said.

"My pleasure," Lattan sneered, rolling his eyes.

"As you know, we're running a story tomorrow on charges that Glasnost Girls coerced underage women into its service. Because I have been unable to reach Mr. Tavista, could you confirm that report?"

"Those charges are not true. No one proved anything. The fact is that Mr. Tavista's company turned away girls who weren't old enough. Some of those who were rejected then cooked up this outrageous story."

"I see," Link said, typing hurriedly. "Do you think this will endanger your support from religious conservatives?"

"I don't see how baseless allegations that don't even involve me have any relevance," Lattan declaimed. "If Al Tavista's guilty of anything, it's not choosing his investing partners as carefully as he should have."

"Anything else you'd like to add?"

Macro drew his finger across his hefty neck.

"No," Lattan said. "That's it." He hung up.

"That was fine," Macro said. "The best that could be expected under the circumstances."

Lattan's brain was boiling. He'd better be right.

Chapter 33

The Showdown

After reading the latest press report and watching Lanny Dearthofwits vilify him on national TV, Lattan knew he had to do something.

But what? How would he neutralize as a campaign issue his association with Al Tavista, his donor who had invested in Glasnost Girls, the Russian matchmaking service accused of forcing underage females into its employ?

So — a call to Al Tavista. What for, he didn't yet know ...

"You're lucky I answered the phone," Tavista said. "All these damned reporters keep calling. I was about to unplug it."

Lattan pictured the Tavistas and their kids hunkered down in their Boise home, besieged by the media. "I'm sorry about that."

"Not as sorry as I am. Christ, an old story based on hearsay and innuendo from crazy Russians who don't even speak English. I still can't understand why it's such a big deal."

"Politics, that's all. Media hungry for a story."

"So hungry they're willing to disrupt people's lives, ruin their good names?"

"It's the nature of the beast." Lattan took a deep breath, tensed his shoulders and grimaced for the next sentences. "I know this has been rough for you. Maybe I should — give you a refund of sorts."

A pause. "What are you trying to say?"

"I'm sorry, but—"

"Dammit, be straight with me. You want to return my contribution to save your ass, say so. Don't patronize me."

Lattan closed his eyes. This conversation was harder than any he'd had in 20 years in politics. "It would be better for both of us, you and my campaign, if you were no longer an issue. I wish it didn't have to be this way."

An awkward moment of silence.

"I understand," Tavista said. "I know how important this race is, and our friendship is strong enough to withstand this. Sure, I'll accept a refund on my contribution."

"I appreciate it more than you know." Eyes open again.

"Actually, it's kind of a relief."

"I'm glad to hear that." Lattan sighed languidly, then rubbed his eyes. "This campaign is draining me. It's an emotional black hole. I can't keep track of when I'm talking to friends and when I'm talking to voters. I feel like I have so few friends, so few people I can be honest with."

"It's politics, like you said."

They exchanged perfunctory farewell salutations, then Lattan hung up ... feeling worse after the conversation than he did before.

"Good," said Macro, hanging up the phone on a table across from the candidate's desk. "We're safe."

"I hope you're right," Lattan said, the machinations in his head clicking and whirring ... what had this little fiasco gotten him? He'd just agreed to give back a thousand bucks from one of his few maxed-out donors, this campaign manager hadn't even had the foresight to see this as a potential problem, and all the media he'd gotten so far as a presidential candidate had been because of this fiasco.

"I hope you don't mind my candor, Alex, but I think you bungled this ... badly." He folded his arms on his chest.

"Hey, boss, I didn't know —"

"That's exactly my point," Lattan thundered, suddenly overcome with rage, as if the Glasnost Girls episode suddenly uncorked the stopper on his anger. "It's your goddamn job to know. What have you done right for me lately? Glasnost Girls — this is only the latest thing. Before that it was those damn phonies in Las Vegas. Before that I couldn't find my damn voting card to impeach the hillbilly pervert. Before that I got thrown out on my can from the National Press Club. Before that —"

"Boss, I don't think you need to remind me of some of the little bumps in the road we've had along the way. That's the nature of a presidential campaign."

"Which we haven't even formally begun!" Lattan bellowed. "For chrissakes, I haven't even made my official campaign announcement yet, thanks to you!"

"Hey, I wasn't the one who walked out of the Bardo Rodeo before I had the chance to give my story to that reporter—"

"The Washington Moomoo paper? Give me a break," Lattan sneered. "They crib practically everything from the wire services anyway!"

"Charlie, just get a hold of yourself," Macro said feebly. "I think this is just stress—"

"The hell it is," Lattan said. "It's your fault."

A long, awkward pause. Then Macro broke the silence. "I know you're pissed off. I'm sorry about that. I swear things will turn around soon."

Suddenly Lattan was calm and composed. As if he knew exactly what to do.

"I blame myself for this," Lattan said evenly. "I put you in a position you weren't ready for. Maybe you can't handle the pressure of a national campaign."

"What the hell are you sayin'?" Macro demanded.

"I think it's time we went our separate ways."

Pearls of perspiration appeared on Macro's forehead. He remained silent, thunderstruck with disbelief.

"I'm sorry," Lattan said. "This is a tough business. After the campaign, I'll help you find something."

Macro looked down, as if examining his shoes for scruff marks. He'd sensed it earlier, but had held out hope for clemency. Without looking up, "What are you going to do for a campaign manager?"

"I might have Kentrell take over," Lattan blurted, although he knew as soon as the words escaped from his mouth that the prospect of putting his media guru in charge of the whole operation was preposterous.

"So that's it? You're just firing me?" Still looking down.

"I am sorry it had to be this way."

"Isn't there anything I can do to make it up? Stay on the campaign in another role? It'll look bad."

Lattan's paternal patience vaporized. "We were taken by surprise by a frigging' story we should have known about! *The Washington Past*, Lanny Deathofwits, Web Link! Do you want me to give you a list?"

Macro's mind flashed to when, at sixteen, he was fired from a waiter job because he kept spilling drinks on the customers. He swore he would never get fired again, never allow someone else the satisfaction, the power over him. Especially not a parvenu like Charles Lattan.

Suddenly he had a burst of effulgence. An idea that would save him from having to suffer the embarrassment of losing his job, the humiliation attendant to having his dreams of working for President Charles Lattan dashed. He glared into Lattan's bullish eyes, and spoke without the familiar squeakiness in his voice.

"Web Link might like to know a few other things than just the bad investment of one of your donors. Don't you think? I might be able to help him with a few more stories."

Lattan stared back at him. Macro didn't break eye contact. Then he laughed. "You're not stupid enough to think you can blackmail me into keeping your job."

"Call it what you will. Call me what you will. You fire me, I go to Link. You keep me, I keep quiet. You pick." Unexpected confidence, a feeling that momentum had shifted. He smiled defiantly.

"I'm going to pretend you're kidding, because I don't want to see your career in politics end. Now, as I said, I'll help you land a job after the election. But don't test my patience anymore."

"So that's a 'no' on keeping me?" Macro's words and stare were frigid.

Lattan leaned forward, exhaling coffee breath into Macro's face. "You're goddamn right that's a no. A big fat no. I got news for you, you piece of crap." He pointed his finger, jabbing the air in front of Macro's nose. "No one, not even MSNBC, is gonna give a rat's ass what a bitter, terminated, ex-campaign manager has to say. No one cares about whatever wild story you try to tell. And even if they did, it would be your word against mine, if it comes to that. So you better think long and hard about whether you want to sabotage yourself. You've got nothing to gain, and everything to lose." He backed off, walked around the desk toward the window. His back to Macro, he ran his fingers through his thinning hair.

Macro felt warm puddles under his arms staining his shirt. "I guess we've got nothing left to talk about," he said, voice again squeaky. He got up and walked out. Lattan didn't turn around.

Chapter 34

Fired Staffer Says Lattan's A Fake!

Washington Past copy aide Web Link switched on his computer to work on the story budget for the new week. He lit a cigarette, and smoked as he waited for the machine to warm up. The phone rang.

"Hey Web, it's Alex Macro. How are you?"

"Fine." Why did he sound so friendly? "Et Tu?"

Macro laughed uneasily. "I was wondering if you wanted a scoop."

Web Link straightened in his chair and placed his cigarette on the edge of the metal desk. "Sure, if it's the right kind of story."

"I'll tell you, but only as an anonymous source."

"Lemme guess. Trent Lott likes Russian teeny-boppers too."

"No, nothing like that."

Web Link leaned back, putting his feet on the desk. He sensed a sales pitch. "I'm in the dark here, so why don't you help me out. Why would Charles Lattan's campaign manager try to feed me an anonymous story?"

"Let's just say that The Honorable Charles Lattan is no longer my boss, and I'm going to tell you why. Provided you agree to my condition of anonymity, and you don't call the Lattan campaign for comment. It'll give me away. I don't want to jeopardize my post-Lattan career."

"Agreed. Provided you have a story."

"Oh, I do. I most certainly do."

Lattan and his newly promoted campaign manager, Kentrell "Alt" DeLeet, lunched in their Cedar Rapids, Iowa campaign headquarters, enjoying a much-needed break from campaigning. They had started in Waterloo at six a.m. that morning, shaking hands with an early shift of factory workers. Then visits to Sioux City coffee shops, schools and an editorial board meeting at *The Cedar Rapids Gazette*. Not one voter mentioned the Glasnost Girls situation, though the editors at the paper focused on it almost exclusively. But Lattan, emboldened by the firing of Macro, had an answer for every question. He left feeling upbeat.

Now, over roast beef sandwiches and potato chips, Lattan and DeLeet read the day's papers. Happy that no more Al Tavista meant no more Glasnost Girls stories.

"Nothing in any of the nationals, either," DeLeet said, wiping mayonnaise from his chin with the back of his hand. "That's all the publications. Looks like we're finally in the clear."

"And not a moment too soon," Lattan said. "There's still enough time for everyone to forget this by caucus day, right?"

"Hell yes. The attention span of the average voter isn't much more than a few minutes, much less days or weeks. One year from now, I'll be calling you Mr. Republican presidential front-runner."

A knock at the door. "Come," Lattan said.

A spindly, blemish-faced college intern came in, clutching a fax. "I'm sorry to interrupt your lunch, sirs."

"Quite all right, m'boy," Lattan said, putting his sandwich down on a piece of delicatessen wax paper. "What's your name, son?"

"Serge Engine, sir." Standing still. "I'm a French foreign exchange student."

"Well, it's a pleasure to have you here, Serge. We appreciate all of your fine work."

"Thank you, sir."

Lattan's eyes shifted from Serge's face to the papers in his right hand. Picking his sandwich up, "What do you have for us?"

"Fax, sir. I was told to bring it to you."

"Fine, fine. Thank you. Keep up the good work, Serge."

Serge handed the fax to the candidate and disappeared. Lattan looked at the paper. He dropped his sandwich.

"What? What is it?" DeLeet demanded.

Lattan handed DeLeet the fax, his hand shaking. He got up, crumpled his napkin, discarded it on the desk. Walked over to the window. Stood silently and stared.

"I'm gonna' kill that fat bastard," Lattan said.

The fax copy of the *Washington Past.com* story read:

LATTAN QUOTES IN PRESS RELEASES ARE FAKES, FORMER AIDE SAYS

The staff of GOP presidential candidate Rep. Charles Lattan (ID-17) has for years issued press releases, constituent letters and other statements containing phony quotes attributed to Lattan, a former top-level Lattan aide told the Washington Past in an exclusive interview.

The aide, who resigned in protest over the practice, said that Lattan is a puppet of his staff, and that he frequently relied on others to put words in his mouth to help craft his image and package it for the voters.

"Lattan doesn't even see the stuff that goes out under his name most of the time, much less say it or write it himself," the source said. "He's been hoodwinking the voters for years, who think they receive a personal response to their letters, and he's been fooling the press, who think he's actually said the quotes contained in his press releases. Ever wonder why his grammar is so perfect in those statements? It's because the staff writes them!"

This latest revelation comes as Lattan seemed to be putting the Glasnost Girls scandal behind him. Last week, the Past revealed that Al Tavista, a Lattan top-level donor, had been an investor in an overseas company that brings Russian women to the United States to marry American men. Then, the Washington Past revealed that the firm, Glasnost Girls, faced allegations of attempting to force underage girls into its service. The Lattan campaign dismissed the allegations, but Lattan did return Tavista's $1,000 donation to his campaign.

"Clearly, this latest episode gives the voters a very good idea about Charles Lattan's character," said veteran political analyst Lanny Dearthofwits. "In one instance, we see him tied to all sorts of questionable business investments. Now, we see that he's not been honest with the voters or the media by overseeing a conspiracy to have his staff fabricate all sorts of documents on his behalf. When you add this to everything that has happened up until now, voters have every right to express serious doubts about Charles Lattan's integrity."

DeLeet balled up the fax and threw it across the room. "God dammit!"

Lattan continued to stare out of the window. Without turning around, "What in God's name did we do to our old friend Alex?"

Lattan spent the afternoon answering press calls from every television station, radio station and newspaper in Iowa, some he hadn't even heard of.

Denial, denial, denial. No, we will not elaborate because these accusations are so outrageous that commenting on them would only give them credibility they do not deserve. Alex Macro was an incompetent bumbler. He's bitter and angry, he's lashing out. The Washington Past never called us to verify anything.

By the time the six o'clock news came on, Lattan was winded. He sat in his office, remote control in hand, watching himself deny, deny, deny all over the screen. Stories began with "New revelations rocked the Lattan campaign again today," "Yet another scandal is unfolding in the battered Lattan presidential campaign," "When it rains, it pours, and controversy is pouring once again in the dark-horse Lattan campaign."

Lattan expected his sound bites to be followed by snippets from his rivals. But the other announced Republicans were conspicuously absent from the newscasts. Why should they say anything? He recalled Napoleon's advice: "Never interfere with the enemy when he is in the process of destroying himself."

Macro wasn't to be found, despite Lattan's careful recitation of his name for every interview. Probably terrified that the press found out who he was. How typically stupid of him to think he could remain anonymous.

Every newspaper reporter who called Lattan that afternoon faithfully wrote a story for the next day's editions. Lattan couldn't buy press coverage when he spoke to a high school, but when the media detected scandal, he couldn't escape it. It was as if they wrote articles to spite his denials, the abnegations adding to the sense of conflict, making it a better story.

But then DeLeet got a mysterious phone call that caused his eyes to ignite with passion. What could it be?

"Good news!" DeLeet said, slamming down the phone. "MSNBC just called! They want you on TV tomorrow night."

"Really? Did they say why?"

"I guess they want to give you a forum to put forward your side in all of this. They said something like chatting about the news or something, and they gave me some question. But it doesn't matter. You're on for a whole hour. They're sending a car and everything. This may be your chance to tell your side of the story on national television before a live audience!"

"A whole hour to myself?" Lattan asked incredulously. "Are you sure?"

"They didn't mention any guests," DeLeet said. "So I guess so."

"Excellent!" Lattan said, trying in vain to disguise his glee. Just what he had been waiting for.

Chapter 35

Fighting For Air Time On MSNBC

Lattan sat in the back seat of the NBC Lincoln Town Car as the driver made his way through DC's rush-hour traffic. When MSNBC had booked him for "News Chat," they'd said he could do it from a remote studio in Iowa. But Lattan said *that's quite all right, I'll be more than happy to do it at your studios in Washington.*

So he'd hopped on a flight back to DC, gone over his message and talking points all day with his campaign manager and media guru, Kentrell "Alt" DeLeet, and now, at 5:30, enjoyed the pomp and circumstance bestowed on him by a network who finally realized the value of having him on a guest.

The driver lurched and then stopped in front of 400 North Capitol St. "OK, there you go, sir," he said, turning back to face Lattan. "You on for half hour or hour?"

"The Congressman is on for a full hour," DeLeet said haughtily, winking at Lattan.

"OK," said the driver with a weariness that suggested he'd ferried more than a few gasbags to TV appearances here. "I'll be waitin' right here."

DeLeet popped out and held open the door for Lattan, who stood up jauntily and strutted across the plaza into the building. He buttoned his coat, checked the knot in his blazing red tie, smoothed the collar on his crisp new blue shirt.

"Congressman Lattan for MSNBC," DeLeet said to the receptionist after they walked through the revolving door. She nodded and waved them past.

Lattan followed DeLeet into the elevator, and watched the numbers light up one after the other until they reached the eighth floor. "This is going to be great," DeLeet said. "Finally, a national forum."

Lattan nodded and followed DeLeet through the double doors to the NBC studios. "We're here for our 6 o'clock appearance," DeLeet announced to the receptionist.

"And you are?" she asked.

"Congressman Charles J. Lattan of Idaho!" Lattan said.

"I'm sorry, I just didn't recognize you," she said. "You're a 6 o'clock chatter?" she moved her finger down a page on her list. "Yes. Here you are. You're the only one we were waiting for. Please join the other two guests in the green room."

"What do you mean, other guests?" DeLeet demanded.

"For News Chat," she said. "You'll be on with political consultant Nick Thimmesch and pollster Kellyanne Fitzpatrick Conway."

"At the same time?" DeLeet asked.

"Of course," the receptionist said. "Is this your first time on News Chat?"

"Well, er, it's not the Congressman's first time on TV," DeLeet spluttered. "We weren't aware that—"

"Don't worry, you'll be fine," the receptionist said. "You'll get plenty of air time. I think John Gibson's a little subdued today."

"Thank you," DeLeet said, grabbing Lattan's arm. "We'll go to the green room."

"What the hell is going on, Kentrell?" Lattan tried to whisper as they walked. "I thought this was *my* time."

"I'm not sure," DeLeet said nervously, struggling for a way to spin it the best he could. "This is just TV procedure. They change things around all the time. We just have to roll with it. At least you didn't get bumped for JonBenet Ramsey. You, Congressman, are on national TV in minutes. That's the important thing."

Lattan strode into the green room to see one fellow sitting and watching the big TV as he smoked a cigarette, and a pretty young blonde woman talking on a brown cellular phone ... which perfectly matched the chocolate acetate color of her dress! How coordinated! How calculated!

"Hello, I'm Congressman Lattan," he said, reaching to shake the fellow's hand.

"Nick Thimmesch," the fellow said, shaking his hand without standing up or making eye contact. "That's Kellyanne on the phone," he said, gesturing with his smoldering cigarette.

At which point the woman turned toward Lattan and smiled and waved, listening intently to the phone cradled on her neck. Wow! Such white teeth! Such blonde hair! Such a made-for-TV ensemble!

"Congressman, we're ready for you in make-up," said a woman who peered into the door.

So Lattan was led out of the green room and into the make-up room, where he was seated and draped in a smock. Then he was blotted and smeared with all sorts of mush while DeLeet continued to prep him on his message. He followed a technician to a small room, where he was seated and hooked with a microphone and nearly blinded by white hot lights.

He stared at the TV monitor, which appeared to be showing commercials. "Ay, I can't hear!" he yelled.

"Don't worry. It's silent during the commercials," the technician said. "Just listen to the feed into your ear, and stare straight ahead. Don't look at the monitor, or you'll get confused because of the sound delay."

"Right," Lattan said, thinking about all of the points he wanted to make.

Then the music started, and he could hear it in his ear. "Hi I'm John Gibson, and welcome to the second hour of New Chat. This hour we take a break from our team coverage of JonBenet Ramsey and look at the issue of politicians using their staffs to fabricate phony quotes. Our News Chat question this hour is, 'Phony Quotes — As Bad As Cliff's Notes, Or OK Way To Get Votes?' We'll be joined by our guests shortly, but first, we have a caller on the line. Bill in Rochester, go ahead."

"Yeah, John, I want to know why you're not talking about Juanita Broaddrick ..."

"That's for InterNight," Gibson shot back. "And then for Equal Time, and then McLaughlin's Special Report, and then the Ruse With Brian Williams, and then Countdown With Keith Olbermann. But not for this hour of News Chat."

But Lattan wasn't listening. What was going on? A question of the hour? Callers? Other guests? What kind of crazy program was this?

"OK, caller, that's 20 seconds," the host said. Lattan watched him on the monitor ... this animated blond fellow with upswept hair, flailing his arms every which way. ...

"And now we go to the news with Patti Anne Browne. Patti?"

And Lattan watched, and watched, as they read the news, and did the weather, and more commercials, and it was nearly quarter past the hour already, and he hadn't even gotten a chance to speak.

"OK, I want to go to our guests," Gibson said. "All three are in Washington. Congressman Charles Lattan is the man who has been accused of issuing press releases with phony quotes he didn't even say. Nick Thimmesch is a political consultant who says writing press releases for his clients, phony quotes and all, is standard practice in politics. And Kellyanne Fitzpatrick is a pollster who will give us some insights into whether this is something that could resonate with voters."

Lattan couldn't see anything more than what the average viewer got at home. He was alone in the studio, staring into a camera lens, waiting for a chance to speak.

"Nick, I want to start with you," Gibson said. "You say this is much ado about nothing, right?"

"Oh, absolutely, John," said this Thimmesch fellow, in a deep baritone, as his face appeared on the monitor. He looked middle-aged, though his head of full brown hair gave him a more youthful appearance. Lattan instinctively ran his hand over his own combover. Thimmesch continued: "Hell, if politicians wrote their own press releases and speeches and letters to the editor, a guy like me would be out of business. It's all standard operating procedure."

"Kellyanne, what about the average voter who writes her Congressman and gets a response signed in his name, even though that letter was written by some staffer on the Hill. Isn't that a little dishonest?" Gibson asked.

"Well John, the practice may be standard in Washington, but to the little old lady in Peoria who wants to communicate with her Congressman, it might come as a bit of a surprise."

"OK, I want to go to our Congressman next, but I gotta do this break first. Stay with us."

And then it was more commercials ... and then the weather ... and then the international news ... and then more callers ...

And then, just as Lattan noticed the clock on the monitor saying 6:35:43, he heard through his earpiece, "Congressman, what's your take on all of this?"

"Well, frankly, this is not what I came here to discuss—"

"Yeah, I know, you guys on the Hill always want to change the subject," Gibson interrupted, rolling his eyes.

"I want to talk about why I'm running for president, and the issues important to my campaign—"

"Sorry, Congressman, but that's for another News Chat. How do you defend this practice of fabricating quotes?"

Then Lattan remembered DeLeet's advice: no matter what question they ask, give whatever answer you want. "I'm running for president because we need a leader who isn't acting like he's at a high school make-out party. My interns will lick envelopes."

Gibson snickered. "That's a cute quote, Congressman, but it doesn't answer my question. Stand by, and I'll give you another chance after this break."

And there were more commercials, and then some blond woman and some gap-toothed fellow talking about their show coming up at 8 pm, and then more callers, and more banter from the other two guests.

Then Gibson returned ...

"OK, before I forget, let's go to our Internet Analyst, M.K. Flynn, to see what the chatters are saying."

And then some cute little blonde number started talking about some chat room and some numbers flashed on the screen.

"OK, that's all we have time for," Gibson said. "My thanks to our guests and the chatters. Coming up next on InterNight: A former alderman from Boulder, Colorado, gives us his perspective on the JonBenet Ramsay situation."

"Bobba Bowie!" Thimmesch yelled over the closing music.

And then the cameraman came over and unhooked Lattan and the lights went off ... and just like that, it was over.

Lattan walked back toward the green room to meet DeLeet and demand an explanation for this ... *indignity*. But before he could get there, the other guest, this Nick person, intercepted him in the hallway.

"Hey Congressman, I enjoyed being on the show with you," Thimmesch said. "I understand that you've promoted your old media guy to campaign manager, so you must be looking for a new media man. I'd like to offer the services of my firm, USA Media Communications."

"Can you book me on shows where I get to *talk*?"

"C-SPAN, CNN, FOX, you name it," Thimmesch said. "I can get you spots as keynote speaker at every right-wing conclave in town."

"Really?" Lattan said, intrigued.

"Why don't we go out for a drink and talk about it?"

"I'm eager to hear what you have in mind," Lattan said.

Chapter 36

Scrap Social Security!

Minutes after his appearance on MSNBC's "News Chat," Lattan sat with his campaign manager and political consultant Nick Thimmesch in a booth at the Irish Times. Amid this loud, smoky watering hole teeming with Hill denizens, the Congressman hoped he'd found the man who could save his faltering presidential campaign.

"Hearing my advice is free," Thimmesch said, exhaling a plume of smoke from a filterless Camel. "But if you want to put my plan into action, it'll cost you."

Lattan felt a blow to his gut—did they have the money to even hire a new media guru? To do media buys? To even buy bumper stickers and lapel pins? When was the last time they'd even looked at the ledger?

"Let's here what you've got in mind," DeLeet said, taking a pull on an Amstel light.

"Well, as I see it, Congressman, your current slogan isn't going to work," Thimmesch said, taking a drink from his Rum & Coke. "Much as I agree with you on principle, you can't convince voters to support you because *your* interns lick envelopes."

"But they do!" Lattan insisted, slamming his fist on the table, nearly toppling everyone's drinks.

"I don't doubt it for a minute," Thimmesch said. "But that won't distinguish you in the field from the other Republican candidates."

Lattan hated to admit to himself, but this Thimmesch fellow—this grizzled veteran of consulting, this war hero of Republican battles over the decades

—was right.

"You need to do something that will make people take notice," Thimmesch continued. "Now I can develop a theme, and then we can line up the earned media and paid media campaigns to push it. But you ought to know my services don't come cheap."

"We can talk numbers later," DeLeet said. "But let's hear your strategy first."

"OK," Thimmesch said. "Let's take the California convention last weekend. What did you say there?"

DeLeet and Lattan looked at each other, utterly befuddled. California? convention?

"What, uh, *exact*, convention, er, *specifically*, are you referring to?" DeLeet said.

Thimmesch shook his head ruefully. "You're not telling me you missed the Republican meeting, are you?" He chuckled — a deep, tobacco-cured, guttural laugh. "Man, you got bigger problems than I thought." He shook his head like a teacher listening to a student's excuse about missing class.

"But *can you solve my problems* is the question!" Lattan said, angry he'd missed the whatever-it-was in California.

"Well, *that* sounds like an advance team issue," Thimmesch said, motioning to the waitress for a refill. "Too late to do anything about that anyway. Let's look ahead. When is your next trip to New Hampshire?"

Again Lattan and DeLeet exchanged puzzled glances.

"You gotta be kidding me," Thimmesch said. "What kind of a campaign are you running?"

"I, er, well, it's that—" Lattan spluttered.

"Look," Thimmesch said, stubbing his cigarette out in the ashtray. "I could be slick here, and paint rosy pictures about everything I could do for you, and cost you a big chunk of your campaign budget. But I gotta tell you, you've got other problems you need to look at before you're ready to hire me."

"What the hell—" Lattan began. DeLeet kicked him under the table.

"I could be like any other consultant, and take your money. But I couldn't do it with a clear conscience, because it wouldn't be honest," Thimmesch said. "Hell, any other consultant *would* take your money, and convince you that he'd win you the nomination. But that's not how I operate. USA Media

Communications has built its reputation over the years by being candid with its clients. That's how we distinguish ourselves from every other firm in town. We're honest." Thimmesch stood up from the booth.

"So what are you saying?" DeLeet demanded.

"I'm saying ... " Thimmesch began, sighing heavily, "that my free advice to you is go back to Idaho and be a Congressman." He threw a twenty-dollar bill on the table. "Drinks are on me."

He turned to leave, and DeLeet and Lattan just watched in silence as this trenchcoat-clad titan of the right shuffled away. They were thunderstruck. But then Thimmesch pivoted on his heels, and turned around to face them once more. "What district you represent in Idaho again?"

"Seventeenth," Lattan said. "Most people don't think it exists."

"Seventeen, huh," Thimmesch said, rubbing his chin. "I'll tell you later if it exists as a winning keno number."

And with that, the consultant turned back toward the door and walked out.

Lattan didn't know whether to be furious at Thimmesch's prognostication or grateful for his candor.

Neither he nor DeLeet said anything for a long while, each silently finishing their drinks, then peeling the labels off of the bottles. Lattan looked around and gazed absently at the haze hovering above the booths ... the scent of tobacco made him think he was in the break room of a Philip Morris factory.

Finally, Lattan could take the silence no more. "Is it really that bad, Kentrell?"

DeLeet didn't answer for a moment, as though composing an answer that would calm the candidate's fears.

"Worse," DeLeet said. "Even if he'd agreed to be our consultant, we wouldn't have had the money to pay him."

Lattan closed his eyes and rubbed his temples. "How much do we have?"

"About enough for two tickets to New Hampshire, a few nights at a hotel, and a compact rental car," DeLeet said. "If we catch fire somehow, then we can go on. But if we don't, it's back to Idaho."

Lattan stared straight ahead. "All right," he said. "Let's go."

"What about what Thimmesch said — our slogan?" DeLeet asked.

"I guess he's right. We'll have to scrap it. We'll need something else if we're going to fire up the Republican primary voters. Any suggestions?"

"Well, the Democrats seem to have regained control of the agenda by talking about 'saving Social Security.' I don't know how we can use that as an issue, but maybe we come up with our own plan ..."

Then Lattan's eyes ignited. He felt a rush of adrenaline through his veins ... then shivers all over. "Forget saving Social Security," he said. "How's this sound?"

He turned toward DeLeet: "Charles Lattan For President. Let's Scrap Social Security!"

DeLeet smiled craftily. "I like it."

"We'll tell people they can opt out of it. ... Young people know they're never going to see a dime of it anyway ... so a vote for Charles Lattan is a vote for a refund on all the money the Democrats have confiscated in Social Security taxes!"

"Let's get out of here and start packing for New Hampshire," DeLeet said.

Chapter 37

War Is Hell

"Thank you for that warm introduction, and for the opportunity to address your meeting tonight," Lattan said, standing at the podium in the meeting room of the — Christ, which town was it? — local chapter of the Veterans of Foreign Wars. Seated among mostly empty metal folding chairs in front of him were precisely eight people, and that included his campaign manager, DeLeet. But this is how retail politics worked in New Hampshire, right? Or so DeLeet had convinced him. ...

God, the looks on their faces. Would they still be alive on primary day? Immediately he hated himself for such a horrible, horrible thought. ... But look at them! Either on the verge of falling asleep or unable to hear him because of low batteries in their hearing aids. And one meek old fellow who looked like he could collapse under the weight of the countless shiny metals he wore on his chest.

"You're probably asking yourself, 'Who the *hell* is this guy, and why am I listening to him?'" Lattan said, pleased that he's thrown the word *hell* in there. Veterans liked raunchiness. "Well, my name is Congressman Charles Lattan, and I'm running for president."

"Never heard of you!" snapped one of the curmudgeons.

"Well, yes, that's part of the reason I'm here," Lattan said. "I want to tell you a little about myself, and what I stand for, and, more important, I want to listen to your concerns."

"How'd you vote on the last veterans benefits bill?" the small man bedecked with medals asked.

Christ! They were starting in already! Scrutinizing his record before he'd barely begun his stump speech!

"Of course I voted for it," Lattan said, knowing he was safe in a reporterless room. He didn't have the slightest idea how he'd voted on it. "I'm a strong advocate of our nation's fighting men—"

"You ever wear the uniform?" snarled a fellow with a hearing aid, whom Lattan had thought couldn't hear a thing.

"Well, I never was *technically* in the armed forces, that is to say, *directly*, although in Congress I deal with military issues—"

"Well what the hell you got to say for yourself?" asked another man in back wearing some sort of official-looking hat. "You about the 10th one come in here recently saying we should vote for him. Can't even remember anyone's name."

"I'm hoping that my ideas will make you remember my name, and earn your support for my candidacy," Lattan said, already losing heart. God, this was utterly hopeless.

"What ideas you got? I like Bob Smith's ideas myself. He's our Senator, and he'd make a damn fine president, too," said a blowzy fellow wearing an "I REMEMBER OUR MIAs" T-Shirt.

"I'm sure Mr. Smith is a fine man," Lattan said, wondering if he really had anything to lose by leaving right at this moment. "But I know for a fact that I'm the only one who has a solution to the biggest problem facing our country — Social Security."

Lattan was finally able to bridge to the topic he wanted to discuss. Ever since the germ of the idea had struck him in that bar in DC — Scrap Social Security! — he'd been salivating at the chance to use it.

"You see, Social Security has taken money from you your whole lives. But the sad fact is, the system is going broke," Lattan said. "Now I know the Democrats and my Republican opponents all have ideas about how to fix it, but they ignore the truth—"

"Damn right!" said the small man wearing the medals.

"Yeah, and veterans benefits too," said the man with the hearing aid.

Finally, he was reaching them ... just needed to get warmed up. "So my solution is this: Let's scrap the entire system. It's broken. It's bankrupt. It can't pay. So let's get rid of it!"

He braced for more "damn rights!" and hoped for some applause ... but he faced eight stone silent faces.

Then, finally, the man who introduced him, of all people, the chapter president or whatever, spoke up:

"Are you out of your flippin' mind?"

Lattan froze.

"How the hell we gonna survive without Social Security?" asked the man in the MIA T-shirt. "God dammit, we've been relying on that money our entire lives, and you want to end it?"

"No, no, that's not what I'm saying at all," Lattan said, spluttering. "I'm saying that the money isn't there, and you're gonna get screwed, and —" God, what *was* he saying? Maybe this wasn't the best audience to use as a focus group for his new agenda.

Why he hadn't thought of that before baffled him further, until he was imploding into his own mental vortex of despair. ... God dammit, it was DeLeet's fault! He should be talking to some slackers at a coffee house, not some bitter old men!

"What kind of an idiot comes here tellin' us he wants to kill Social Security thinkin' it would get our votes," piped in a man in wheelchair. Everyone else turned to him and nodded in agreement. "Go back to Washington! We're sticking with our man Bob Smith!"

And from then on it was a perfunctory performance, then a blissfully quick announcement from the chapter president that they were out of time, *thanks for coming*, and before he knew it he and DeLeet were standing out on the curb, like two rowdy drunks tossed out of a bar.

"Why the hell did we start with seniors, Kentrell?" Lattan yelled, pacing back and forth as his campaign manager just stood rigid. "Couldn't we have gone to some community college or something?"

"This was the only group who said we could come to their meeting," DeLeet said meekly. "I must have called a hundred organizations."

"Oh, it's just as well," Lattan said. He stopped pacing and leaned against a tree. "Eight people," he sneered, shaking his head. "Hell, there wasn't even a vote for each Republican candidate in that room."

"Don't worry," DeLeet said. "I'm still waiting on a bunch of people to return calls. We'll have plenty of chances to speak to groups in Manchester, Nashua, Concord —"

"What town are we in, anyway?" Lattan asked, his eyebrows askew. Then he turned to look at the sign on the VFW hall. "Aha! Raymond. Raymond, New Hampshire. Well, at least *that*'s cleared up."

"Let's go to another town, maybe work some pubs or something," DeLeet suggested. "I circled this town called Milford on the map, known for its oval."

"Sounds good," Lattan said, standing straight up after leaning on the tree. He ran his hand over his head, checking the condition of his combover. It felt different ... sticky ... like his hand was sticking to his head. "What the—" He looked at the palm of his hand, which was gummed up with a sticky black goop.

"Oh yeah," DeLeet said. "That reminds me. It's maple syrup season. I read it in a guidebook. Looks like you leaned on some sap."

"Sap indeed!" Lattan said, kneeling and wiping his hands up and down the grass. "Wish I had a goddamn handkerchief!"

"We'll stop at a gas station on the way to Milford and you can clean up," DeLeet said, and began walking toward their rental car: a Dodge Neon. Oh, the romance of running a campaign on a tight budget ... at least he was a proven fiscal conservative, if only by necessity. ...

Chapter 38

Going After The Youth Vote

"A diner. Perfect!" said a beaming Lattan as he and campaign manager DeLeet spied the Milford Diner in Milford, New Hampshire. "There we'll find some people receptive to my message of scrapping Social Security!"

Lattan rubbed his palms together to warm up from the cold and prepare for some good, old-fashioned hand-shaking. DeLeet held open the door and a confident candidate held his chest out and chin up to lumber inside.

At the 7 a.m. prime time breakfast hour, the Milford Diner was teeming with a nice cross-section of people from this blue-collar GOP town. Everyone from laborers to coveted twenty-something slackers seemed to be scarfing down eggs and bacon in between gulps of coffee.

Lattan took a deep breath and headed toward the counter to start working the place. *Just like in Idaho*, he told himself, *just like working a room at the Potato Lodge or the American Legion or the Spudsville Chamber reception. ...*

"Oof!" said a startled man in a suit, bumping into him. "Sorry, pal."

"Don't mention it," Lattan said to the man towering over him.

The fellow looked familiar. Lattan studied the topography of his face. He was tall and lanky, yet, oddly, had several chins ... where had Lattan seen him before? And he was smiling ... this tall fellow. ... so familiar-looking.

Finally, the stranger introduced himself.

"Hi, I'm Bill Bradley, and I'm running for president," the fellow said, reaching out to shake Lattan's hand.

Lattan was stupefied. "Of course you are!" he blurted out, a little embarrassed he had not recognized this respectable member of the loyal opposition. Well, of course he could have a good-natured laugh with this possible general election opponent. That was how *statesmen* acted!

"So, do you vote here in Milford?" Bradley asked, nonplussed. "If so, can I count on your support?"

Lattan was speechless. Why ... the ... *chutzpah* ... surely he had to be kidding ... of course he recognized a fellow elected official, didn't he? Or had he been out of the Senate too long?

"Ha ha, that's a good one," Lattan said clumsily. "No, actually, I'm here for the same reason you are, you kidder you!" He winked and punched Bradley in the shoulder—a little harder than he meant to, knocking Bradley off-balance for a moment. Luckily, Bradley didn't yelp, "I got the foul!"

"I thought this was down to a two man race," Bradley ventured, studying Lattan skeptically. "Who are you again?"

"On your side, maybe," Lattan said. "I'm Charles Lattan, Congressman from Idaho's seventeenth district."

"Ah, I see," Bradley said, nodding, in a manner he doubtlessly used many times as a bored Rhodes Scholar. "Well, good luck," he said, walking over to a booth to start shaking hands with breakfast eaters.

Lattan shook his head and started toward the booths at the other side of the diner ... but already there shaking hands was some young guy in a bad haircut saying "I just got my hair cut over at the barber shop across the oval" ... then the guy said something about being from Ohio and his dad being a mail carrier or something ... *ooh, real smart, fellah, put voters in the mind of guys who walk into post offices with machine guns blazing.*

Lattan turned back toward the counter to talk with folks *there* ... but *another* guy in a suit had stepped in front of him to get to those voters first. ... Nice suit, too, expensive ... but he was carrying a pitchfork ... how odd ... and explaining about the need to defend poor, helpless Nazi war criminals ... while some bored old biddie slurping her tea pretended to listen ... and he had this stupid sort of habit of saying "my friends" ...

Again Lattan turned to locate part of the diner not overrun with presidential candidates ... Christ, were they all up here?

Then his attention was snatched by the huge entourage at the door ... cameras flashing ... reporters scribbling ... Secret Service talking to their sleeves. Suddenly everything stopped ... oh no, not *this guy* again ...

"Hello, New Hamp-shire voter," said the stiff phony as he entered and leaned over mechanically to shake hands with someone inhaling sausage and biscuits. "Did you know that I in-ven-ted the ve-ry sau-sage and bis-cuits you are en-joy-ing right at this mo-ment?" God, what a robot! "And now, if you'll ex-cuse me, I must leave to go to another town to ann-ounce some gov-ern-ment grants."

And then the phony was off ...

Lattan shook his head once more. "Look, more of 'em!" DeLeet said, pointing. Sure enough, at the far corner of the diner, by the men's room, was some fellow in a plaid shirt, bobbing his head up and down as he spoke to some burly guys in neon orange road construction uniforms ... then a short fellow talking about moral values, as if he were a fundamentalist preacher, was boring some poor saps near the cash register ...

"Forget this," DeLeet said. "No generation Xers here anyway. Let's go to the bar downstairs."

They scampered downstairs to the Stonecutter's Lounge, a real drinker's bar, with Sixties style bucket seats, a low ceiling, and a nice view of the river. This was more like it.

Only problem was ... it was breakfast time, and the bar was empty, except for one young man wiping down tables.

"Ay, we're not open yet," he yelled, rag in hand.

But all Lattan saw was that this young man was in his twenties — the perfect receptacle ... er, *recipient* — for his "Scrap Social Security" theme!

"Don't want a drink," Lattan said, smiling a Nixonian fake smile. "Just want to ask you about how you feel about having the government taking your money."

He leaned over and whispered into Kentrell's ear: "Go upstairs and grab some reporter to cover this so it doesn't go to waste."

"Right," DeLeet said, and then scampered back up the stairs.

"Whaddaya wanna ask me?" the young man said.

Lattan walked over, shook the young man's hand, and introduced himself.

"Young man, are you tired of the government thinking it knows how to spend your hard-earned money better than you do?"

"You're damn right I am!" the young man said, his face instantly contorted into a snarl of righteous post-adolescent rage.

"Are you tired of looking at your paycheck and seeing 7.85 percent of it go right off the top to the bureaucrats in Washington for Social Security — when you and I both know you'll never see a dime of it?"

"Goddamn it! I sure as hell am!" the young man said, pounding his fist on the bar.

Lattan sat on a barstool. "Well, young man, you have a friend in Charles Lattan." Damn it, where was the media? He'd be damned if this was going to go to waste!

Finally Kentrell came back down the stairs — but he was all alone. "No one would come down," he said meekly.

"What do you mean no one would come down!" Lattan demanded, turning away from his first New Hampshire supporter.

"I tried to tell them, but they wouldn't listen. I said, 'Congressman Lattan is talking to a young voter about his vision for overhauling Social Security,' but they all said, 'Who the hell is Charles Lattan.'"

"Newman!" Lattan said, gritting his teeth, as though on an episode of Seinfeld.

"Sorry, boss," DeLeet said, shrugging his shoulders.

"Well, we have to go now," Lattan said, shaking the hand of the barback. "Can I count on your support?"

"You can count on me, sir!" he said, nodding and scrunching his eyebrows. "And when the black helicopters come, I'll shoot 'em down for you, yes sir! No more Trilateral Commission, no sirree! Charles Lattan gonna end that! Gonna get me back all the money the government stole from my Social Security paycheck! That's right, mister!"

Lattan looked at the young man as if the kid had just sprouted antlers. "Uh, right."

"You can count on me, sir!" the young man repeated, saluting. "We'll get all the black helicopters for you!"

DeLeet began pushing Lattan out of the bar. "Congressman, let's get out of here."

And as they trotted up the stairs, all Lattan could think of was ... *well, a crazy vote was still a vote ...*

Chapter 39

A Rousing Speech To New Hampshire Voters

The crowd! He couldn't believe the size of it! There had to be thousands of them out there, holding up placards — "GOP Unity," "Let's Elect Someone Who's Unimpeachable," "Slick Willie's Greasy Lies Give Me Heartburn" — and they were cheering! For him! The Honorable Charles J. Lattan, Congressman from Idaho's seventeenth district, Republican presidential candidate!

He knew his tenacity would pay off eventually. And now it finally had. Here, in Nashua, where he was headlining, *keynoting*, the GOP Unity convention, the adulation of the cheering throng pulsed through his veins like some wondrous narcotic.

OK, so he was a little fuzzy on the details. He admitted to himself that, as was his nature, he hadn't *quite* been listening to every word as his campaign manager DeLeet explained how he'd wrangled this particular speaking engagement. For all he knew, there might even be other speakers, other presidential candidates, the flotsam of New Hampshire Republican politics, slated to have their share of time at the podium tonight. But right now, he *owned* this podium — and the crowds were cheering!

"I want to tell you about a man with a vision for America," he'd been saying. "I want to tell you about a man who's got a solution to our problem of what to do about Social Security. I want to tell you about a candidate who may not be a topic of conversation yet at your dinner table, or the subject of a strident editorial in the *Nashua Telegraph*, but who nonetheless is someone you should be paying attention to!"

The man to whom he was humbly referring, was, of course, none other than Charles Lattan. But he'd decided to dispense with speaking in the first person. It was just so — so — egomaniacal, self-absorbed, arrogant. In a word, Clintonesque. So he'd decided to invoke the device of the royal "we," and talk about himself as if he wasn't there, to lend some statesmanlike stature to his campaign. And, as evidenced by the crowd response here, it seemed to be working.

"Fellow citizens, haven't we had enough of lies, prevarications, and just plain insults to our intelligence from the lying, impeached pervert hunkered down in the White House?" Lattan was declaiming. And they were loving it! How far he'd come from that small VFW meeting in Raymond mere days ago!

"Haven't we been hoodwinked enough?" Lattan continued. "You know, Lenin used to have fun insulting the intelligence of the American public much the same way Slick Willie does now. That's right, New Hampshire, I don't think it's too much of a stretch to say that Bill Clinton is taking his cues from Vladmir Lenin. You see, Lenin used to say, 'We spit in America's face, and they call it dew.' Well, I think that's how Bill Clinton thinks of the American people!"

Was that the exact quote? Lattan wasn't sure. DeLeet had fed it to him, and he'd probably filched it from *Bartlett's Familiar Quotations*. But did it matter? They were shaking their fists, furling their brows, yelling "Hell yea!" He was working them into quite a dither about how Clinton had screwed them, and they were all too ready to listen to more! They were eating it up like Idaho potatoes au gratin!

"That's right, good people of New Hampshire," Lattan continued, on a veritable roll, like a southern fundamentalist revival tent preacher stirring the soul of the crowd. "Slick Willie has used your Oval Office — that's right, yours, the one your tax dollars pay for — to get serviced by a subordinate government employee while he talked on the phone with my colleagues. And just last week he joked about the whole episode at the White House correspondents dinner. I mean, for Godsakes, he was impeached! ... Now he's bombing Kosovo just to deflect attention from the China scandal. That slick liar has no shame, no sense of remorse, no sense of right or wrong. Just a profound sense of self-indulgence at *your* expense!"

"Fire the liar!" came a shout over the cacophony of the crowd.

"Slick Willie — You Make Me Sick, Willie!" read a new sign being waved by an angry white male.

"Now I'm no psychiatrist," Lattan continued, "and I certainly don't play one on MSNBC, like some people." Titters in the crowd. "But I think we know enough about ol' Slick to say that he's a classic sociopath: No sense of how he hurts anyone, whether that poor little fat intern girl or the American people; no sense of responsibility for his actions, as shown by his penchant for blaming the people who tried to bring him to justice for *his own criminal behavior*; and when it comes down to looking back on the havoc he has wrought, the wreckage that he's done to the precious institution of the presidency, all he can think about, all he can talk about, is his own pain, as if *he* were the victim, rather than you, or the credibility of the American criminal justice system! The arrogance!" Lattan pounded his fist on the podium. "The shamelessness!" He pounded his fist again. "The sheer, unmitigated gall!" He pounded his fist yet again. "Or, as my friends in the Jewish community would say, 'the chutzpah!" A final pounding of his fist for emphasis.

Now he just stood and nodded, basking in the crowd's cheers! Yes! By all means! GOP unity! Behind this man, Charles Lattan!

"But my fellow Americans, enough about that pervert," he said, shifting rhetorical gears.

"You're damn right we've had enough!" came another shout from the audience.

"Good people of New Hampshire, I want to talk about some positive things," Lattan said. Now he would ever so subtly shift into his third-person mode, referring to himself obliquely, and let the crowd infer that he was their man for the Republican presidential nomination.

"I want to tell you about a man who has principles," he began. Immediately the crowd roared in anticipation of learning more about the Boy Scout who would restore the honor of the presidency, make them proud, and scrap Social Security! "I want to tell you about a man from the West, who stands for family values, who knows that it's the people of this great land of ours that produce the wealth, and it's not the government's right to confiscate it!"

The cheering became louder, more intense. God, this was intoxicating!

"This is where we Republicans differ with the Democrats most profoundly," Lattan continued. "We believe that *you* know how to spend *your* money better than anyone else. After all, it's *your* money! But Slick Willie and his accomplices—you know who I'm talking about—that phony who says he invented the internet, and the other phony from Missouri who changes positions on every issue every single day—they believe that you, you poor, stupid, little people, are like children who need guidance from the government. They believe they know better than you how to spend YOUR money! Talk about arrogant!"

"It's our money!" came a shout.

"That's right, it is YOUR money. It's not the government's money, although the Democrats seem to think they have a divine right to take it from you by confiscating it in taxes and spending it on their own pet projects. No, my friends, it's not their money, it's yours ..."

Lattan continued, rising to a crescendo ...

"And so, let me close by telling you about a man who respects you, respects the office of the president, and who will make you proud once again to tell your children it's OK to want to grow up to be president ..."

All of a sudden the crowd burst into applause. The lights in the hall flamed to a blinding glare. People jumped from the seats, clapping and cheering. Yes! It was happening! Charles Lattan was being coronated Republican front runner! Right here and now! History being made!

"And the name of that man is ..." he began his final oratorical flourish—

"George W. Bush!" came a booming, stentorian voice over the PA system ... and then came some pushing and shoving ... Lattan being jostled offstage ... his countenance violated! ... he was yanked from the podium by two burly brutes in cowboy hats—*gawd, they looked like sides of beef!*—and jerked off stage.

And as he looked back over his shoulder, confused and flabbergasted, he watched the familiar face of the governor of Texas take the podium and thank him for that wonderful introduction, one of the best he's ever received ... why couldn't all of his opening speakers, his introducers, be as wonderful as the man who just spoke ...

So that's what he'd neglected to listen to during DeLeet's instructions ...

yes Congressman, you are confirmed as a speaker at the Nashua GOP Unity Conference, but only as the introducer for George W. Bush. ...

And at that moment, Charles Lattan knew what it felt like to be one of those children whom the Democrats thought they needed to make wards of the state. ... At least he'd saved himself the additional embarrassment that would have resulted from mentioning his own name during his speech.

Chapter 40

Passover Seder Gaffer

For Congressman Charles Lattan, it started as a slight slipping sensation on top of his head, as though his combover was about to flop down to the side, revealing to the world his bald pate. He'd experienced it plenty of times before — usually in the wind, or at the end of the day, when his hair glop had crusted and flaked off, leaving only an oily resin too weak to hold his few remaining tufts of hair in place.

But there was no explanation why now, as he sat at the Passover Seder table at the home of the Beersteins, New Hampshire's Jewish Republican gurus, he should be experiencing combover flop. There was no wind, and moments before, driving over with DeLeet in their rented Dodge Neon from the Manchester Motel 6, he had showered and shaved and dressed and pasted his viscous hair down until it had hardened into a kevlar shell.

And yet ... he felt the slide on top his head ... no doubt about it now ... something on top of his head was slithering down the back of his skull, then onto his neck —

"Congressman, your yarmulke fell off," said Phil Beerstein, his host.

"My what?" said Lattan, wondering if his host was using some secret code to indicate his combover had failed him, and that his head now stood naked to the entire table.

"Your yarmulke," Beerstein repeated. "It's on the floor. Pick it up and brush off the *schmutz*. Then kiss it before you put it back on your head."

Again with the foreign language. Lattan obeyed, craning over to retrieve his hat. He rescued it from the floor and read the inscription inside: "Bar

Mitzvah of Alexander Portnoy, 1946." He then kissed it clumsily and placed it back on his head.

"Now, we continue," said Beerstein, returning his gaze to his copy of the *I Gotta*, or whatever it was called, that everyone had in front of them, and reading the story of the Jews' exodus from Egypt.

Beerstein was a slight, bespectacled man in his mid-sixties, the leading Jewish Republican in New Hampshire. Of course, being the leading Jewish Republican in New Hampshire was a bit like being ... well, the top *anything* in Idaho. But Lattan knew he wasn't exactly in demand as a guest much these days — particularly after that confusion over his introduction of George W. Bush — so he tried to be humbled by the invitation.

After all, Beerstein had been effusive in his praise for Lattan. "I'm particularly impressed by your strong support of Israel," Beerstein had said on the phone just two days ago. "In a race where at least one of the Republican candidates seems to be obsessed with defending accused Nazi war criminals, your voting record in Congress is a welcome tonic."

Lattan had never thought much about the Middle East. It was all simple enough to him; Israel was the region's only pure democracy, and it was a strong strategic ally of the United States. To him, supporting Israel was not unlike supporting U.S. ties with Canada. But then it had occurred to him why the American Jewish community thought more of his support for Israel than he ever did: When your people have been persecuted as much as they have throughout history, you don't take your allies for granted.

So a foreign policy position that had been slightly more than an afterthought had landed him at a Seder table this lovely spring evening, surrounded by two dozen other guests, platefuls of large crackers, and bottles of syrupy sweet red wine made, he was told, especially for the occasion. Thankfully, there were no other candidates tonight.

"Why is this night different from all other nights?" Beerstein asked, reading from his *I Gotta*. Lattan looked at his own copy of the *I Gotta*, or whatever it was called, and could only think, *heck if I know*. The words on the page were in weird shapes, the writing going in several different directions. Already it seemed as if the night had gone on interminably, with a lot of reading, asking of questions, uncovering and then recovering of the big crackers, raising and then lowering the cups of wine — all without eating!

But then Lattan remembered to mind his manners. He was a guest. He should be honored to share in this ritual, this festival of freedom. He was surrounded by people who had a culture, a set of mores, valued traditions, to which they'd adhered in the face of unspeakable horror. And what kind of a man of faith was he? Scarcely went to church, rarely prayed — the last time was back on election night — and hardly ever thought about the big questions. Oh, he invoked God and Country and all the rest of the platitudes people expected of politicians, but did he really believe any of it?

"And now, to symbolize the bitterness of the Jews' hardship in Egypt, we eat the Hillel sandwich ..." Beerstein was saying.

Finally! Food! Lattan watched the woman to his right smear some purple mush on a big piece of the cracker ... so did DeLeet, on his left. Lattan took the cue ... but, God, was he hungry! Hadn't eaten all day, had been sitting through the recitation of the Passover story for two hours ... so naturally, he took a big glop of the stuff and slathered it on his cracker.

"Careful with all of that horseradish, Congressman," said the helpful woman sitting next to him.

He nodded and smiled as he took a bite —

Then he immediately realized why the woman had warned him. His mouth was aflame! It started on the tip of his tongue and then spread like a brushfire to his gums and the roof of his mouth. He felt his face flush, his nostrils flare, his eyes puddle, his forehead spangle with sweat. The cracker did nothing to buffer the punch of the horseradish. His whole head was ablaze.

Panic-stricken, he reached for his glass of wine, knowing he was violating one of the rules, though willing to suffer the consequences in the name of dousing the inferno. He guzzled it in one gulp, the sickly sweet taste only momentarily slaking his thirst. More!

He reached into the middle of the table for another cup of wine that didn't seem to belong to anybody —

"Congressman! That's Eliahu's wine!"

But it was too late, as Lattan guzzled that one, too, feebly attempting to drown the bonfire in his mouth and throat. Whoever this fellow Eliahu was, he could get a refill. ...

"Whew! That's hot stuff," Lattan said, trying to laugh it off, as the pain subsided.

Then he noticed the entire table glowering at him, one big collective state of disapproval for this ill-mannered *goy*—

"What? What did I do?" Lattan said, like a little kid baffled by the anger of his parents at his behavior.

"Congressman," Beerstein began scolding, "that was the cup of wine for Eliahu." He said it with a tone of formality that suggested Lattan *should have known better*.

"Sorry about that, chief," Lattan said. "I'm sure he can get another cup. Where is he, anyway? Did he go to the bathroom or something? I don't believe I've had the pleasure of meeting him yet."

The whole table continued to singe him with their stares. Beerstein shook his head ever so slightly, like the disappointed father. Then he resumed reading aloud from the *I Gotta*, and everyone pretended to proceed as if nothing had happened.

But Lattan had the familiar anvil-in-the-gut feeling that he'd done something horribly, horribly wrong, and from which he would never recover, no matter what he did the rest of the evening. No, Congressman, now you will pay your penance, you will serve your sentence, by sitting here and enduring the rest of this ritual, with the full knowledge that no one in this room will ever consider voting for you.

At that moment, he swore to himself that if he ever got invited to another Seder, he would study up on his Jewish history ... or at least rent the video of "The Ten Commandments."

Chapter 41

Campaign Dreams And Caviar Wishes

"Hi, *how are you* ... Hi, *nicetoseeyou* ... Good morning, *howdoyoudo*."

The bromides were swift, the smile wooden, the candidate's enthusiasm forced as Lattan stood this crisp spring morning on the median strip on the main drag in Nashua heading toward Boston. When the cars stopped for the traffic light, he walked up to each one to shake hands with the driver. His campaign manager followed behind, handing out literature and recruiting volunteers.

It was nearly eight o' clock, and he'd been at it for an hour. Already his jaw was sore from smiling so much, and he found his mind wandering back wistfully to the peaceful slumber from which he'd roused himself ninety minutes before.

Getting up this morning was harder than it had ever been during his month in New Hampshire. Sure, he'd gotten his first good night of sleep in months, and he'd been particularly exhausted last night. But for the first time, he'd felt just a hint of *hesitation* this morning.

The questions caromed around in his head: *Do I have a chance? Even if I did, do I really want to be president? I never thought I'd admit it to myself, but I actually miss Idaho. And Washington, of course. God, I need a vacation.*

Yet he continued, as if driven by some primordial need he couldn't identify.

"Hi, I'm Congressman Charles Lattan, and I'm running for president," he muttered through a phony smile to a nice old biddy in a Lincoln. She smiled, pointed to her ear, and stared at him. It seemed an eternity as he stood there and listened to the *whirrrrrrrrrrrrrrr* of the power window as it lowered.

"Hi. Good morning, ma'am, *how are you*?" he said, reaching to shake her hand. Her palm was sweaty.

"Good morning, Congressman," she said. "I'm glad you stopped to talk to me."

Finally! A woman who'd waited for him to stop and talk to her! *Of course* this was a worthwhile exercise! *Of course* he was making progress! *Of course* he'd just had a momentary attack of the doubts—

"You see, Congressman, I think you're wasting your time here," she continued. "The majority of the people driving this road don't even vote in New Hampshire. We're Bostonians."

She continued talking, but he, typically, was no longer listening. All of a sudden his doubts from this morning came roaring back, throbbing in his skull like a bad hangover that wouldn't quit. She closed her window and continued on her way, waving a friendly *goodbye*, as if she was saying, "*I hope I was helpful, you Idaho ninconpoop*."

"Kentrell!" Lattan yelled across the median strip, where DeLeet was trying to foist campaign pamphlets and other paraphernalia on bleary-eyed *Massachusetts* voters.

"Yeah, boss," DeLeet said, scampering over the grassy knoll, dropping leaflets and *Scrap Social Security* talking points and *LATTAN 2000* bumper stickers.

"Kentrell," Lattan said, hands on his hips, "how many volunteers have you signed up this morning?"

"Volunteers?" DeLeet answered, as if he'd just been asked to translate Chinese. "Well, we've given out a lot of—"

"How many people have said they want to work on the campaign, or even put up a yard sign?"

"Well, a lot of people smiled and said they'd love to help, except that they vote in Massachusetts."

"Is that right," Lattan said.

"Yeah," DeLeet said. "Normally, I'd recommend we go somewhere else, but I think we're going to do well in Massachusetts as a result of this."

"You do, do you?" Lattan said. Cars were now whizzing by, the wind blowing his combover to the side of his head. He saw a little girl in a minivan point to him and giggle. "Kentrell, the Massachusetts primary isn't until a week *after* New Hampshire! If I don't finish in the top three *here* we won't be going *there*!"

"I guess I didn't think of that," DeLeet said sheepishly.

"You didn't think ... you didn't think ..." Lattan clasped his hands behind his back and began pacing on the median strip. He stared up at the sky. Cars honked. He waved absently. "Thank you," he sneered.

"Well, it's still early in the day," DeLeet said. "We can go to Manchester and campaign among the French Canadians. They're big potato eaters. They have this dish called poutain, which is potatoes smothered in gravy and cheese —"

"All right!" Lattan snapped. "Save it. Let's just go."

He stepped in front of the cars stopped at the intersection's traffic light. DeLeet trotted past him across the road, headed toward where they'd parked on the shoulder. He opened the passenger door to their rented Neon, and Lattan grunted as he sat down.

DeLeet tried to make conversation. "In Manchester, we can —"

"Just shut up and drive," Lattan snarled, rubbing his eyes.

By lunch time they were in a Cajun restaurant (the name of which Lattan couldn't pronounce) on the west side of Manchester, across from the Merrimack River, going after the French Canadian vote.

"Bonjour, cher!" Lattan said to a diner at the restaurant.

"Bonjour," the diner said. "Como tally vous?"

"Pardon?" Lattan said.

"Como tally vous? Je me souviens festival du homard!" he shouted, spitting souffle crumbs in Lattan's face.

"Merci," Lattan said, smiling the wooden campaign smile, then stepping away.

"I take it you don't speak French," said another diner, a porcine old woman hovering over her French onion soup. God, she was a cow! Her polyester stretch pants were strained to their physical limit; her complexion was like spoiled cottage cheese. "You look like another one of *them*—"

"Who are *them*?" Lattan asked, though he feared the answer.

"Aw, *come on*," the woman said. "You're running for president, right?"

"OK, you got me," Lattan said. "I admit it. But I am an honorary Canuck, I assure you," he said, winking.

"Ya don't say." And with that, the woman turned back to her soup, carefully spooning it into her mouth, staring at it intently, obviously waiting for Lattan to make a graceful exit. Again, he had the feeling he'd committed a horrible breach of the candidate-voter social contract. But, as usual, he had no idea which clause he'd violated.

Canuck was a term of endearment, wasn't it? For godsakes, the National Hockey League had its Vancouver Canucks, and their games were broadcast all over Idaho's seventeenth district. No one ever complained about *them*, like they did the Redskins in Washington.

Just then, DeLeet lost an argument with the restaurateur over placing a *LATTAN 2000* placard in the window. He marched back over to reunite with Lattan.

"I've had it, Kentrell," Lattan said wearily.

"OK," DeLeet said. "We can go somewhere else to campaign. I can't believe these people — can't even speak English, half of 'em, yet they can vote."

"Not so loud!" Lattan barked.

"Ah, they can't understand anyway," DeLeet said, taking out his filofax. OK, maybe we can head to Dixville Notch next. Then Durham. Or Concord—"

"No. I've had enough of this crap," Lattan said, walking out the door, DeLeet chasing him.

"But we don't have the luxury of losing the rest of the day," DeLeet said, flipping to another page in his pocket organizer as they trudged through the slushy parking lot. "We can't be like the egomaniacal movie director who will scrap a day of shooting and eat the costs if the sunset isn't the right shade. By my calculations, we only have enough money to last us ... uh oh."

"What's uh oh?" Lattan stopped in the middle of the lot.

"We, uh, are a little short on funds," DeLeet said. "Maybe I forgot to carry a number. Hang on a sec." He mumbled frantically and scratched his head as he recalculated their budget.

"Well?" Lattan said, his arms crossed on his chest.

"Er ... we, uh ... " DeLeet said. "Oh crap."

"Crap?" Lattan scowled. "I hope you're referring to Gore's latest fabrication!"

"We, er ... we have to leave ... uh oh ... we have to leave tomorrow." DeLeet looked at him helplessly.

Lattan closed his eyes and rubbed his temples. He was beyond anger. By now, he was accepting the kicks in the solar plexus as routine. He was at the point where one concedes the ability to foster any residual rage at the world for its many injustices against him. The point at which numbness to everything collapsing around you is a welcome sign of relief. At last, he would get to leave this godforsaken place.

"Let's get a good night's sleep and blow this joint in the morning," Lattan said, opening *his own* door to the car — a sure sign he was losing interest in even the most mundane aspects of being a candidate.

The next morning, Lattan and DeLeet stood at the lobby of the Raymond Comfort Inn to check out. Lattan glowered into his coffee cup as DeLeet handled the paperwork with the front desk clerk.

"Uh, boss, do you have any cash on you?"

"I'm tapped until we get back to DC. Why?"

"Uh, well, we're a little short here," DeLeet said. "I forgot to calculate room taxes and a few incidentals into our budget."

"Taxes, always taxes," Lattan said, conjuring a mental image of Slick Willie biting his lip and feeling his pain. "Yet another legacy of the impeached lying pervert, no doubt, higher hotel taxes!"

"I know," DeLeet said, eyes darting nervously between Lattan and the front desk clerk. "But we still need to pay the bill."

"I told you, I'm tapped," Lattan said. "Put it on your credit card."

"I'm, uh, over my limit," DeLeet said. "Can we use yours?"

"I maxed it out on the goddamn rental car and all of these fancy meals, you nitwit," Lattan said, trying to whisper, but managing to yell.

Just then, a strapping young man sauntered into the lobby, around his neck a press pass reading *Manchester Union Leader*.

And all Lattan could think was: *reporters, never there when you need them, always there when you don't want 'em!*

Chapter 42

Paying The Hotel Bill With Dishpan Hands

Lattan felt the familiar shards of ice surge up the spinal cord as he spotted a *Manchester Union Leader* reporter. Now, his little problem of paying his hotel bill at the Raymond, New Hampshire Comfort Inn would be amplified on the pages of the state's most influential newspaper.

Lattan and DeLeet were silent, holding their breaths in unison as they watched the approach of this unassuming young man with the press pass jangling around his neck. The hotel desk manager, sensing their shock, momentarily suspended his demands for money, if only to gaze in wonder at the visage that had so stupefied his customers.

The reporter — handsome, in his late twenties — gamboled toward the front desk. "What room is the McCain event in?" he asked.

"John McCain for president press conference. Roosevelt room," said the desk clerk, unaffected. Lattan and DeLeet stood frozen like two ice statues.

The reporter gave them a quick once-over, then returned his eye contact to the desk clerk. "Thanks, chief," he said, and walked toward the McCain event.

"Whew, that was close," said Lattan, watching the young man saunter off.

DeLeet scratched his head, then cupped his chin between his forefinger and his thumb. Lattan knew the look: media guru hatching a scheme.

"As I said, sirs, you must reconcile your bill before checking out," the guest desk attendant said. "That's our policy. Same for Congressmen as it is for everyone else."

"And what if we can't pay?" DeLeet said.

"That, too, is the same for Congressmen as it is for everyone else. Kitchen duty, six bucks an hour, until you work it off."

"We'll do it!" DeLeet said, a crafty smile overtaking his wan face.

"Are you out of your mind?" Lattan barked. "Excuse us for a moment, please."

He grabbed DeLeet by the triceps and yanked him away toward a far corner of the lobby. They huddled over the remains of the complimentary continental breakfast, a stale tray of sticky buns with grease stains under them.

"What the hell are you thinking!" Lattan tried to whisper, but the anger in his voice raising the volume of the interrogation. "You think it's presidential to wash dishes to pay off a hotel bill — while Mr. War Hero is holding a press conference? I'll be a laughingstock!"

"No you won't," DeLeet said confidently. "Think about it! While Mr. War Hero talks about a conflict in a European outpost most people can't even pronounce, you'll show your ties to the common man by washing dishes. I'll go get that young reporter to cover it, and it'll be a great story!"

Suddenly Lattan felt the imaginary light bulb above his head blaze to life. Yes! It *would* be a great story! DeLeet was earning his keep after all!

"I think you've stumbled onto a great way to turn lemons into a vodka tonic!" Lattan said. "I'll make kitchen duty arrangements with the proprietor, and you go get that reporter!"

Minutes later, Lattan was standing over a huge food service-sized industrial sink full of greasy pots and pans, a scrub brush in one hand, a egg-coated plate in the other, and an apron over his frayed polyester-blend shirt and suit.

He scrubbed a little, feigning interest in this little sham, as the other kitchen workers' attitude turned from momentary disbelief to long-standing disinterest. When DeLeet burst through the swiveling doors from the dining room, with the same young reporter in tow, Lattan started whistling and scrubbing the plate intensely.

"Congressman, this is Matt Reed of the *Manchester Union Leader*," said DeLeet. "I was able to pull him away from Senator McCain with the promise that he would get a story none of the other thirty reporters in that room would get."

"Thirty reporters!" Lattan said, splashing water as he dropped the plate. "That's ... well, we all can't be war heroes, can we?" he said, smiling his phony campaign smile at the reporter. "I'd shake your hand, son, except it's full of soap suds."

"That's OK," Reed said. "So, Congressman, I understand you're running for president."

"That's right, m'boy," Lattan said, scrubbing away on a pot. "Did you bring a photographer? This would be a great shot for your front page."

"Well, if it merits one, I can call in for a photog," Reed replied, unfazed. "Of course, with all due respect, Congressman, it has to be a good story, you understand."

"Of course it does, Matt!" Lattan said. "Well, I'll tell you why this is a good story. You see, young fella, I'm not like my distinguished opponents. I come from a blue-collar background. I didn't have a rich family or a well-known family name. I wasn't appointed to all sorts of high-profile posts. I wasn't in Vietnam as a POW for six years. No sir, I'm just a plumber, a common man, who's interested in the interests of the common man—"

"So, if you don't mind my asking, Congressman, why are you washing dishes?" Reed asked. "It seems to me you'd be better off unclogging drains."

"An excellent question!" Lattan said, a little too enthusiastically. "I'm washing dishes because I'm not afraid to roll up my sleeves and get my hands dirty."

"Dirty?" Reed asked incredulously. "It seems to me that you're getting your hands *clean* by washing dishes."

"Ha ha ha!" Lattan laughed. "That's a good one. Boy, you reporters are tough!" he winked. "But seriously, Matt, did you know that the average American has to work nearly three hours out of every day just to make enough money to satisfy all of his federal, state and local tax obligations? Tax Freedom Day, the day Americans earn enough money for the year to pay all of their taxes, is May eighth. That means you are working for the government over four months every year before you get to earn money for yourself. I don't think that's right, and as president, Charles Lattan's first priority will be to cut your taxes!"

"Sir," Reed replied, "Again, with all due respect, I believe you have said as recently as a month ago that your first priority was to Scrap Social Security. And before that, I believe you wanted to distinguish yourself from the current office-holder by adopting the slogan, 'Charles Lattan's interns lick envelopes.' Are you planning yet another shift in your message, and, if so, is this shift caused by your last place standing in the polls among likely Republican primary voters, as well as your lack of campaign funds?"

"Wow, you've done your homework," Lattan said, laughing nervously. He focused on another pan, this one streaked with gravy and butter. After a moment, he looked again at Reed. "I don't believe my campaign message has shifted as much as it has *evolved*..."

"And another thing, Congressman," Reed said. "Do you think your failure to vote on impeachment undermines your credibility as a critic of Bill Clinton?"

Christ! Where had this kid come from? Lattan scrubbed and scrubbed and rinsed and soaked and grabbed another pot. What a live one! What the hell was DeLeet thinking? What a horribly idiotic idea this was! Here I am, an honest man, and I have to explain myself while that impeached lying pervert continues to wage his illegal war in the Balkans! God, the injustice!

"I don't think my credibility is undermined one bit, no sir!" Lattan said. "You want to talk about credibility, let's talk about Slick Willie. Let's talk about using subordinate government employees young enough to be his daughter to cater to your sexual perversions. Let's talk about perjury. Let's talk obstruction of justice. Let's talk about bombing sovereign nations without a formal declaration of war. Let's talk about giving military secrets to the Chinese. Let's talk—"

"Congressman, do you think your message of just attacking Clinton is enough to run a campaign on?"

"That's not my only message!" Lattan said, reflexively pounding his fist on the table but splashing it in the sink instead. Water doused his apron, got into his eye, sprinkled the reporter.

"Oh, jeepers!" Lattan said. "Sorry about that." He clumsily grabbed a towel and reached to wipe off Reed. "As I was saying —"

"That's OK," Reed said, stepping away. He looked at his watch. "Well, gotta go. Thanks for your time, Congressman."

"Wait!" Lattan pleaded. "We haven't talked yet about—"

"That's OK," Reed said. "I've got all I need."

"Well, I trust you'll be fair," Lattan said.

"Oh, not to worry," Reed said. "I don't think there'll be any story. You haven't really given me any news."

And before Lattan could protest, he caught himself—quickly concluding that *no* story would undoubtedly be better than anything that would come out of this little aborted photo-op. He watched Reed walk out of the kitchen, and his thoughts turned, more quickly than he'd care to admit, to the more non-political concern how much more time he had to work in order to pay the bill.

Chapter 43

All Fiascos Must Come To An End

"Are you sure," asked DeLeet, as he caucused with the candidate in a cramped Capitol Hill studio apartment.

"I'm more sure about *ending* this now than I was about *starting* this disaster in first place," said Lattan, spiraling into a vodka coma.

"Oh, come on, boss, it hasn't been a disaster—"

"Save the spin," Lattan barked. "The time for spin is over. I may not have been very statesmanlike during this campaign, but I can have some dignity *now* in deciding not to prolong this fiasco. It'll distinguish me from the rest of the also-rans. If I can't be president, at least I can lose with class."

DeLeet had no riposte for that nugget of candor, for Lattan knew it was completely out of character for him to be so prescient about his own political fortunes. But during the interminable wait caused by US Airways screwing up his return ticket from Manchester, and on the plane ride back to Washington, during which he'd finally had the chance to review his poll standings and cash on hand, it became apparent what he needed to do.

At first he'd been reluctant to accept the obvious. While he plowed through a brigade of Johnnie Walker Black miniatures, he explored countless alternatives: third-party candidacy. Suspension, but not termination, of the campaign. Running explicitly for *vice* president. Loaning the campaign money from his plumbing businesses back in Idaho. Adopting a new slogan, such as "Vote Lattan To End The War," or "Lattan For President: He's In Contempt — Of Higher Taxes!" It didn't help that the haze of self-denial seemed to be thickening because the campaign manager was sleeping next to him, rather than acting as foglight.

But as the empties distended the seat pocket in front of him, Lattan realized that if he'd had a chance, he wouldn't be sitting on a plane *returning* from New Hampshire. So, confident on scotch, he allowed his mind to entertain the possibility of dropping out. Instead of the body-wrenching depression he'd expected, he felt instantly liberated.

He worked out the checklist in his head, perfectly able to organize the process while his strategist slept. First the talk with the family. Then with the donors. Then with the Idaho people. Then to the loathsome, biased media that had conspired against him from the start.

So it was now, after the taxi from Reagan airport to his tiny DC apartment, that he broke the news to DeLeet. His decision had been made. Now all that had to be worked out were the details.

"I feel a bit absurd in asking this," Lattan said, as he sat in his ripped recliner, gripping a tumbler of vodka in his fist. His tie was askew, his combover flopped on the side of his head, his polyester blend shirt was crinkled like tin foil. "But what is the proper way to withdraw from a race?"

"Well, I would advise against a press conference," DeLeet said. "All those bastards in the press who've been ignoring you until now will gleefully pack a room to document your demise. Let's not give them the satisfaction. I recommend we fax a press release."

"Yes, yes, I like that idea," Lattan said, nodding, then taking a long pull of vodka. "I'll appear statesmanlike, not wanting to make a big media splash out of my decision. Not being so completely self-absorbed, thinking every little stream-of-consciousness thought I have is of national significance. Not deluding myself, trying to spin my way out of bad fundraising numbers and poll position, like that plaid-shirted phony from Tennessee. No sir, Charles Lattan will be dignified, like Benjamin Guggenheim on the Titanic, dressed in his evening best to go down like a gentleman!"

"Er, sounds good, boss," DeLeet said meekly. "Except maybe I'd scrap that part about the Titanic."

"Of course," Lattan said, waving one hand as he used the other one to bring the drink to his wizened lips. "I was just reminded of that part in the movie."

"Well, I have to say, you sure are taking it well," DeLeet said. "I can tell you've done a lot of thinking since we left New Hampshire."

"Ah, who wants to be president anyway?" Lattan said, rising from his chair and tottering over to the kitchenette, where he retrieved the bottle of Stolichnaya from the small freezer. "After all of the frat parties Slick Willie's had in the White House, I'd have to spend my first hundred days fumigating the Oval Office." He clunked ice cubes into his glass, then poured vodka over them. "And then I would have to have Clinton arrested and jailed — I mean, I'd be shirking my responsibility to the public and the Constitution if I didn't — and who wants to start that way, you know what I mean?"

DeLeet just sat on a folding metal chair and nodded.

"Who wants to start his administration having to clean up the mess left over by the tyrant who savaged the place?" Lattan asked, pouring tonic water into his drink, then stirring it with his pinky.

"Why don't you call your wife and the steering committee members, and I'll draft us a press release."

"Yes, why don't I do that," Lattan said, shuffling toward his fold-out couch. DeLeet grabbed a legal pad and began scrawling:

FOR IMMEDIATE RELEASE

CONTACT: KENTRELL ALT DELEET

LATTAN WITHDRAWS FROM PRESIDENTIAL RACE

WASHINGTON — Congressman Charles J. Lattan (R-ID-17) today announced he is withdrawing from the presidential race.

"I have enjoyed the opportunity to meet with voters in Iowa and New Hampshire," Lattan said. "And I have enjoyed listening to their concerns. But with such a large Republican field, and with at least two candidates dominating the media coverage because of their fortune to have well-known family names, I have concluded that I cannot remain as a candidate and compete effectively to deliver the messages about which I believe so passionately.

"Therefore, I am hereby terminating my presidential campaign, effective immediately, and I will return to serving the people of Idaho's seventeenth district, who I have had the privilege to serve for nearly three years.

Lattan did not endorse any of the current candidates, but did say he would unequivocally support the eventual Republican nominee.

"I am not throwing my support behind any particular candidate," Lattan said. "I urge my supporters to search their consciences and work to elect the candidate they believe best represents their position on issues." Lattan added: "The most important thing is that we return integrity and honesty to the institution of the presidency. The current occupant of the White House has sullied and degraded our precious institution for his own shockingly self-absorbed reasons. Indeed, even members of his own party called his behavior 'reprehensible,' former top-level members of his staff have publicly questioned his fitness for office, fully half of the United States Senate voted to remove him from office, and even now each American surely questions whether he has one shred of credibility to be waging an undeclared war."

Lattan concluded: "Fortunately, our democracy is strong enough to withstand the assault on our values by this petty man, and I believe our next president — and she or he *will* be Republican — will be able to restore the institution to its proper place as an office of stature and respect."

DeLeet read over his press release, and nodded with satisfaction. Not a bad piece of flackery, if he did say so himself.

"Hey, boss, why don't you take a quick look at this before I type it up and fax it out," DeLeet said without turning around. "Boss? Boss?"

DeLeet turned to see Lattan passed out on the couch, a half-empty vodka tonic balanced perilously in one hand and the cordless phone in the other.

DeLeet smiled to himself. How long it had been since he'd seen Charles Lattan at rest. "Well, not to worry," DeLeet said to the sleeping Lattan. He rose and straightened his cotton tie, then put on his sports jacket. "I'll just send this baby out myself. Nighty night, boss," he said, as he folded the press release in his jacket pocket and closed the door behind him.

Chapter 44

The Transform Party

The jackhammer drilling away in his skull woke Lattan from a fitful sleep. He tumbled out of bed onto the floor and lay there for a few moments in the vain hope that remaining motionless might lessen the throbbing.

Now he knew why they called scotch and vodka *hard* liquor. Its liquid form was deceiving. Once ingested, and given hours to incubate in the body, it calcified into heavy machinery that churned and lurched and pulsed within the brain.

He surmised that walking to the bathroom to get some Advil was worth the momentary discomfort for ameliorating the long-term pain. So he dragged himself to the medicine chest, choked down four tablets dry, and then retrieved the *Washington Past* from outside his door to read at his little kitchenette table.

He scanned the front page, then inside of the A section ... Nothing! Then, finally, on page A16, he saw it in the "Politics" column ... the last entry! He began reading:

GOP Field Narrowed By One

Rep. Charles Lattan (R-Idaho) last night withdrew from the presidential race. With little fanfare, reporters were notified via a press release, which, although brief, managed to take some desperate parting shots at President Clinton. Despite spending more than a month in New Hampshire, Lattan failed to make any significant progress in any of the Republican polls, was hampered by poor fundraising, and seemed to constantly shift from slogan to slogan without ever defining a coherent message.

He closed his eyes, leaned forward with his elbows on the table, and rubbed his temples. Now the throbbing was augmented by dizziness. The memories came back. Descending into a vodka coma ... mumbling about the injustice of it all ... the inevitable drunken screed against Slick Willie ... the last sight before passing out was his campaign manager scrawling a press release on this very table ... What the hell had DeLeet written?

Oh, it didn't matter. He should have just been happy to have it over with. Now he could concentrate on returning to the burning issues facing Idaho: the ever-present threat of a french fry tax, among other things.

Suddenly the phone erupted. The ring was so shrill when it pierced the skull of a hungover drunkard!

"Congressman Lattan," he said, trying to sound alert.

"Congressman Charles Lattan! Answering his own phone! Well I'll be," said the unidentified yet somehow familiar voice disembodied through the line. "That's a good sign, answerin' your own phone, see. Makes you closer to the people, see. Not one of these prima donnas. I like it. And that's why I like you."

"Why, thank you," said Lattan, trying desperately to figure out who it was. God, the voice was *so* familiar!

"Now, listen here, Charlie," said the voice, continuing in its rapid-fire southern accent. "I just read on the wire about you pullin' out of the Republican race. And I gotta tell ya,' I'm not disappointed, see. Don't get me wrong — I'm not happy you're out of the race. I'm only happy you're out of the *Republican* race. Because I'm a big fan of yours. Oh, you bet I am. I been followin' this race *very* closely, see, and I like what you've been saying. Scrap Social Security. Well, by God, it's about time someone had the guts to say that. And attacking Clinton's lack of character. By golly, that *should* be an issue. American people got the right to expect decent behavior from their presidents. Yes, sir!"

"I'm glad to hear it," Lattan said, rifling through his mental memory bank to put a face to this high-pitched southern voice, which sounded like a weed-whacker cutting through tree trunks.

"See, we need a candidate like you. America needs you, Charlie. But you couldn't see it because your message got lost in that field of blue-bloods and pretenders. You're running in the wrong primary," the mystery caller continued. "That's right, the wrong party."

"And the right party is?"

"The Transform Party, you ninny!" came the voice. "Hell, I'd run again, but I just don't have it in me. But you got it in ya', boy! And with my backing, and my girl Bessie's backing, you'll win it! That's a sure a thing as an armadillo dead in the middle of I-10 in Texas in August!"

Finally Lattan pieced it together. Of course! It was that little buzz-cut billionaire, Hoss Bordeaux!

"Now see here, Charlie," Bordeaux said. "I want you to go and meet with our highest elected Transform Party official in the country, see, and you can map out a strategy to run nationwide with her backing. You go to Michigan, see, and meet with Governor Bessie 'The Snoddy' Bravura, see, and you talk with her. Now, Bessie's approval ratings are sky high. Sky high. You want to know why? Because she's a straight talker, see. Just like you. Not like all of these precious prima donnas, see. You go meet with her, talk about the Transform Party platform. Make a big deal out of it. Get a lot of good media. That would be a nice change of pace for you, wouldn't it, Charlie? And with her blessing, we coronate you the Transform Party nominee."

"I'm flattered," Lattan said, trying to absorb it all through his hangover. "But if you don't mind my asking, why are you so concerned about this race?"

"I feel responsibility for Slick Willie, see. If I hadn't run in ninety-two, he wouldn't have been elected. And the presidency wouldn't have been in the sorry state it is now, see. With only forty-three percent of the vote, he would have lost, see. I mean, that's even less than that Greek fella got in eighty-eight. So I feel a personal responsibility to make sure his wooden deputy isn't elected. I mean, I'd love to show that phony fella what it's like to work on a Texas farm in a hunnerd-n?ten degrees blazing heat in July! Lordy, it ain't like the air-conditioned halls of St. Albans!"

"I'm truly flattered," Lattan said, rubbing his temples. "But I need some time to think about it."

"We ain't got time," Bordeaux said. "But I'll tell you what. I'll have my people schedule a meeting for you with my girl Bessie Bravura for next week. That'll give you time to think about it. But I can assure you Bessie will talk you into it. And if that don't work, I'll have her mud-wrestle you like she used to do in her Gorgeous Ladies of Wrestling days!"

"I'll talk it over with my family and my campaign manager—"

"And you will answer yes!"

Chapter 45

Nerd On The Hill

After showering, shaving, dressing and guzzling a large bottle of Perrier to rehydrate, Lattan sought stability in the familiar confines of Capitol Hill. Perhaps the shaky foundation of his statesman's facade would be buttressed with the reliable mortar of a Congressman's duties. He hoped that anchoring himself in the Congressional routine would ultimately serve as an investment in regaining his momentum, and would pay dividends later in his House re-election campaign.

And at this point it was *only* a House re-election campaign. Once he'd regained his post-hangover equilibrium — and harnessed his common sense — he'd called back Hoss Bordeaux and respectfully declined his invitation to meet with that vulgarian wrestler-turned-governor Bessie "The Snoddy" Bravura. Running as a Transform Party candidate would make him even more of a laughingstock than he already was, if for no other reason than it would forever link him to that national punchline, Hoss Bordeaux.

Now Lattan, undaunted by his most recent troubles, would once again attempt to recover some of his eroded self-confidence through executing his responsibilities as Congressman. The safe environs of Capitol Hill would be a sanctuary, the one place where he wouldn't be bracing himself constantly in the expectation of being battered with questions about events of the recent past. Kiwanis, Knights of Columbus, taxpayer organizations, gun zealots, any part of his base of supporters would likely focus on his disastrous presidential campaign. He had no more patience for such encounters. So he resolved to spend time on the Hill — meeting with lobbyists, back-slapping his colleagues, attending committee hearings. Acting as if nothing were amiss in the world of Charles Lattan, *Congressman*. Perhaps if he imagined it, perchance if he acted on such a belief, it would become true.

At that moment, on the steps of the Capitol, Lois Cahmin was incredulous that her peers could appear to be so uninterested in what their tour guide was saying. Here they were, a select group of high school scholars in Washington under the auspices of the National Youth Leadership Conference to learn more about careers in public service ... the student elite, winnowed from thousands of applicants for the annual Washington Week Seminar, a select few whose essays on Why I Want A Government Career had aroused the judges' interest ... and they looked positively bored.

They were yawning. They were giggling at whispered jokes. They were playing with their hair. They were looking off into the distance, as though they wanted to be anywhere but on the steps of the U.S. Capitol, learning about the machinations of government.

Sure, it had already been a long day, what with the 7 a.m. White House tour, then a trip to the Lincoln Memorial, the Smithsonian Museum, then the National Archives, and now a tour of the Capitol. But late morning fatigue was no excuse! They were in Washington, for goodness sake! The epicenter of the political universe! Part of a select few lucky enough just to be here!

Yes, after years of dreaming about traveling to Washington, seventeen-year-old Lois Cahmin was finally here, half a continent away from her home in Wichita, Kansas. On the steps of the building housing the greatest deliberative body in the world!

Did no one else share her awe? Certainly they must! She was willing to forgive their inattention and seeming lack of interest, chalk it up to exhaustion, if only she had an indication that they were as awestruck as she was just to be in Washington. Just so she wouldn't embarrass herself with her schoolgirl alacrity.

But if she was alone in her enthusiasm, at least she knew it was a familiar place for her to be. Politics had been an obsession from a very early age. While others had read comic books, she had read the *Almanac of American Politics*. While other girls had watched MTV, she had been enraptured by C-SPAN. Now, the place she had dreamed about visiting while other girls coveted trips to Disney World, hitherto accessible only through photos and textbooks, was all around her.

Her straight A's, her essay — "The Positive Role Government Plays in People's Lives" — had earned her a spot in the group. She'd been apprehensive about coming, worried that her expectations of the nation's capital were so high they couldn't possibly be fulfilled. But the real Washington had, in her mind, exceeded her expectations. Now it was clearer than ever — one day, Congresswoman Lois Cahmin, the honorable gentlelady from Kansas, would gambol up these marble steps, representing her constituents, voting her conscience.

The tour guide, a greasy-faced graduate student, continued his explanation about the history of the Capitol. OK, he was less than scintillating. Soon she found her gaze wandering, absently watching overweight Capitol police officers, Congressional staff members and tourists shuffle in and out of the building. So far, no Members. Let others swoon over rock bands and movie stars. Lois wanted to see someone she recognized from C-SPAN.

Then — could it be? She spotted a wiry, middle-aged man — no, older — in an ill-fitting suit, his bad combover flopping on his head with each step he took up the staircase toward the Capitol entrance. A Congressman? No, couldn't be. Not with such a bad suit! But he walked with such urgency, as though compelled by a mission ... he was certainly too old to be an aide.

The man continued toward them, and the lapel pin glinting in the sunlight confirmed her speculation. A Congressman — finally! And headed their way!

Lois flushed with excitement. Let the other girls blush at the sight of singers and sports stars. To a Kansas girl who'd spent her whole life looking at pictures of Congressmen, seeing them on television, it was a magical moment. So what if his suit was wrinkled, his eyes were bloodshot, his face craggy, his hair mussed? He'd probably spent a grueling morning fighting to save a program to help the poor or the elderly.

Now the tour guide was pointing at the marble columns, explaining the building's architectural nuances. Then he, too, spotted the approaching Congressman. As if sensing an opportunity to give the students a special treat — and tired of talking — he acted.

"Excuse me, Congressman," the guide said as the Congressman rushed by them. "I know you're busy, but I wonder if you wouldn't take a moment to say a few words to a group of young scholars in Washington for the first time to learn all about government."

Of course the Congressman would stop for a moment to address the students. Never knew if they were nascent voting constituents, or the sons and daughters of your PAC contributors. Occupational duty.

Lois noticed that his face was tightened, as though he was ruminating on some great national issue. The burdens of serving the people! Or maybe he had a rock in his shoe. Then he turned to the group and smiled. He was obviously excited to have the chance to speak to a select group of tomorrow's leaders!

"Yes, what a wonderful group we have here," the Congressman said. "I'm Charles Lattan, a Congressman from Idaho," he said, his eyes surveying the group one by one. "Any of you young scholars from Idaho?"

No one said a word. How do you talk to a Congressman? A statesman? A leader of the country?

"We've got students from twenty-seven different states," the tour guide said. "No one from Idaho, I don't think."

The Congressman grimaced for a moment, then resumed grinning.

"Well, young scholars and leaders of the future, allow me to personally welcome you to Washington D.C.," Lattan said. "You've made a fine choice in being part of this program. Not enough young people take an interest in public service these days. It makes my heart skip a beat to know that the next generation cares about their country and is eager to work. ..."

And with that glib statement, he rotated and resumed his original course. But Lois was willing to forgive such a brief encounter. He must not be kept from the people's work!

Chapter 46

Almanac Attack!

Lattan stood statesmanlike at the window of his Cannon House Office Building, looking from his fifth floor perch into the courtyard below. Not much of a view, but then again, he knew deep in his solar plexus that he was not much of a Congressman.

His hands were clasped behind his back, his chin was thrust forward, as if he believed that striking a contemplative pose would be the catalyst for weighty contemplation. But in this spring of his failed presidential campaign, the only thing weighty about him was the dozen or so extra pounds he'd put on working the rubber chicken circuit.

What a depressing view he had. Looking toward the center of Cannon, the building appeared to be a ghastly monolith of socialist realist architecture, as if Walter Gropius and his Balhaus buddies had been appointed to some panel by federal bureaucrats.

There was scarcely little vegetation, no discernible scenery. Just slabs and slabs of concrete. Perhaps if he'd win, oh, another five terms, in a *decade* he could have a view of the Capitol. Something to look forward to.

Dare he admit it to himself? At times like this he actually missed Idaho—

"Knock knock," he heard the familiar cigarette-cured voice behind him.

"Come on in," he said to his Congressional chief of staff, Rachel Emmell.

He waited until she was seated in the familiar leather wing chair across from his big oak desk, then he pivoted around and sat down, facing her.

She sat silently for a long moment, as if taking him in. For once, she wasn't playing with the pearls around her neck in her nervous way; her hands rested in her lap, a sheaf a papers clutched between them.

"What?" he asked.

"You look tired, Charlie," she finally said. "And if you don't mind my saying, a little distracted."

"I *am* tired!" he barked defensively. "I'm tired from wasting half a year of my life on that goddamn campaign that flopped."

"Maybe you need some rest."

"You're goddamned right I need some rest," he said, getting angry, though he didn't know why. "I need a rest from Slick Willie's illegal war, I need a rest from Slick Willie's China scandal, I need a rest—"

"Charlie, your Clinton hating is getting a little old," she said. "You're not on the stump in New Hampshire anymore. Give it a rest. Maybe that's why you're so cranky."

"Give it a rest? Give it a rest? What, have you gone soft on me?!"

"No, Charlie, it's just that he's almost gone, and everyone knows Prince Albert can't win, so enough already. You'll be working with a Republican president soon enough."

"I suppose you're right," Lattan said, sighing languidly. "Maybe I should go back to Idaho for a while, take a vacation."

"You mean a district work period."

"Right, a district work period," he said, his mind already wandering to thoughts of being home in pastoral Spudsville, county seat of the lush seventeenth district. "Why don't you get what's-his-name, the intern, to book me a flight tomorrow?"

"I'll be glad to, Charlie," Emmell said, smiling maternally. "But first I want you to do something for me," she said, placing the sheaf of papers in front of him on his desk.

"Oh God, paperwork," he said.

"It's just the survey from the *Almanac of American Politics*," she said, as he rustled the papers in his hands. "Won't take but a few minutes."

"Why the hell can't you do it?" he asked. "Christ, you and those kids answer all my mail. I can't remember the last time I even saw a letter from one of those idiots in Idaho."

"Those idiots vote for you, Charlie!"

"Exactly why they're idiots."

"Oh, are we in self-pity mode," she asked cheerfully, her voice lilting. "Anyway, there are a few personal questions on there, so it's better if you do it yourself."

"Fine!" he said. "Just book me that flight."

Emmell disappeared and Lattan was left alone with the forms. To hell with the damn Almanac! Who cared about those stupid questions? And why couldn't his goddamned good-for-nothing staff handle it? What the hell was his staff for, anyway?

He looked for excuses not to do it. ... He clicked on the TV, and surfed through endless channels ... MSNBC's "Time & Again" featuring archival footage of its attempts to fill the 8 pm time slot ... FOX News Channel's coverage of the aftermath of John Elway's retirement from the Denver Broncos, dubbed "Terror In The Rockies" ... CNN's coverage of its bumbling dismissal of Prince Albert of host of "Larry King Jive" ... bad infomercials, bad soap operas — and that was just C-SPAN's coverage of Congress ... VH-1 "Behind The Music" on Emerson, Lake & Palmer.

He clicked the remote control and the TV flamed out. Grudgingly, he glanced at the *Almanac* questionnaire. How hard could this be?

Name ... that was easy enough ... he scribbled *Charles J. Lattan* ... date first elected ... *1996* ... date and place of birth ... *January 8, 1940, Spudsville, Idaho* ... city of official residence ... *Spudsville* ... education background with years and degrees ...

Well, that's a little personal, isn't it? None of their damn business what his educational background is! Screw them! Just another attempt to remind voters that he wasn't a fancy Harvard boy, that he'd been a working man, a plumber. Well, forget them! He'll show them!

He scrawled ... *Idaho Plumbertechnic Institute, Master's Degree in Septic Sciences* ... then he leaned back and smiled, very self-satisfied. That'll show them! Who would ever know?

Chapter 47

Ending America's Bumpy Ride

"Oh Charlie, you ninny!" said an exasperated chief of staff, even though the Congressman wasn't in the office. She shook her head *tsk tsk tsk* and crinkled in her hand the scrawled survey for *The Almanac of American Politics* filled out by Lattan. She was his employee, yes, but at this moment — as at so many others — she was more like the frustrated mother who learns that her incorrigible son has fudged his homework yet again.

"Master's degree in septic sciences, *really*," she sneered to the silent office, still shaking her head, and blotting the survey with a White-Out brush. The old man couldn't even fill out his own biography without setting himself up for trouble. But mop-up operations were an occupational duty for her, wasn't it? If the Congressman didn't need his staff to save him from himself, she'd be out of a job.

At that very moment, Lattan was a dozen or so miles northwest of Capitol Hill, lurching and bobbing as he drove over the countless speed bumps on his way back from addressing a meeting of the Montgomery County, Maryland Young Republicans. Speaking invitations were so scant these days that he'd jumped at the chance to speak to the group. Even if only thirteen people had showed up, he'd still reached *someone*, hadn't he?

His Buick Brushfire rattled and shook on the bumps. There was just no way to navigate the nuisances. If he sped up to act is if they weren't there, his car would shudder and shake and go *ka-thunk*, and his ribs would rattle and his combover would flop down on the side of his head. If he slowed to the pace envisioned by the social engineers who used public funds to construct these slabs, he'd never get where he wanted to go. And worse yet, he'd be letting them win!

There seemed to be at least three on every street. And a stop sign on every corner! What kind of crazy socialist nanny state was this? There weren't even any kids playing or dogs galloping or whatever other appurtenances of suburban life speed bumps were supposed to protect. This was just another excuse for the liberals to run people's lives!

There ought to be a law against these goddamn things!

Wait a minute—

Now *there* was an idea.

Yes! That was it! All at once it came to him, and he subconsciously floored the accelerator. Damn these speed bumps!

And he bounced and shook and the car chugged and lurched and bobbed over them —

And then he waited at a stop sign for oncoming traffic that never came —

And finally, after God knows how many dozens of speed bumps and twists and turns and deserted suburban streets, he was finally back on a main thoroughfare, where the road was smoother and he had the chance to collect his thoughts.

Anti-speed bump legislation — why hadn't he thought of that before? The genius of it! He needed a title: "The Mobility Liberation Act." No, too bureaucratic sounding, as if those overpaid, self-important legislative counsels had written it. Hmm. "The Freedom To Drive Act." No, too general. "The Anti-Street Obstruction Act." No, too negative. "The Roadway Smoothing Act." That had a nice ring to it. ...

"You're kidding, right?" said Emmell the next morning, as she sat across from him in his Cannon Building office, slurping coffee.

"No, I'm not kidding," Lattan said, pounding his fist on his big oak Congressional desk. "Why must you sneer at every idea that isn't yours — especially if it's minc?"

"I'm not sneering, Charlie," Emmell said, outlining the ring of her styrofoam cup with her finger. "It's just that some of the things you've been doing lately—"

"What! What things?" Lattan demanded.

"Well, *The Almanac Of American Politics* survey, for one thing."

"Oh, that," Lattan said, turning up his nose and waving his hand dismissively. "You've got to be joking. No one reads it."

"Yes they do, Charlie!" Emmell said. "For God sakes, it's the political bible — updated every two years! Newspapers across the country, especially *The Washington Past*, lift from it verbatim when they're too lazy to do research about Members' backgrounds themselves. Earnest policy wonks keep at their desks as if it were holy writ. Meddlesome interest groups pore over it for voting records. It's serious, Charlie, and you just can't make stuff up about your educational background!"

Lattan sighed and looked away. "So I take it you ... *corrected* ... my embellishment?"

"Of course I did, Charlie! Jesus, do you realize what might have happened if you faxed that back to the careful people at the *Almanac*? They're very thorough over there!"

"Whatever," Lattan said blandly. "That's what I pay you for, right? Keeps you on your toes!" He winked and forced a chuckle.

"Oh, Charlie!" Emmell said. "Sometimes I feel like you're a little kid. And that's what this speed bump idea makes me think of. Just some kid with his crazy ideas about fixing the world. For goodness sakes, you know the federal government can't — and shouldn't — do anything about speed bumps. It's not even a state issue. It's a local issue."

"But it's something people care deeply about."

"Yes, but if you go into the well of the House and introduce legislation to ban speed bumps, you'll be laughed out of the chamber."

"Will I? Or will everyone be so supportive that it'll get passed on a suspension?"

"Charlie, you're not doing this."

"The hell I'm not," he said, slamming his fist on his armrest. His combover flopped on to his forehead. He quickly scooped it up with his right hand and flopped it back on top of his head. "I'm the Congressman. You're my aide. I want a speech. I want a press release. I want those lazy bastards at leg counsel to draft it. And I want the whole package ready to go by next week. Got it?"

Chapter 48

In Congressional Left Field

Lattan felt his eyes burning as he glowered across his big oak desk at Emmell. If she wanted a showdown over the speed bump legislation proposal, she would get it! Who did she think she was, threatening him? *He* was the Congressman, and if *he* wanted to introduce a bill to ban speed bumps, make it a federal issue, *she* would obey him!

"*Really*, Charlie," she said in a tone sprinkled with just a hint of condescension. "Of course, we'll do everything we can to back you a hundred percent if you want to go forward on the speed bump thing. But as your top adviser, I must say I think there are better issues to focus on right now."

"Like what?" He wasn't going to be talked out of it, but he was curious what she had in mind, what devious tactic she would employ to try and make him talk himself out of The Roadway Smoothing Act.

"Well, for one thing, the president's poll numbers are his worst in three years," she said flatly. "You're always so eager to attack him, now might be the perfect time."

"On what?" Oh, how he hated to admit to himself that she'd piqued his interest! How she knew which buttons to push!

"The war, you ninny!" she said, as if he were an insolent student. "The way he's bungled this thing has the country turning on him. The fiasco with the Chinese missile technology transfers is only compounding the issue, showing the American people what happens when a frat boy draft dodger tries to pretend he's a statesman."

"I like the sound of it," he said, a crafty smile coming over his wan face. "So what do we do?"

"Well, some of the real lefties in the Democrat party — God, politics makes strange bedfellows — are supporting a demonstration on the Memorial Bridge this afternoon. You know, they're doing the human shield thing, wearing bulls eye targets on their clothing as a symbolic gesture, to show solidarity with the people of Serbia against the NATO bombings. Maybe you could go out and join them, be the first Republican to cross the line, as they say."

"The first Republican?" Lattan asked incredulously. "There are plenty of Republicans out there opposing the war."

"Yes, but not as part of demonstrations against it," Emmell said. "You know your colleagues. Those buttoned-down stiffs aren't about to join hands and sing 'Give Peace A Chance' with a bunch of aging hippies."

Lattan winced at the thought of it. And what made her think he would want to hold hands with those unkempt longhairs! Reflexively he smoothed his combover. Those were the same people he so gleefully sneered at during the eighties as Soviet dupes for the Stalinistas in Nicaragua. And now he would demonstrate against U.S. military policy with them?

"I don't know," Lattan said. "It could backfire, don't you think? I mean, just picture it — me with my suit, wearing a bullseye with all of those granola eaters. I don't think it's a good idea."

"Well, ah, that could be ..." Emmell said nervously, as if she suddenly realized it really was as bad an idea as the speed bumps bill, and she didn't have a good plan B. She shuffled through some papers on her lap, tugged at her pearl necklace, obviously rifling through her brain for another suggestion.

"What other ideas you got?" Lattan asked, like a kid eyeing a tray of brownies that his mother just removed from the oven.

Emmell flipped through her copy of *Roll Call*. "Well, you could endorse someone in the New York Senate race," she said. "Maybe Tina Woley, that Congresswoman thinking about taking on Hillary."

"What?!" Lattan said. "Why would I endorse one liberal tax-and-spend Democrat over another? And what kind of crazy, arrogant move would it be for an Idaho Congressman to take sides in the New York Senate race?"

"And what kind of crazy, arrogant move would it be for a first lady from

Arkansas *to run* in the New York Senate race?"

"Hmm ... good point," Lattan said. "But if I endorse someone in that race, won't I be seen as no better than the carpetbagger herself?"

"Hmmm ... good point," Emmell said.

"Hey, speaking of endorsements, did McCain get back to us on my decision to back him for president?"

There was a long, swollen pause, and Emmell again began shuffling the papers on her lap, as though it were some sort of nervous tick. "Uh, yeah, Charlie, I, uh, meant to tell you," Emmell stammered. "We, uh, got some less than completely successful news—"

"Come on!" Lattan said. "Don't spin me!"

"OK," Emmell said, exhaling. "McCain declined your endorsement."

"*Did* he?" Lattan said, thunderstruck. "Well." He sighed languidly.

"There's ... uh, more."

"More?"

"Well, we went down the list. I mean, certainly someone would want the endorsement of the first candidate to withdraw, right?"

"Of course," Lattan said. "So who do you think I should—" "Bush already said no."

"That blue-blooded phony," Lattan harrumphed. "After my glowing introduction of him at that rally in New Hampshire!"

"And so did Elizabeth," Emmell continued. "And Quayle, and Bauer, and Smith, and Kasich."

"I don't even like those phonies!"

"We could still try Forbes and Lamar."

"No!" Lattan thundered. "We've got to draw the line somewhere. We've got to have *some* standards."

"Fair enough," Emmell said. "I guess I don't even need to mention the Nazi-coddling ex-CNN host."

"You're damn right you don't!" Lattan said. "Anything else."

"Oh," Emmell said. "I almost forgot. There is one more thing."

"What's that?"

"Hollis Roper, the head of the Committee Representing American Plumbers, wants to offer you something. He didn't say what. But I scheduled a meeting with him next week."

Chapter 49

What A Load Of CRAP!

Lattan removed his voting card from the slot and gamboled up the aisle of the House floor. He glanced briefly toward the C-SPAN camera, jutted his jaw and thrust out his chest. Make sure they get a shot of his good side, not the one where he parts his hair midway down his head to swoop it over his bald pate in a combover.

Once outside, he skittered down the steps of the Capitol. God, it was hot! Humid, swampy, a dampness lingering in the fetid Washington air, not like the cool breezes of Idaho. He made his way across the promenade back toward Cannon. Out of the corner of his eye, he spied a camera crew and a young lissome blonde sticking a microphone in the face of one of his colleagues. Instantly he shuddered, a chilly sweat dampening his polyester blend shirt as he braced for ambush. What the hell had he just voted on? Appropriations, government operations, spending bill, taxing bill — who could keep track? All he knew was that the chief deputy whip had flashed him a thumbs-down, and so he'd voted no, just like the caucus wanted.

He walked past the interview — and when his quotes were not demanded, he exhaled an audible grunt of relief. Just another MSNBC girl interviewing another Member dreaming of raising his national profile on an unwatched cable channel. ...

He skipped up the steps to Cannon, nodded a Congressional *howd'yado* to the guard, and walked into the waiting elevator piloted by his favorite operator.

"Hi Congressman," said Noreen Clause, seated at the elevator control panel. "You look nice today."

"Why thank you," said Lattan, beaming. He knew she said this to everyone, but for a balding Congressman almost sixty, it never failed to brighten his mood.

"Have an nice day," she said, depositing him on the fifth floor, right around from suite Five Forty-Five.

"Good morning, all!" he said as he lumbered into ... an empty office. No receptionist, no intern logging in constituent mail, no lobbyists or constituents, or even earnest young scholars on their first trip to Washington to see how the government works, were sitting in the waiting area. How odd. He poked his head into the legislative assistants' room — no Legislative Director, Legislative Assistants, Legislative Correspondents ... not a soul.

He turned back toward his personal office, the door of which was closed. Strange. He gripped the handle and twisted.

The door opened easily. Then he saw them. A whole room full.

"Hello, Charlie," said his wife, Ariel. "Sit down, dear." She motioned toward his desk, and his big congressional chair was the only seat not occupied. On one leather wing chair sat his chief of staff, Rachel Emmell. On the matching chair, his campaign manager and media guru, Kentrell "Alt" DeLeet. On the couch — the traitorous fat bastard! — his former campaign manager, whom he fired, Alex Macro. And fanned out like silverware at a fancy place setting were his official and campaign staffs — Don Root, Dot Com, his old pal and disgraced donor Al Tavista, even the intern, Serge Engine. And then Hollis Roper of the Coalition Representing American Plumbers (CRAP), along with a couple of high-priced trade association flunkies.

"Well, it isn't my birthday, but thanks for the surprise," Lattan said, laughing nervously. The room was silent. He tiptoed gingerly toward his chair and sat down.

"Charlie, we're all here because we care about you," began Emmell. Every eye in the room fixed on him. He was beginning not to like this one bit.

"What, are you all here to tell me to stop drinking?" Lattan asked feebly, his stentorian voice cracking. "For chrissakes, a couple three scotches a night to take the pressure off—"

"It's not that kind of intervention," Emmell said. "We're all here because we care about you as a Congressman. And a person."

Lattan was stupefied. What was this about? He began to feel beads of perspiration spangle his forehead.

"Well, I'm flattered," Lattan said sarcastically.

"Please, Charlie, this is for your own good. Your family is on board. The campaign is on board. All of your friends and supporters —"

"What the hell are you talking about!" Lattan demanded, pounding his fist on his desk.

"Charlie, please calm down and listen," said his wife soothingly. "This is exactly the kind of outburst we're trying to stop."

"She's right, Charlie," said Hollis Roper, speaking for the first time. "Listen. We think you'll like what you hear."

"Fine!" Lattan said, slumping back in his chair, playing with his tie.

"Charlie, as of last night, you have an opponent. And a pretty formidable one at that," said DeLeet, rising from the leather sofa and placing the most recent *Idaho Informer* on the desk in front of him. "Her name is Maureen Hurley—"

"What! You gotta be kidding me! Who the hell is that?"

"All we know about her is that she just filed."

"What kind of nonsense is that?" Lattan demanded, his combover flopping down the side of his head. "For chrissakes, is that what this is all about? You know a Democrat can't win in my district!"

"She isn't a Democrat," DeLeet said. "She's running against you in the Republican primary. Says you're out of touch."

"Oh, Christ!" Lattan said, smoothing his combover.

"We have a way out of this, Charlie," said Emmell. "Listen to the plan."

"Let me guess," Lattan said. "I begin working the phones and fundraising tonight, and we start running the 'Hi I'm Mr. Wonderful' ads next week!"

"No," Emmell said evenly. "The good news is that the plan doesn't involve you campaigning or fundraising or faking a smile or pretending to be interested in any voters ever again."

"Well, I think I like that!" Lattan said brightly. "Go on."

Emmell nodded to Hollis Roper, who nodded back and stood up from his seat. Roper buttoned his coat and ran his hand over his slicked-back, high-viscosity silver hair. He wore horn-rimmed glasses, a perfectly tailored Hugo Boss three-button suit, an Armani tab-collared shirt and a guacamole-colored Hermes tie.

"Congressman, thanks for having us all in like this," Roper began. "As I'm sure you already know, we at the Coalition Representing American Plumbers are going to be honored tomorrow night to present you with our Golden Plunger Award in recognition for your service to America's septic tank maintenance community, and to show our respect for you as this nation's highest-ranking ex-plumber."

"Why, no, I didn't ... thank you," said Lattan, glowering momentarily at his chief of staff for failing to give him a heads up.

"But that's not all," Roper continued. "Our annual convention also includes the election of a new president."

The room was silent. "And? Who do you want me to endorse?" Lattan asked simply.

"We want you to be our new president," Roper said, smiling, as if he was a game show host offering a contestant a *brand new car!*

"We all do," said Mrs. Lattan. Emmell nodded and smiled maternally. Others also nodded, or signaled a thumbs up.

Instantly his mind was spinning ... an AA intervention might have been more fun.

"Now, before you say anything, we want to complete the package offer," Roper said, miming a picture frame with his hands. "We've taken care of everything. Salary — mid sixes, with benefits and stock options, expense accounts and use of our corporate condos in Vero Beach and Aspen. Bankers' hours. Everyone in this office comes over with you, your whole staff. Chief of staff becomes executive director. Legislative assistants become policy analysts. Press secretaries become communications managers. No more votes, no more elections, no more campaigns, no more constituents, no more headaches of politics. You get to keep all of your friends on the Hill, talking to them only about the issues you and we care about — plumbing legislation. You, Charles Lattan, the next President of CRAP. Whaddya say?"

Lattan was dizzy. What were they asking him to do? Resign? Admit failure and quit? Give up his political dreams? —

—But still—

It *was* an attractive offer ... who would have thought that a working class man—a plumber!—could become a Congressman and then The President Of A Major National Industry Trade Association. Making mid-sixes ... Christ, what the hell did that mean? And why did he blurt it out like that? Mid-sixes? Like $500,000? Or $300,000? Or $700,000? And the benefits—

Aspen. Didn't ski. Could learn, right? Would certainly have the time, wouldn't he? Vero Baton ... Or Was it Boca Beach? Ah, didn't matter. Florida! Sun! Stock Options ...

Time to be serious here, Charlie ... what would he ever ascend to in the House? Chief deputy assistant to the majority undersecretary of holding the line on government spending ... never achieving a salary greater than $145,000 and change for the COLAs ...

What about a Senator Charles Lattan? Christ, after the presidential campaign, wasn't it painfully clear how poor his prospects on the political social promotion circuit were?

"Charlie, it's really the best thing for everyone all around," his wife said, walking over toward him and putting her hand on his forearm, then stroking it gently. "After all you've been through, you deserve a break. We deserve to have our Charlie back."

It was all too much to digest so suddenly ... but the prospect of feigning interest in the voters again for another 18 months, the thought of shaking hands and kissing babies and glad-handing and palm-pressing and gripping-and-grinning and asking for your $100 which will help me bring back common sense to Congress ... Gawd, it seemed awful!

And here was his chance to gently tug at the silk string that would inflate his very own customized golden parachute.

He steepled his fingers, put his elbows on his desk and looked out at his team for a long moment ... then he rose and turned toward his window overlooking the concrete slab of the Cannon courtyard, and clasped his hands behind his back.

"OK," he said without turning around. "I'll do it."

The next evening, Lattan waited apprehensively to be introduced at the CRAP dinner. He peered out from the dais, where various CRAP executives were investigating their mesclun green salads as a prelude to their roasted chicken with new potatoes and julienne vegetables. In front of him in the Hinkley Hilton Ballroom, seated around two dozen tables like petals on sunflowers, were five hundred roaring septic tank experts, plumbing pioneers and assorted other commode analysts.

God, what a sight the lot of them were! So many polyester sports coats stretched over distended beer bellies barely contained by pants with buckling waistbands, ties with assorted food stains, and shirts with polyester sheens that shouted Low Class. This would be his new constituency, the Congressional District Of America's Voting Plumbers.

Lattan navigated through dinner silently, grateful that the people to either side of him had gotten caught up in conversation with people seated on their other sides.

Soon the outgoing CRAP president clinked his glass and got up to make the perfunctory opening remarks, welcoming old and new friends to our nation's capital and expressing his profound gratitude for the opportunity to meet like this at such a critical time in our industry's history.

"And now, I'd like to introduce to you the winner of this year's Golden Plunder — I mean Plunger, haha — award, and the next president of the Coalition Representing American Plumbers. Charles Lattan is a man who has served us admirably as Congressman, fighting for the interests of our industry in a sometimes hostile legislative environment, and who will continue to serve us as our chief spokesman and advocate, working with his Congressional colleagues to continue his fight for our interests as the president of CRAP. You know, I remember when I first supported Charlie's campaign years ago. He said he was running for Congress because a man who'd earned his living unclogging drains and commodes could certainly unstop clogged legislation. Well, now, what goes around comes around, and I think we can all say with great confidence that Charles Lattan will be an admirable unclogger of commodes once again — figuratively speaking, of course — because of his experience unclogging stopped-up legislation in the House! Please give a warm CRAP welcome to the Honorable Congressman, and our next president, Charles J. Lattan!"

With that the audience ignited with applause, and Lattan placed his napkin atop the chicken carcass on his porcelain plate. He buttoned his suit coat and smiled his reflexive wooden smile. He stood and waved, and then turned and shook the hand of his introducer, stepped behind the podium, and adjusted the microphone.

"Thank you for that wonderful introduction," Lattan said. "I am indeed honored by your words, and humbled by your deeds, both for presenting me with the Golden Plunger Award and for bestowing on me the privilege of serving as your next president," he said, reading from the text prepared by the CRAP public affairs office speechwriting division.

"We stand at a crossroads in the history of the plumbing industry," Lattan said, continuing from the script. "Various legislative proposals now pending before Congress could, if enacted, drastically alter the business environment in which we operate, and negatively impact our collective bottom lines. ..."

Oh, God, what a load! Not even the speeches written by *his own staff* were larded with such horrible bromides!

"... the task before us, therefore, my colleagues — and the task before all of us in the septic community, including those who couldn't be with us tonight — is how we manage to stand up for our interests as we glide from the cusp of the new millennium into the new millennium itself."

For chrissakes! Who was writing this garbage! Lattan had no Master's Degree in Fine Arts, but he could spot cliches and mixed metaphors and purple prose when he saw it! And maybe these pork chops in the audience couldn't identify the flaws of this particular address in a clinical way, but they knew bull when they heard it! *Cusp of the new millennium*, indeed! Which Harvard puke in the CRAP PR office penned *that* one? *How we manage to stand up for our interests* ... what a cliche! Was there a speech delivered anywhere in this town that didn't include that line?

God, the rest of the speech certainly had to be worse, didn't it? It had to go downhill from here, didn't it?

"But, my friends, I'm sure I'm telling you nothing you haven't already heard before," Lattan said, looking up from the speech and deciding to go off-the-cuff. "You go to any conference in this town, meet with any elected official, they'll all say they're 'working for your interests.' Well, let me ask you a question. If *everyone* is working for *their own* interests, doesn't someone have to lose? Not everyone can have their interests met!"

Lattan gripped the sides of the podium, then hunched over it. Only absent throat-clearings and coughing broke the silence. He thundered forward: "And that's not the worst of it! When we can't dismiss each other with a simple 'I'm on your side,' that's when we start bending the language, mouthing gibberish as if it were public policy, hoping we'll confuse each other enough to get away with whatever malfeasance we're foisting on an unwary public!"

Now he could see a couple people in the audience whisper to each other, a few others look at him incredulously.

"Let's look at our abuse of the language. For chrissakes, we've gotten so far away from saying what we mean that none of us means what we say!" Lattan inveighed, banging his fist on the podium.

Now the whispers were more audible, and he noticed some animated shaking of heads. To hell with them!

"Just look at the jargon and phoniness in this text I have in front of me, and from which I'm supposed to be reading," Lattan declaimed. He rattled the paper-clipped speech in his hand. "Pro-active tactics! Grassroots mobilization! Grasstops activism! Strategic objectives! What the hell does any of that mean? I'll tell you what it means. It means nothing!" he bellowed, and flung the speech, all thirty-four pages of it printed in eighteen-point-type, at the audience in front of him. The papers cascaded down like fat flurries of snow on TABLE 3 RESERVED. People caught them or scooped them up from the floor, as if part of orchestrated stagecraft.

"It's all — pardon the use of your beloved acronym — a load of CRAP!" Lattan said, again banging his fist on the podium. "Part of the reason I agreed to accept your gracious offer — and leave Congress — was because I was sick of all of the pretense. Who can even understand what the hell Congress does anymore? Ways and Means, Appropriations — that's half a dozen more syllables than needed to describe taxing and spending! Continuing resolution — that means we've been lollygagging around and haven't got our work done, so now we have to pass — and this is my favorite — an emergency spending bill! *Emergency* spending! The only emergency is the number of Members of Congress getting loaded at receptions instead of doing their goddamn jobs!" He pounded the podium again with his fist.

Now the fellow who introduced him, and seated next to him, kicked Lattan, though he maintained his gaze straight ahead at the audience, so no one would notice. Lattan glowered at him. "I'll get off this stage when I'm good and ready!"

Lattan turned back to the audience, who were mumbling to each other and looking at him with skewed eyebrows. His combover had now flopped down to the side of his head, but he resisted the urge to plop it back on top. Lattan in the raw!

"And let me tell you another thing," Lattan said, his face contorted in righteous indignation. "All of those letters you all have sent me over the years —and which I pretend to remember when you thank me for answering them —they're all fakes! I've never seen one! I let my staff handle 'em, some snot nosed twenty-something puke with a head full of naive idealism about changing the world has entered your name into a database and clicked on a command to send you a form letter. I don't know what you think, I don't care what you think, and no one on Capitol Hill does! You're all an equation— the amount of time you get, the attention you receive, is directly proportional to the money you cough up. Simple as that. 'Oh, this is Flip Screen. He maxed out for a thou in the last cycle. Treat him nice, Congressman!' That's how we deal with you."

By now he could feel himself sweating through his shirt, the perspiration beading on his forehead and then sliding down the side of his face, soaking his shirt collar. The audience was in full rumble, as if contemplating a revolt.

"Oh yes, don't act like this is all a *surprise* to you!" Lattan snarled. "You're willing accomplices, if only to ensure that your little piece of the porkpie is preserved, and to hell with the rest of the country. Public service? HA! People's House? HA! Elected representative? HA! It's all a ruse, and you're as guilty as I am."

Now they were shouting: "Get off the stage!" "Shaddup and sit down!" "You're the problem, not us." Others were on their feet, cupping their hands over the mouths, booing and hissing.

"Don't get me wrong," Lattan said. "I know I'm culpable. Oh sure, I came from Idaho, where we believe in things like public service and elective democracy and all that warm and fuzzy stuff. And when I learned how it all really works, I did nothing to stop it, just tried to adjust to the game as best as I could so I could someday play on the varsity squad. But I'm saying to you now, 'Enough is Enough.' The lies, the prevarications, the phoniness has to stop. We've been doing it all so long we don't know what is true anymore and what is spin, what is pretense and what is real, whether we're acknowledging our real feelings, or whether our response to certain stimuli is learned and pre-programmed based on the latest polling data. Well, I can't live like that anymore. I need to be real. I need to pay attention to how I feel, not how it's best that I feel in order to win votes. If that means going back to my country bumpkin' Idaho ways, then that's worth it to me!"

And with that he swung the microphone down to the podium and leapt off the stage, nearly crashing onto the floor. But somehow he kept his balance, and, after regaining his equilibrium, rushed through the crowd, enduring boos, hisses, and even the occasional chicken bone bouncing off his shoulder.

He dashed through the lobby and out the door into the horseshoe driveway, then ran up toward Connecticut Avenue, working up a ferocious sweat. Running, running, his wingtips clomping on the pavement, his suit clinging to him as he sweated like a potato farmer after twelve hours in the Idaho fields. Finally, after three blocks, he felt compelled to stop running. The scene where he now stood, overlooking Rock Creek Park atop the Taft Bridge, was oddly calming, if for no other reason than it was free of any indications that he was still in the middle of Washington DC.

And at that moment, as he stood and panted and gazed at the horizon at the very end of the long summer day, it all came clear. He would return to Idaho and feel again what it was like to be real.

The End

Printed in the United States
50860LVS00004B/1-102

9 781413 783483